APRIL RAiN

AM Grout

APRIL RAiN

By

AM GROUT

AM Grout

1.   Fiction-Crime Thriller   2.Fiction- Mystery Murder
3.   Poetry/Lyrics   4. Grief/Healing

Printed in United States of America

Dedicated to the lives lost

before they were made known.

AM Grout

Books also by AM Grout:

An Angels Journey

Dear Baby, Get Out!

Prologue

Besides my close friends and family, no one really knew me until my picture emerged in the headline of the local paper. GIRL MISSING, was all it read. The rumors of why I disappeared and the possibility that I was kidnapped sent shivers up the spines of everyone in town.

Heads swirled with thoughts of how I could be missing. You don't misplace a person. My last known whereabouts confused the investigators and the public even more. Greenways Alterations and More, the local dry cleaners in Tymingsly, looked completely normal except when the owner arrived to begin business as usual and discovered I left the door unlocked. The mystery of why began to disturb more than just the owner, as the discovery of clues began an investigation to find me.

Everyone including the police were suspicious. Foul play must be involved. A responsible hard working beautiful young lady like Jessica Briggs doesn't just walk away into the future unless she was abducted by aliens or a sinister intruder.

I don't believe in aliens, and I certainly don't like to think about sinister intruders except if it involves an April Fool's Day prank. And this isn't a prank. My body was missing.

A few days after my disappearance, my body was found. Dead. It was Easter Sunday, a day catholic's celebrate Jesus's resurrection but that gloomy rainy April day didn't celebrate the resurrection of my life, it forever immortalized the reality that I was dead.

AM Grout

The newspaper headlines read MISSING GIRL'S BODY FOUND. Jesus's body wasn't found which made his mystery sweet, he rose, was healed and now resides in heaven body and soul. My body did not go to heaven, it went to the Medical Examiner's office. The earthly mystery surrounding my death wasn't given peace when my body was found. The drama of why and how I ended up in those woods just down the street from where I lived needed to unravel.

Before I share this story, I need to you to know that I did enter heaven's gates at the moment of my death. The love, hope and faith of heaven is real, however the fact that our conscious mind can linger made me feel like it was a dream. I hoped it was a dream.

It felt like a dream as I sat by the edge of the water listening to the waves lap against the shoreline. I found myself flying over mountaintops in a mystical form of my own imagination. Corny Unicorns surrounded me. All my childhood memories and dreams were in the breeze that carried me until I landed upon a blue cloud. It was magnificent. It is magnificent.

As I touched the cloud, a lady appeared through the veil of the sunlight. It was Mother Mary. So often I had prayed to her and now I was graced with her presence. It was real. It is real.

Mary, dressed in blue, reassured me then and now that I am okay. I asked what happened and how I came to be here with her in this magical dream built from my own realities. She gently wrapped her arms around me and together we made a journey home to discover the grief, sorrow, pain, and fear that my departure caused.

The why, when, where, who and how are the questions everyone needs answers to. Everyone but me. Not only do I not need them, I do not want them. Mother Mary shared with me that there is a state of grace given to all and a fall from grace is less than pleasant for those on earth and thus makes us in heaven fear the judgement of those who consider themselves God.

I am not God, nor the energy which moves the words you read, but the energy behind this story is gifted from God. The God of creation, the one true God that first created the day and the night from which we all originate from.

There is no right or wrong reason for death, it happens. The web of friends that I have never left gives me great comfort. Their unconditional love of me is something I treasure still today. For it is true that LOVE lasts forever. Forgiveness, acceptance, wisdom and even fear does not last forever, but love does.

Death happens; and I did die too young. My life was just beginning but mistakes happen. Accidents aren't intended, and people make uneducated choices; but in the end, we all do the best we can to forgive, move forward and live.

I want to forgive but that is not for me to do. I need to accept, accept the change that death alters this world into being. My death caused fear and to end the fear has been difficult because we all need to believe superheroes are real, and that superheroes would never create a mystery without a happy ending. But they did create a mystery around my death because they wanted to protect me.

I do not need to be protected anymore. Heaven's door welcomed me home. I've heard the prayers contained in the thorns around your heart. You will know the truths that share a piece of me with you.

In the end, no secret is worth keeping when a life, a spirit, a soul, created by God is near.

AM Grout

April 1992

AM Grout

~1~ BACKYARD TRAIL

Sitting on a stool pushed against his kitchen counter, Bob Jensen takes a bite of his toast and adjusts the fold in the newspaper to finish reading the front page article about the missing girl. It is all the town has talked about over the past three days. News reports indicate she vanished from the dry cleaners she worked at around closing time on Wednesday. It is now Sunday, Easter Sunday. Bob's dog nudges his nose into Bob and barks.

"Baxter, you want to go for a walk?" Bob asked.

At the words "Want to", the dog raises his eyebrows and wags his tail. Bob puts the newspaper down on top of the toast crumbs. He puts the butter knife in the sink and replaces the butter to the refrigerator before slipping on his boots, and reaching for his coat. Baxter wags his tail and barks with approval.

Bob pats him as he opens the drawer next to the door and pulls out a leash. Bending down slightly, he attaches the leash and said, "Ok Buddy, let's go!"

Baxter heads down the wet stairs as Bob holds the railing. Bob adjusts his hood to repel the mist in the air. As they head towards the wooded corner of the backyard, Bob releases Baxter from his leash.

Baxter dashes around with his new found freedom, then stops in the back corner of the yard and looks into the wooded area. His nose twitches as his senses become alert. He looks at Bob, then takes off running into the woods.

Bob calls after him, "Baxter!" but Baxter ignores him. He walks quicker towards the woods calling Baxter's name. The dog has run out of sight. "Baxter!" He yells louder. His eyes searched faster than his pace, Baxter's bark grows further into the woods.

Discarded beer cans, cigarettes butts, and muddy footprints litter the ground as he tries to catch up to Baxter. He carefully walks through the muddy tire tracks that run down the path and thinks of the keg party he had heard in the woods a few nights earlier. He hadn't called the police like he had in the past, because they were respectful, and kept the music lower than previous nights.

Baxter stopped running and was barking and sniffing at a tree. Bob approached the tree to see what Baxter is so obsessed with. Within a few feet of the tree his own nose discovered a foul smell. He put his hand over his nose and moved closer. The smell was coming from a piece of clothing that wasn't covered with snow.

Baxter begins to tug at the green fabric, exposing what Bob assumed would be a dead animal. Last summer, Baxter discovered the remains of a cat that someone dumped wrapped in a blanket. This wasn't a cat. It was a leg, a human leg and attached to it was the body or the body parts of a woman. Her shirt was filthy with larva and bugs squirming over what appeared to be dried blood. There were parts of her body that resembled the look of spoiled hamburger. Bob looked away and instantly threw up.

There was no one to hear him as he let out his own yelp. Bob didn't have to touch her to know she was dead. He tried wrangling Baxter but he would not let go of her sleeve. Bob couldn't pull Baxter off her without seeing the damage to her body. Baxter whined and began pulling her limp body off of the snow covered mound under the tree, uncovering dried blood smeared beneath her.

Baxter continued to sniff her up and down. His tail stood at attention as he cautiously licked the dried blood on her. Dew stood still in her motionless palm. Baxter lapped it up. "Woof!" he barked as the wind blew a lock of her long curly hair in his face.

Bob took the leash and whacked Baxter, "STOP!" Then he quickly attempted to put Baxter back on the leash. Baxter growled. Bob grabbed him by his collar, fastened the leash and forced him to walk towards the house.

Opening the kitchen door, Baxter raced in and shook the dew off himself scattering droplets over the kitchen floor. Bob reached for the phone on the wall and dialed 911. The cord was short, forcing Bob to stand next to the wall.

"911, this line is being recorded, please state your emergency."

Out of breath and shaking, he stuttered, "Hello, This is Bob Jensen. I live at 1489 Stafford Street, and I just found that girl." Baxter barked as he looks out the lower window panels of the kitchen door.

"No, she isn't okay. She's dead. Yes, Yes, Yes, I will be here."

Baxter pulls at Bob's sleeve. Bob hangs up the phone and pushes Baxter off him. Tears began to flow out of his eyes. He kneels down and hugs Baxter.

~~~

The man is six feet tall. I see a tattoo under his shirt.
I don't know how I know this.
It says USMC.

He is wearing glasses and construction boots.
A hood covers his head to protect it from the rain.
The white shirt under his jacket is tucked into his jeans.

He calls out to his dog, Baxter; a German Shepard.
Baxter is running loose and running towards me.
"Baxter, Baxter" I yell.

He is barking and sniffing me.
What a good dog.
The man continues to call him.

"Sir, he is with me."
I put my hand out and he licks it.
It tickles.

The man is approaching me.
Now dressed in shades of blue.
He looks down on me and I see he is a woman.

A lady to be exact.
Her long hair looks like mine,
Her eyes shine with a light that knows me so well.

She takes my hand and we fly over the trees.
I can see buildings of the city, the river and the bridge.
The rain is misting but we are not getting wet.

The blue lady keeps her arms wrapped around me.
We become one flying in the rain.
~~~~~

AM Grout

~2~ SUNDAY MORNING

Detective Dave Rolland was having a cup of coffee looking out his kitchen window as his wife retrieved a few carrots from the refrigerator. The dining room table was set for ten. An elongated floral design of yellow lilies, purple tulips, orange sunflowers and pink roses sat between a pair of taper candles.

Suzanne Rolland fastened an apron over her floral printed dress and began diligently peeling the carrots over the sink.

"Joanie called, said the kids woke them up at 4:30. She said she understood why we made her and Jeff wait until the clock said 6am when they were little." Dave smirked and shook his head, "That was early enough to search for plastic eggs filled with junk."

"I never understood how you could let them eat candy that early." He said, sipping his coffee. Suzanne shook the carrot peeler at him, "Now wait a second, you know I didn't let them eat any of the candy until they had breakfast. You were the one that didn't even let them open their baskets to get the toys out until all the eggs were found."

Dave chuckled, "Searching for all those eggs at least stopped the candy gorging episode until closer to 6:45 and that was even after your lovely feast of hard boiled eggs, toast, and jam." He winked at her.

She placed the peeled carrots inside a pan filled with the water on the stove. Closing the lid she said, "Good thing the Easter bunny left a note telling us how many eggs were hidden." Dave reached for an orange bag on the counter which had protected the newspaper from the rain. He removed the orange bag and put it in the trash, a small amount of water remained on the counter. He grabbed a paper towel and wiped it up.

Removing the sales flyers from the newspaper, he placed the paper on the kitchen table and walked over to pour another cup of coffee. "I am still in awe that we made it to 8:00 mass each year."

"It always worked out. As you saw today, if you don't get there twenty minutes early, you'll never get a seat at the 10:30." A pan on the stovetop was bubbling over, he removed the cover exposing boiled potatoes. "Do you want this burner on?" Suzanne placed a fork in the potatoes. "You can turn it off."

"What time is dinner?" Dave asked.

"Joanie and Jeff both said they would be here after the 12:15 mass, so I am hoping for 2. When they get here, you can start carving the ham." She handed him a cutting board and a block of cheese. "Will you slice this please?"

Returning to the sink to drain the potatoes, she said, "I hope Mikey and Lisa haven't had too much candy. That poor child who sat a few rows up from us in church really was on a sugar high. Good thing his mother had some quiet candy to calm him."

"Quiet candy?" His eyebrows raised above his glasses.

"Yes. You know, tootsie rolls and starburst. Candy that doesn't involve loud unwrapping and they don't sound like a rock collection. Remember when Jeff dropped those Skittles when he was four?"

"How could I forget?!"

Suzanne carried two egg printed cellophane baskets to the coffee table. A pink and a blue bow topped each one of the baskets. Inside were Tonka trucks, batman coloring books, a Barbie doll, hair accessories and chocolate bunnies named Happy.

Dave was standing in the window looking out at one of the deer that frequently visited his backyard. The doe stood frozen staring back at him. A hunter couldn't get so lucky to have a doe look you in the eye for this long he thought. He hardly ever even looked his wife in the eye this long, at least not lately.

Yesterday he could barely look Jessica's parents in the eye. He could only imagine what was going on at their house. Would they even celebrate Easter? When he was there yesterday, the counters were filling up with casseroles and baked goods. They definitely had enough food for a large feast, but would they even eat.

The cheese sat unsliced on the cutting board. He didn't have an appetite; he imagined they wouldn't either. The doe turned and pranced back into the woods.

"Honey?" Dave was startled by his wife's voice. He took his gaze off the window and looked at her.

She gestured for him to take the phone. "What?" he said. "The phone, it's Chief Robinson." Placing his coffee cup back on the table, he took the phone from her. "Hi Chief, what's up?"

He tried to walk into the dining room but the cord tangled, stopping him in his tracks. Suzanne starred at Dave knowing something was up. He closed his eyes, and bowed his head, "Where?"

Suzanne's hands came together as her eyes closed in prayer and listened. "Ok." He said followed by a long silence. "I'll be right there."

Handing the phone back to his wife, he looked out the window hoping to see the doe again. He couldn't look at his wife. He hung his head and sighed, "They found her."

Her hands clutched her mouth as she mumbled, "Alive?" He shook his head. She knew he couldn't give her any more details. He didn't actually have any except for the location.

Tears streamed her face as she handed him his hat, "Do her parents know?"

"No. Robinson wants me to tell them." She hugged him hard and he held her in his arms. Wiping her tears, he swallowed his own. She pulled away and quickly filled a thermos with the remainder of the coffee.

Tightening the lid on the thermos, she said, "This is not the Easter miracle I was hoping for."

"I know." He said las he looked in the mirror by the door and he put his coat on. He adjusted his hat. "Tell the kids, I am sorry. I will call you as soon as I can." Taking the thermos from her, he leaned down and kissed her on the forehead.

~~~

Softly landing on this lush green hill.
I want to roll down it like a child.

Where am I?
Panic sweeps over me.

I want to go home, I don't know where I am.
Am I lost?

Words echo through my soul, "Found her."
Closing my eyes I recite my prayer.

Hail Mary, Full of Grace, the Lord is with thee.
Blessed are thou among women and
Blessed is the fruit of your womb Jesus...

The Blue lady reappears.
Angelic voices burst through the clouds.

The melody lifts my soul.
The words echo and say, "Can you hear me?"
Whispering softly, it calls my name.

The blue lady gently whispers,
"Some things are hard to understand,
when life doesn't go as planned"

Reflecting through a window I hope to see God's plan but all I
see are the eyes of a doe staring back at me.
~~~~~~

AM Grout

~3~ DAVE ROLLAND

I live less than ten minutes to any given point in this small town. Lived here all my life. I love the small town community where almost everyone knows your name, at least in the neighborhood that your supermarket is. There used to be three supermarkets but the need for three dwindled to two, when one of them closed a few years ago.

The town of Tymingsly is a great place to live. People are friendly and always smiling, until four days ago. Now there is one less smile in the population of 11,617 that we will never see and as I make my way to her parents' house, I know I will be greeted with a smile of hope but just as quickly I will erase any smile they may ever have again.

Delivering news like this doesn't get easier with the job. The first time I notified the next of kin was to Mrs. Stephens. The reality of telling her that her only daughter died in a car accident just miles from her house forced me to imagine if it was my own daughter.

My shift was to be over in thirty minutes when I got the call to respond with an ambulance to an accident at the corner of Stafford and Market Street.

The driver of the oncoming car hadn't judged his speed nor the accuracy of his left turn when his truck collided with her small Toyota. She had the right of way, traveling eastbound over the bridge. The driver of the truck slammed into her door. There happened to be a nurse in the car behind her. Her assistance at the moment of impact was heaven sent but by the time I arrived, the girl had died.

The nurse hung her head knowing there was nothing she could have done. She explained in detail what she had witnessed. We identified the girl, booked the driver of the truck for vehicular manslaughter, DUI, and gross negligence. As the responding officer, it was my job to inform the next of kin.

Mrs. Stephens opened the side door as I stepped out of my car. Her curiosity rose when she saw the police car traveling down her dead end street, and parking in her driveway.

"Is there a problem, Officer?" She said politely, standing on her porch with a pitcher of lemonade in her hand. Taking off my cap, I responded, "Hello ma'am, I apologize for the intrusion."

There was no easy way to tell her. I verified that she was the mother of the girl in the car; then without choking on my words, I said; "Ma'am, I am sorry to inform you that your daughter was involved in an accident this evening."

Without hesitation, she opened the door and placed the lemonade pitcher on the kitchen table. The table was set for two. She and her husband were about to enjoy their dinner. The juice from the steak was inching its way around the serving plate. Her husband had just sat down, eager to dig in, when they spotted the cruiser pulling into their driveway.

"Where is she?" her father asked. "Is she okay?" Taking a deep breath, I repeated the words that I had been practicing on the 4000 feet it took me to drive here. "Ma'am, Sir, I am sorry to tell you that she was involved in a fatal accident."

"What are you saying?" her father demanded, pushing his plate into the center of the table. His wife walked over to him and held his hands as they listened to me explain.

Standing in the doorway, I explained a few of the details. I told them there was a nurse at the scene and she did all she could before the ambulance arrived. Her father looked at me like I was the one that caused the accident.

"Sir, I am very sorry." I said; knowing there were some questions I needed to ask, including if he would identify her at the hospital. After sharing the details, he followed me to the hospital, leaving his wife home with a neighbor praying I was wrong.

Every tragedy that I have had to be the messenger of bad news, has become embedded in my memory. The faces of the next of kin are images that haunt me. The department offered counseling, which I refused until the day I found that Lakewood boy hanging in the woods.

I became a police officer to protect and serve. I did not want to deliver news of death, and especially not suicide. The counselor explained that people absorb tragedy in different ways. The exposure police officers witness on the front lines often can bring on an array of psychological issues. The unstoppable crimes and traumatic

AM Grout

events can create anger that could get in the way of them doing their job.

I assured her that it wouldn't get in the way of my job. I wasn't angry, I merely sought counseling because seeing that boy hanging was not a description that I wanted to share with his family, nor my own.

A psychological evaluation is normal during contract negotiations, and mandatory after engaging with an armed suspect. Passing a psych evaluation is serious business. Most officers are aware that nothing said to a counselor, or even a peer is confidential, unless it is in writing prior to the conversation. "Off the Record" only goes so far.

The police academy gives minimal training for death notifications to next of kin. I suspect it was a subject no one wanted to teach. When the subject came up, we often would discuss the matter of discovery because in cases of homicides, it was important to listen to clues that could help solve the investigation.

This was exactly how we solved the death of Mrs. Medalis on Maple Street. We didn't have to inform her husband of her death. He actually called us. Seems she fell down the stairs and died. Sounds like an easy report to file but as any good detective will share, a crime scene needs to be evaluated for many reasons.

When we arrived at the house, her body was laying at the bottom of the stairs, covered by a blanket. Her husband draped it over her because he didn't want to see her that way. He explained that he heard her fall down the stairs and when he got to her, she had no pulse.

I lifted the blanket. Her bathrobe had fallen below her shoulder but remained tied at the waist. She had no slippers on, and the way the robe gathered around her, shared with us that she was naked. Blood seeped from the back of her head, her fingers twitched as I checked her eyeballs for signs of life. She was dead alright.

We called headquarters to secure the scene and I proceeded to take Mr. Medalis's statement. As I scanned the room, it did look accidental but the fact that she was naked under that blanket made me consider it could be more.

Mr. Medalis composed himself professionally to give me the facts. He was in the basement working, when he heard a loud noise. He yelled up to her, assuming she dropped something down the stairs. After a few minutes of not hearing her respond, he came upstairs to look for her. That's when he saw her on the ground. He ran over to her. Her head was bleeding, her arms twisted beneath her and she just laid there lifeless.

He immediately called 911. The dispatcher told him they would send an ambulance and an officer was on the way. She asked if he knew how to perform CPR. He said he did. He put the phone down and tried but she wasn't breathing. He told the dispatcher to hurry.

I asked why she was naked. He told me she had been in the shower. He mentioned she had complained of a headache earlier and she must have passed out as she walked past the stairway to her room.

Back at the station, we reviewed our notes. The officers that observed the scene, as well as the statement and observations I made when I arrived were recorded. The deadly fall down the stairs may have looked accidental but we all agreed it could be more.

The bed was neatly made. The bathroom neat and tidy. Nothing seemed out of the ordinary except for an opened box of sexual toys found on the bed. The Medical Examiner rolled her over and discovered bruising on her backside not consistent from just a fall. One of the investigators noted a neatly twirled scarf and a pair of nipple clamps in the kitchen trash barrel. We awaited the autopsy.

The autopsy revealed a blow to the side of the head, and two broken ribs. Sure all that could have happened from the fall, but further analysis indicated blunt force, like a foot. So with careful investigation, and close grievance support for the widower, we realized we had a cover-up.

The couple was engaged in their own private world of sex. Consented or not- is not ours to judge but discovering the scarf in the trash that was used as a blindfold, the markings on her nipples, and the handprint on her back, was all we needed to investigate further.

Perhaps, the scarf had been removed after she was pushed down the stairs, a forceful blow to the head furthered any damage she received from the fall. Throwing a blanket over her before calling us, enlightened us to his cover up.

He told us he grabbed the blanket off the couch and covered her before we got there because she was only in her robe, fresh out of a shower, yet upon that investigation we discovered the tub hadn't been used. That's an easy test, no water marks on the shower door, or on the floors. There was no wet towel to indicate she dried off, and no sign of anyone else in the bathroom.

We discussed he most likely blindfolded her to lead her on an adventure. Dressed in nothing but a robe and nipple clamps, she followed his commands. He walks her to the stairs, and with one forceful surprising move, he pushes her down the stairs.

Her hand tried to grab the railing but missed, breaking two fingernails in route. Tumbling over herself, her neck breaks, perhaps she tried to cough, to breathe, or even scream, but she couldn't, she died instantly. We imagine Mr. Medalis removed the scarf to see her eyes staring at him. He removes the nipple clamps, walks away with the scarf and rolls it up before placing it in the middle of the trash barrel.

Picking up the phone, he hears a gurgling sound. Thinking she is alive, he walks back with the phone in hand and sees her body twitching. Just nerves reacting. He kicks her twice in the ribs then once in the head. No movement. Her eyes still open but only the whites showing. He calls 911 to report his wife has fallen and is unconscious.

The dispatcher instructs him on CPR. He says he can't because her mouth is closed. She gives him more instructions, he says he is doing it but all he does is prop her neck back so that an attempt looks like it was done.

Hearing the sound of the cruisers, he walks to the door and cries to the dispatcher, "Please hurry, she is not responding."

A warrant for his arrest was never made because the District Attorney said it was too circumstantial. There was no record of domestic violence, and even though the evidence pointed to murder. It simply could be a cover-up to an accident.

Jessica's death certainly wouldn't be ruled an accident. She has been missing for four days now. Her dead body located three miles from where she disappeared, two miles from her parent's house and less than a half mile from her own apartment. All the questions needed answers. And I had the one answer her parents didn't want to hear.

~~

Peeking through a rainbow. I wonder...
Who was she? Where is she?

Praying for a miracle.
Will she return regretting leaving as she had?

I search for my keys, I cannot find them.
I search for my purse, I do not need it.

There is breaking news on the screen.
I readjust my eyes to the news being reported.

Searching alongside everyone, the tears flow.
Praying and asking the question why?

I want revenge.
An eye for an eye.

But, this is just a dream.
I am among the beautiful flowers on the altar.

My pain is gone.
The need for revenge has ended.

Then a painful thought pierces my soul.
It is undefinable.

Questions swirl in so many heads.
Fear builds.

The horror of reality makes me question.
Who is this girl? Could it be me?
~~~~~

AM Grout

~4~   NIGHTLY NEWS

Dave Rolland had been a fixture at the Brigg's home since Jessica was reported missing. When he wasn't at their house, he was following up on the leads the department had been receiving; including one about a white van being outside Greenways a few hours before closing time, the night Jessica was last seen.

Dave found the white van thanks to one of the business that had purchased supplies off its traveling showroom. The man owning the van was questioned, and the van inspected. He and the Chief determined the man was not involved in her disappearance.

Another caller reported Jessica was seen at a fraternity party that night at Hinsdale University. Some officers went over and checked it out, but it seemed to be mistaken identity.

Chief Robinson sent officers to check the bus stations, the airports, and the train stations. No one reported seeing Jessica. The chances of her leaving town without any identification or any of her belongings seemed farfetched. Her parents, Mariam and Walter Briggs agreed.

That shoe print on the door at Greenways indicated someone could have been lying on the floor and kicked the door. The forensics team determined it came from a sneaker and according to Kathy, Jessica's roommate; Jessica wasn't wearing sneakers.

AM Grout

The owner of Greenways, Carol Stypeck, had never noticed the mark on the door before. The question was when was that mark made and by what.

Carol had been renting that location for less than four years, so it could have been there that long. The state forensics team was continuing that investigation.

Dave interviewed Jessica's roommate, Kathy Fern. She was shocked to learn Jessica was missing. She informed Dave that she had just seen her the night before. She told him about how she brought Jessica a change of clothes around dinner time. He asked for all the details.

Kathy said, "I called Jessica a little after five to see how she was feeling. She hadn't been feeling well earlier. She told me she got her period and asked me if I would bring her a change of clothes. I did. I dropped her off a green skirt, a pair of black underwear and two maxi pads. I offered to get her something at McDonalds, so I stopped and got her a sprite and hamburger. She was appreciative when I got there and quickly changed her clothes. She joked about being able to wash her clothes while she worked. She seemed fine, complained of some cramps and of possibly catching a bug from school."

Learning about Kathy stopping at McDonald's explained where the soda on the counter came from, and the burger wrapper found in the trash. It also provided Dave and the other detectives to consider that Jessica may have put her bloody underwear in the grocery bag and tossed them to into the dumpster out back, missing the dumpster and landing next to it. Dave didn't share that information with the Briggs, nor that a 911 call came in; nor that there was a cruiser across from Greenways an hour before closing.

Sargent Scott McKylie was on duty that night. Scott said he was going to respond to the 911 hang up call from Greenways but by the time he got there, he got a call to respond to a domestic dispute on Northland Street. He drove by Greenways, saw Jessica working at the counter so he assumed it was a false alarm. He was embarrassed he didn't go in so he asked Dave to keep that on the down low.

Dave left a message for Jessica's boyfriend Joe Dyer to call him. Joe had been away working on location in Winslow, ninety miles north of Tymingsly since Monday. When he came home Thursday night, he called Detective Rolland. Dave immediately met Joe at his house to question him.

Joe was nervous as he talked, but seemed honest. He told him the last few weeks Jessica had been pushing him away. Joe was suspicious she was seeing someone else.

He said, "About a month or so ago, Jessica and I broke up for a week and a half. We made up, but this past weekend at Buckley's we did have words. On Sunday, Jessica left me a message on my machine. She said she needed time to think and that we would talk on Friday, which is why I haven't heard from her. I wanted to call her but she said she would call me. I left early Monday morning and just got back now; and I haven't heard from her."

Dave asked him about the fight on Saturday. Joe said, "Mike Piccard walked into Buckley's Saturday night around midnight. He made eye contact with Jessica and I made a comment asking her what was up with that. She

37

started to tell me that Mike flirted with her at the coffee shop the other morning. I got upset and accused her of liking it."

Joe continued, "It isn't the first time, Mike's flirted with her. Jess told me that Mike gave her the creeps but I was drinking and she got mad at me. She screamed at me to leave her alone. That is when Mike came over and walked me out the door. I would have punched the fucker but being in uniform makes him untouchable. The guy is a dirt bag. Teddy was there that night, he came out to calm me down. I asked him to make sure Jess got home alright. I called her Sunday, but she didn't answer. She called me later and said she would call me Friday."

He couldn't replay the message on the machine because it had been recorded over.

He asked Detective Dave Rolland if Mike was working that night that Jessica was last seen. Dave checked and found that he was, but on the other side of town. Jessica's parents didn't suspect Joe of foul play, but he was on the short list of suspects. Admitting they had been arguing was a red flag.

The other suspect was Teddy Teggotta. Joe's friend and Jessica's ride home on Saturday night. Teddy was possibly the last to see her before she was discovered missing. Teddy came immediately to the station when Dave called him. He was so concerned and worried about Jessica. Dave warned him that he was a suspect since he was the last to see her.

Teddy was nervous but he shared all the details of last seeing Jessica. He had stopped by around 8pm to pick up a chair cover that his mother was having repaired for their banquet hall. The Teggottas owned Rosewood Thyme Theatre, a unique dinner theatre style restaurant. Teddy's father Jack Teggotta inherited it in 1974, three weeks after he turned 21. His parents and his only sister died in a horrible car accident on the Interstate; leaving Jack sole owner.

Rosewood Thyme Theatre opened in the early 1950's as a summer theatre. Jack's sister ran a summer theatre camp for kids when she moved home after having minimal success as an actress in New York. Jack's parents received requests to host weddings a few years later and thus began the use of the barn as a banquet facility. They hosted small weddings, Christmas parties and many family reunions.

In 1968, a large pavilion was built to accommodate outdoor weddings and the addition of two modern ballrooms and a commercial kitchen was built on the far end of the pavilion. The barn still holds the original country charm and Teddy's parents continue the tradition of children's theater in the summer.

Teddy told Dave that Jessica seemed fine when he was there. "When I first got there I didn't see her, she was in the back room so I ducked in front of the counter. When she came out, she obviously heard me. I didn't say anything but when I heard her pick up the phone, I jumped up and surprised her. She freaked and tossed a box at me. We laughed. She told me she was about to call the police. Then I asked her if she and Joe made up. She said they had." Ted paused before he added, "She really seemed fine."

Dave detailed everything in his notebook, and proceeded to ask more questions

"How long did you stay at Greenways?"

"About twenty minutes or so."

"Did anyone else stop in?"

"No. A few women walked by headed to the Korner Pocket but no one came in."

"You said it was around eight?"

"Yes. I think so. It could have been 8:30, I don't know. I had to run a few errands for my mother. I got back to the Theatre around ten and then went to Buckley's for a few drinks until closing."

Dave knew the 911 call came in at 8:08, so he wasn't sure what to make of Teddy's lapse of time, but he knew Teddy's family and didn't see any reason for him to lie about the time. The rest of the questioning involved where Teddy went and who was at Buckley's. Dave knew he would have to verify all of this information to rule Teddy out as a suspect.

"Can you tell me about Jessica and Joe's relationship?" Dave asked.

Teddy admitted that Joe and Jessica fought when they were drinking. He said that happened a lot but they always made up. Teddy confirmed the argument Jessica and Joe had at Buckley's Saturday night. He said he gave Jessica a ride home that night.

"When I got to her apartment, she opened the passenger side door of the Jeep and fell onto the sidewalk. She didn't realize how high my Jeep was. She scraped her hand on the sidewalk and it was bleeding. We laughed. I helped her into the house and got her a Band-Aid and some water. Her roommate Kathy was there with her boyfriend."

Dave kept Teddy for over three hours for questions. As Teddy was leaving, Dave asked, "Do you happen to have a receipt for the chair cover you picked up?" Dave had reviewed the slips at Greenways and hadn't seen it.

"Uh, Jess couldn't find it. She said she would ask Carol about it and have her call my mom. We have a house account so it wasn't a big deal."

Once Teddy's interview was over, Dave began to type his notes from the morning Jessica went missing. Making notes that when he arrived at the shop, the door was unlocked and the place was empty. He had shouted "Hello" then poked his head into the three doors behind the counter. One led to a dumpster behind the building, another to the bathroom and the third to the back room where the rotating rack of finished dry cleaning hung, each covered in plastic with the Greenways logo imprinted at the top.

When Carol returned to the shop, she told him she had gone next door to Gallo's Pharmacy to see if Jessica was there. She wasn't. Carol told Dave that Jessica's purse and jacket were still in the store. She pointed to the white Toyota outside and said, "That is her car. I can't understand where she would be. She is very responsible and always closes properly. I called her apartment, there was no answer. Her mother said she hasn't seen her either."

Dave listened to Carol's worry as he made notes of the condition of the shop. The money was in the register untouched, the shop looked neat except for a water bottle and crumpled paper towels on the floor. Carol said, "Jessica said she didn't feel well last night when I left but she assured me she was fine to work. I had to teach a sewing class at the library so I didn't have much time to talk with her."

Dave asked Carol details about Jessica. She was twenty-three, average in height and weight and always happy. She hired Jessica two years ago when she started teaching sewing classes. Carol said, "Jessica contemplated quitting Greenways when she enrolled in the master's program at Hinsdale University but she agreed to stay on for Tuesday and Wednesday nights so I could teach my sewing classes. Truth is she needed the extra money too."

Jessica worked the front counter taking in dry cleaning and small loads of same day laundry. The small shop had two sets of washers and dryers, as well as all the proper dry cleaning and tailoring needs.

Carol told Dave when she arrived at work, she saw Jessica's car in front of the shop and figured Jessica had forgotten something from the night before. The door was unlocked.

Carol hollered, "Hey Jess everything okay?" There was no answer.

Carol knocked on the bathroom door. No answer. She opened the door and saw crumpled paper towels on the floor in there and under the sales counter. "Jessica?" she called out again. Still no answer.

She could see Jessica's purse under the counter on the shelf where she always kept it and her coat was hanging in the backroom.

Carol then opened the door leading to the dumpster, Jessica wasn't there either. She decided to call the police.

The dispatcher told her a cruiser would come over to take a report.

Carol then reached under the counter and retrieved a rolodex. She looked up Jessica's apartment number and dialed it. There was no answer. She then dialed Jessica's mother's number.

"Hello Mariam, this is Carol at Greenways, Sorry to bother you but is Jessica there by any chance?"

Mariam told her she hadn't talked with her since the weekend. Carol shared her concerns. Mariam agreed that it didn't sound like Jessica to just leave everything like that. Carol told her the police were on their way. Mariam said she would be right down.

Carol walked over to the pharmacy. They were just opening up for the day. She shared with them her concerns that the store was unlocked and Jessica's car was in the parking lot. The girl working the counter had her excessive amount of hairspray holding the fluffy style to her hair.

The girl only knew Jessica as the counter girl that arrived when her own shift ended. She suggested Jessica could have gotten a ride home but leaving the door unlocked was weird.

When Dave arrived, he and Carol walked the around the shop looking for anything out of place. Carol said it all looked okay. The front counter was clean, a poster with pricing and dry cleaning policies hung above the back counter which held metal bins with invoices.

Dave opened the bathroom door the crumpled paper towels on the floor that had missed the trash barrel.

Carol said that was a little unusual, especially since there was some on the floor under the sales counter as well.

Dave walked into the bathroom. An unopened pack of toilet paper sat on a small shelf across from the toilet along with some cleaning supplies. Behind the door was one of those mops they sell at the fair, a corn broom, and a dust pan.

Dave made a mental note of everything as he walked into the backroom. Jessica's coat was hanging on the hook next to the door. A mechanical clothing rack held laundered clothes ready for pick up. The only desk was against the wall next to the doorway that held stacks of invoices for dry cleaning supplies from Brown and Pratt. Assorted pens and special markers were in an open cigar box; and colorful twisty ties and cohesive paper bands used to wrap the tops of the hangers were spilling out of the plastic bags that had been ripped opened. Next to the desk were open boxes filled with new hangers, and plastic sheets customized with Greenways logo.

Carol apologized for the room looking disorganized but she assured Detective Rolland nothing was out of place. Then she spotted a black mark on the outside of the bathroom door. She said she had never noticed that before. Dave examined it and said, "I'm going to call forensics to determine exactly what that is." He clicked his radio receiver and said, "Requesting ten-twenty-five, over".

A few minutes later three police cruisers pulled into the parking lot. One cruiser parked in a parking spot and two others were left running in front of Greenways. Carol explained to the neighbors gathered outside the plaza that she saw a black mark at the bottom of the bathroom door. She was afraid she was making something out of nothing but Dave reassured her that until Jessica was located, they needed to investigate every detail.

The officers began securing the property when Mariam Briggs arrived. An officer at the door tried to stop her from entering. Carol immediately told the officer Mariam was Jessica's mother. Detective Rolland nodded to let her in and he introduced himself to her. "Mrs. Briggs, I am Detective Rolland, I appreciate you coming down here."

"Have you found her?" she asked.

"No, Ma'am. I assure you were are looking into her whereabouts but at this time, we are considering she may have been forcefully taken sometime between closing last night and now."

"What are you saying?" Mariam looked around the shop; "She was kidnapped?"

"We don't know ma'am. All I can tell you at this time is, I will be running this investigation and I promise we will do everything to find her."

Mariam asked Carol if she could use the phone to call her husband.

When Walter Briggs, Mariam's husband arrived, a photographer from the police department was taking photographs of the entrance of Greenways. His camera lens focused on the sales counter and the counter behind it which contained dry cleaning policies thumbtacked to a corkboard, invoices arranged neatly in a metal desktop wire sorter, and a pad of unused Greenways Alteration and More invoices.

A single yellow sunflower in a glass of water was on the back counter, barely visible over the height of the register on the front counter. Nothing looked out of place from that angle. On the shelves below the register was a cabinet, housing a small safe, a few office supplies and Jessica's olive green purse with the shoulder strap tucked underneath. Two rolling carts sorting incoming laundry were neatly tucked next to the cabinet under the counter.

The officer took photographs of the paper towels on the floor and in the waste basket. Using his gloved hand, he moved the paper towels around in the barrel and discovered an uneaten McDonald's burger and vomit. He took more photos; then opened the door leading to the dumpster. The door closed behind him.

Dave was looking through Jessica's purse when Walter Briggs arrived. The small pocket in front contained a few receipts, a pack of spearmint gum, and a business card from the Blue Lily Florist in Tymingsly. The card had the words "Something to Brighten Your Day" written on it; and her car keys. Two of the receipts were for coffee from Coffee Partner.

Dave frequented Coffee Partner, it was the closest place to the station to get good coffee. One of the receipts was from last Friday for a coffee and a cinnamon raisin bagel with strawberry cream cheese. The time stamp on the receipt was 7:14. The other receipt was too worn to see the date. A gas receipt from the station next to Coffee Partner was folded with a bank receipt indicating her bank balance was $1322.91 was also from yesterday. The time stamp from the bank was 16:36.

Inside Jessica's purse was her wallet, a makeup kit, and a floral covered datebook. A small zippered pocket inside the purse contained a tampon, some folded tissues, a memorial card from her grandmother's funeral, and a lot of loose receipts, including one from a department store where she bought a skirt in December.

Paper clipped inside her datebook were a few business cards. One indicated a hair appointment at The Dellaria Hair studio on Main Street in Hinsdale on May 10, and another was for a dentist appointment on June 3 with Dr. Theo Bolan. Behind Dr. Bolan's card was a pamphlet for the Hinsdale Planned Parenthood Clinic.

A coffee lover's bonus card from Coffee Partners fell out of her wallet as he removed her license. She still had six more coffees to buy before earning a free one.

Detective Rolland quickly put all the items back into her purse and zipped it when Walter Briggs entered. Dave made a mental note to finish the inventory of her purse.

He introduced himself to Walter and expressed his empathy for the situation. Walter embraced his wife. For over two hours, investigators photographed every corner of the shop, including inside each washer, dryer, trash barrel and shelf.

Mariam went into the pharmacy next door and asked to use the phone. She called Becky Connors, the owner of Helping Hands Therapy, the place Jessica worked on Mondays, Wednesdays and Fridays. Becky hadn't seen Jessica since dismissal yesterday and didn't plan to see her until Monday since it was a long weekend.

Becky was shocked to learn Jessica was missing. She had known Jessica since she was nine and knew her to be a very responsible girl. Becky hired her when she was in high school to work her summer programs and eventually hired her part time during the school year. It was a perfect fit for Becky and Jessica. Jessica received college credit for working at Helping Hands and was scheduled to get her Masters in Behavioral Science in the fall.

An officer reentered from the back door and motioned for Dave to come outside. An inexpensive pressure treated fence surrounded the dumpster. Officers were standing around a discarded plastic grocery bag next to the dumpster. On the ground was some loose plastic and a few hangers that seemed to have missed the dumpster.

"Sir, the dumpster is empty except for a few bottles of laundry detergent, however we found this." He pointed to the bag they were all looking at. "We haven't moved it but we did look inside." Dave bent down, and opened the bag exposing a pair of flesh colored underwear covered in blood.

The officers began to speculate if they belonged to someone from the Korner Pocket. Dave had them take it into evidence, not knowing if it was part of the crime scene. But when Kathy came forward with her information about dropping off a change of clothes, it made sense that perhaps Jessica just tossed them herself. Dave decided to exclude that from his notes, since it was private information.

~~~

Good St. Michael
Protector of our law enforcement
Watch over them, their families
and the community.

Keep them safe,
Give them courage,
Protect their lives,
Forgive their faults.

Navigate them to overcome all obstacles.
Guide righteous actions,
Nudge gentle compassion,
And in temptation remind respect
and honor.

The oath is as real as the air unseen.
Integrity, Character, Courage and Accountability.
Serving Truth and providing Trust.
Providing what is virtuous and right.
~~~~~~

AM Grout

~5~ NO PEACE AT THE DOOR

Walter Briggs was laying on the couch in his living room on Sycamore Drive. All the homes on Sycamore have the same mudroom and two car garage attached to the frame of the two story houses. The Briggs' driveway was curved in front so one could make a U-turn or park in the garage. The parts of the front yard that weren't paved were filled with meticulously placed perennials which prided the neighborhood with curb appeal in the summer.

The front door opened, Walter and his wife exchanged eye contact. His wife had been staring at the newspaper on the kitchen table. The headline read, "Girl Missing". Mariam Briggs carefully circled the words over and over again until the words were scribbled away. A set of rosary beads and a lit candle remained in the middle of the table.

Samantha Reese, Mariam's sister, walked in carrying a tin foiled covered casserole dish marked Baked Ziti. "Mrs. Marsh dropped this by last night." says Samantha.

"I'm not hungry." Mariam replied.

Samantha turned on the oven. Mariam turned the paper over. The top of the newspaper had a picture of a bunny and some colored eggs. It was Easter.

"I haven't missed a mass on Good Friday or Easter Sunday ever. But I just couldn't go. I wanted to, but I can't have everyone looking at me wondering what I am thinking. I don't even know what I am thinking!

I've been praying all night; incessantly saying St. Anthony's prayer. "Tony, Tony turn around something is missing that needs to be found. And this something is my daughter!" Mariam screamed, slamming her hand on the table. "Why aren't they listening? Where could she be!?"

Samantha was just as worried as her sister but knew she needed to comfort her. "Mariam, God will hear our prayers, he is working on getting her home."

Mariam looked at her sister and said, "What if someone did something to her?"

Samantha said, "We can't think like that. I can't think like that! Let's just pray."

Together they held hands and prayed an Our Father. Mariam added, "And please, please, please bring Jess home safely."

Mariam put her head into her hands as her elbows rested on the table. Samantha gave her a side hug and said, "He will. He has to."

The oven alerted Samantha that it was preheated. She retrieved the casserole and placed it in the oven setting the timer for thirty minutes. She then took a set of keys out of her purse on the counter and went outside to her Pontiac Sunbird parked in the driveway.

She unlocked the car, leaned in and retrieved something small in the cup holder. It was a stone. The stone was slightly bigger than the onyx she was wearing on her right hand. She had found it on the ground as she walked into work on Thursday morning. She always enjoyed finding flat rocks on the beach as child. This stone wasn't flat but it was covered with mica, which allowed the sunlight to reflect off it like a mirror.

Samantha held it up to the sun. The mica held all the colors of the rainbow but the blue was most dominant. She put the stone in her pocket and went back in the house.

A few minutes later, the doorbell rang. Walter jumped up from the couch. Out the window he could see the police cruiser. Mariam asked her husband, "Who is it?"

"It's Detective Rolland." He said. Mariam quickly walked over to the door as Samantha began to make a fresh pot of coffee.

Four days has passed since he told the Briggs that he would find their daughter. He felt nauseous as Walter opened the front door. He removed his hat and said, "I have some news."

Mariam looked at him and said, "Where is she?"

Dave blinked his eyes to stop the tear that was forming. He cleared his throat and said, "We received a call an hour ago. A body was discovered by a man walking his dog in the woods on Stafford St."

"Her body?" Mariam began to shake, then she shook her head and moaned, "No, no, no."

Samantha came over and put her arm around Mariam. Tears couldn't come fast enough.

Walter didn't let go of the door handle as Dave explained that he was on his way there. He didn't have many details but he wanted them to know before the news began speculating.

Walter squeezed the door knob with all his strength. He wanted to punch Dave but he knew he was just the messenger.

"Would you like to sit down?" He asked Walter, gesturing to the couch. He shook his head no. Mariam was sitting on the stairs leading up to the second floor. Samantha sat with her.

Mariam's heart had been pierced. She wanted all the details but then she wanted none. She shook her head repeating the words, "No, no, no!"

Walter took a deep breath and asked, "You think it's her don't you?"

Dave said, "It fits her description but I cannot confirm anything at the moment."

"What if it isn't her?" Mariam asked.

"Mariam, I hope it isn't, but all indications are that it very well could be. It could be hours before we collect all the evidence and remove her body. I just want you to know what is going on." He gestures to the street where a Channel 6 news truck had pulled up.

Dave closed the front door. "As you can see the media is anxious to get a statement. And at this time there is none."

Walter reached for his jacket on the banister, "Should I go with you?"

Dave shook his head, "No. It's better if you don't go to Stafford Street. The media will follow and make confirmation before we do. I will call you if I need you to identify her, if it is her."

Walter nodded his head. Before opening the door, Dave said, "I strongly advise you not to talk to the press until you hear from me." He looked at Mariam on the stairs and said, "Mariam, this might not be her."

The timer went off in the kitchen. Samantha went to turn it off. Walter put his arms around his wife and said, "He's right, it might not be our Jessica."

Mariam wanted to believe those words but her spine shivered with a reality that her daughter could be dead. She closed her eyes and just let Walter hold her.

Outside, Detective Rolland addressed the news reporters quietly and said, "We have no comments at this time. Please respect the family's privacy."

The news reporter nodded as his crew setup for a live broadcast.

AM Grout

~~~

Extending a hand, I do not hesitate.
The wrinkles on her forehead concern me.
But her voice reassures me that I am safe.

In the back of a car we ride into my driveway.
I am so excited.
I am home.

I want to lie in my bed but the recliner replaces where it once was.
The blanket Gram made me is on the backside of the chair.
It wraps around me effortlessly.

The sound of a bell rings.
The lady holds my hand as I hear a sound I have never heard before.
A whimper, a moan, a cry comes from below.

One hand muffles her mouth.
Her eyes stare blankly at a man with a hat in his hand.
She tries to catch her breath.

I put my hand on her trembling shoulder.
She puts her hand over her heart.
I consider she might be frightened by me.

The man holds back tears in his eyes.
I ask, "What did you say to her?"
He doesn't even look at me.
He doesn't even acknowledge me.

Gesturing towards the couch.
Tears stream inside my father's eyes.
My arms stretch wide placing another hand on his shoulder.
I want to wave a white ribbon but there is none.
~~~~~

~6~STONEWOOD EXTENSION

Stonewood Extension is an undeveloped portion of land owned by the town. The city planners have discussed creating a new neighborhood in the wooded section across from Stonewood Place. The development began and just stopped over ten years ago, installing drains under the path to section off the underground stream that rises each spring. The future road could connect Stafford Street to the private airport on the other side of town but most likely the city councilors will approve the sale of the land to a private builder.

The ground is muddy as Detective Rolland is guided by the officers securing the path to where the Chief and more officers are investigating. Yellow caution tape has been linked around trees, brush and other natural weeds.

Tire tracks form a mini ravine that Detective Rolland and the others need to step over to get to the location of the body. There are puddles within the path that lie dormant from more than the rain. Melted snow holds the reflections of the trees above which continue to drip with dew.

Looking to his left, Detective Rolland remembers the call from last summer, there was a car that was stuck in the mud. Detective Rolland recalled the story the responding officer shared at Buckley's. Many officers stop by Buckley's Bar & Grill after their shift, the owner sets aside the back room for officers only. Shop talk doesn't need to be spread like gossip but even the Chief knows we need to share to be informed. Chief is a regular there too. The general public knows not to enter that room.

"The poor kid didn't know what to say. It was obvious he went there to go parking but when the car couldn't get unstuck, he had to walk to the pay phone to call for help. I asked him what they were doing out there. The boy said he was following friends that led him off the road as a joke, and they took off on him."

The officer used the winch on the front of the Chevy Blazer cruiser and pulled him out of there. The kid thanked him and asked if he was going to call his parents. The officer winked at him and said, "Listen kid, go park on a paved street next time."

Detective Rolland stopped walking and took out his notebook and began to make some notes.

1. Trucks here?
2. Wyatt's crew?
3. Last patrol check?

On the right side of the path, a little dirt road paved by trespassers led his eye to see blackened firewood in a makeshift fire pit. Beer cans, cigarette butts and discarded packs of chewing tobacco littered the area.

Sergeant Scott McKylie picked up a large plastic ski rack made by Sport Mates. One ski was missing from the holder. Scott had a similar rack he used when he went skiing.

His often got stuck in the roof rack, making it difficult to remove. Scott handed it to another officer. "We should mark this as evidence."

The officer took it and asked, "What is it?" Scott said, "It attaches to a mount placed on the roof or trunk of a car to carry skis."

"Looks like junk to me." the officer said.

"It probably is." Said Scott. "I have one similar, they never click onto the mount on the roof properly. I usually carry mine in the back seat but I should just toss mine too. No matter, mark it as evidence."

Scott bent down and picked up a beer can. "This too." He looked in the beer can, "There are cigarettes inside, and maybe forensics can test for prints."

"What are you doing?" Dave yelled. "Put some dam gloves on and be careful!"

"Uh, sorry sir." The officer responded and headed back to the parking area to get his collection kit.

Chief Robinson heard Rolland's voice. He motioned to him to come over to the 13x13 canopy tent that had been set-up within the yellow lined area. Scott followed. A sheet was draped over the body.

"How are they?" Robinson asked Dave.

"Upset. They are hopeful that this isn't her but they are realistic to know it probably is. How are you guys?"

McKylie combed his hands through his thick gray hair and said, "Someone did a number on her. I don't know what to think. She was such a beautiful and nice girl. I knew her from Buckley's. This is hard. I'm casing the area for clues.

Someone had to have seen something back here. Maybe we can get fingerprints from some of the beer cans."

Rolland said, "I agree, but we need to be careful. You guys didn't even have gloves on. We don't need anything to get contaminated. We need to make sure this is done right."

Chief Robinson looked around and saw other men collecting evidence without gloves on. He shouted, "Get some gloves!"

McKylie said, "I get it. But shit, I think the animals already contaminated a lot."

The chief nodded his head in agreement. The white sheet covered what no one wanted to see. Dave lifted it to peek. Chief Robinson said, "The animals did do a number to her. She had to be out here for a few nights."

Rolland raised his hand to his mouth and shook his head. With a hard swallow, he took it all in. Her face, especially her eyes had nymphs and larvae on them. Her clothes, what she had left of them, were wet from the rain. Several holes in her shirt showed where a knife jabbed through her skin. Her waist was twisted such that her legs crossed at the ankles. She laid naked from the waist down with no shoes, no socks and no underwear around.

Detective Rolland turned to McKylie and asked, "Is this exactly how you found her or did someone move her?"

"That was draped over her covering her legs." he said, pointing to the green cloth that was soaked and stained with blood. "I believe the dog moved it off her. Check with Mike Piccard, he was the responding officer."

A few mayflies swarmed around the corpse, as well as the investigator's eyes. Rolland waved his hands in front of his face to shoo the flies away. "Was she killed here or do you think someone just left her here?"

McKylie shook his head, "I don't think she was killed here. I would think if she was alive, she would have run for help. It doesn't make sense."

Just then another officer came over and said, "Sir, the District Attorney is here."

The Chief looked down the path and there was Jack "Sully" Sullivan, the three time elected District Attorney. Chief Robinson walked in his direction and shook his hand.

"Hey Sully."

"What do you think, is this Jessica?" he asked. The Chief nodded.

"Initial thought is she was dumped here after being raped and stabbed somewhere else. I don't think she was attacked at the dry cleaners. There is no sign of struggle. Someone kidnapped her, raped her, and killed her. That's what I think."

Sully walked over to the tree where Rolland was observing Jessica's corpse. He winced at the condition of her body, then touched her arm to feel the density of skin and said, "The Medical Examiner can get the time of death, and what wounds might be post mortem. There isn't a lot of blood which could mean she was stabbed after she was already dead."

Officer Mike Piccard walked over, pointed to the green material and said, "That material is a skirt. It was just laying on top of her, covering her from the waist down. The man walking his dog said his dog pulled it off."

"Were you first on site?" asked Sully.

"Yes sir." Mike put his hand out and introduced himself. "I was headed back to the precinct at the end of my shift when the call came in. Do you want me to stay or go write up my report?"

The Chief grabbed Mike by the arm and said, "Buddy, we all stay here until the body is moved. This ain't no shift work anymore"

Mike replied, "Yes Sir."

Dr. Dianne LaVallee, the chief Medical Examiner for Tymingsly arrived and headed to the canopy. Scott and Mike were talking a few feet away. "I'll fucking kill the bastard myself, who did this to her." said Mike.

The District Attorney stopped his conversation with Dr. LaVallee. Media trucks were setting up at the end of the trail. "Piccard, watch your language and stay professional." he warned.

Mike looked at the media antennas on the vans and said, "Yes Sir, sorry Sir."

~~~

The car turns off the road.
Bumping my head on the door.
Where are we going?

I called out to the nurse but she wasn't there.
I didn't see anyone.
She was so nice. She stopped my pain. I am forever grateful.

The voices are inaudible.
Hello, can you help me?
My legs are tangled in a blanket, I have an itch on my knee.

The door opens and I roll onto the wet ground.
It isn't the lush green grass that I laid in before.
The brittle weeds snap as my weight shifts.

Music is playing up the path. I wander towards the music.
Incense fills the air.
The music gets louder and the voices go silent.

A light flashes and I see a couple in love walk down the path.
They kiss by the tree that was once next to me.
Maybe still is next to me.

She walks fast past the blanket that once held me.
She trips, then screams.
It's a raccoon, not me.
~~~~~~

AM Grout

~7~ CURTAIN CALL

Sixty-five year old Liz Dalker is sitting in front of a cup of tea. A votive candle illuminates the kitchen as she holds prayer beads in her hands. The kitchen clock ticks loudly, and the microwave's glow indicates it is 9:14 pm. Liz is distracted by the activity at her neighbor's house. Two twenty something year old girls live in the house. Neither ever seemed to be home at the same time. Liz knew the girls' names were Victoria Mallard and Kristina Legrand because often the mailman would mix up their mailboxes.

There was more traffic than usual at their house tonight. The police cruiser that often stopped by during the eleven o'clock news silently parked outside the girls' house. Since the baby was born, Liz had seen him walk in through the side door without knocking. She originally thought it was a brother or a friend of the girls until she saw the way he kissed the baby's mother. Their sexual and violent affection made Liz wish they closed the curtains. Liz had retired from the Department of Family Services last year and was trained to help abused women but she knew how difficult it was to help women that didn't want help.

A truck pulled in the driveway, and two people entered Victoria's house. Liz didn't pay much attention until a few minutes later when the cruiser pulled up. The officer went in, they all started talking as a girl sat on the couch.

The cop walked towards the window and pulled the curtains shut.

A few days later, the newspapers reported Jessica Briggs was found murdered. Liz tried to convince herself that her imagination was running overtime but she couldn't get the image out of her mind of what happened Wednesday night. A week after Jessica's funeral she dialed the police station and said, "I may have some information regarding Jessica Briggs."

The dispatcher forwarded the call to Detective Rolland. Rolland was examining a photo that showed the front counter area at Greenways. Carol Stypeck said nothing looked out of place. Jessica's purse sat on the back counter, keys on the front counter. She must have been getting ready to close thought Rolland. He squinted his eyes staring at the yellow flower on the counter in the photo until his phone rang.

"Detective Rolland here" he said into the receiver.
"My neighbor, she is a single mother and I believe she is in trouble." Liz took a deep breath and said, 'I think I have information that could concern Jessica Briggs too."

Detective Rolland clicked his pen. He asked Liz for her name but she said she wanted to remain anonymous.

"Wednesday night I was lighting a candle to begin my evening prayers when I saw a girl in her house visibly upset. She was crying and clutching her stomach. She sat on the couch that was covered with a sheet. I know that the girl that lives there is in a relationship with a police officer. It's none of my business but last night I saw him slap her in the kitchen. She fell to the floor so it was a pretty hard smack.

Her living room faces my house, and the picture window allows a view all the way back to her kitchen. I realize that they may have just been having a conversation but it isn't the first time he hit her. With hearing about Jessica being murdered, I had to call."

Detective Rolland had been taking many statements from all around town. Mostly from wives and girlfriends that were afraid they were going to be next. Not in the sense that they thought they would be targeted by a serial killer, which was also on the forefront of some minds, but these women were accusing their own guys.

"Ma'am, I appreciate your concern for your neighbor but unless it's happening at the moment, I cannot do anything to assist her."

"But Sir, it's more than just him hitting her. It is what I saw Wednesday night before the curtain closed. I watched my neighbor tidying her living room. It wasn't anything out of the ordinary but I noticed she covered her couch in a sheet. She clearly looked upset but I didn't think anything of it until now."

"Ma'am, we are quite busy here at the precinct, I appreciate all these details but I don't understand how this has anything to do with Jessica Brigg's case."

"Sir, Please, I can't sleep until I know I reported this. I want to mind my own business. I tried to look away and finish my evening prayers but when that truck pulled into the driveway, I felt the need to clutch my rosary beads harder."

Detective Rolland wished someone else had taken this call. He picked up his pencil and wrote some notes, "Praying a rosary when a truck pulls in the driveway."

"What kind of truck was it ma'am?" he asked, trying to sound professional and wondering how this could ever be connected to Jessica Briggs.

"It was a four door pickup truck. A guy and a girl went into the house, and I can tell you the girl had on a green skirt, and her hair was the same color as that girl's photo in the paper."

"Was the officer in the house?" Rolland asked, making a mental note to see who was on patrol in that area that night in a cruiser.

"Not then, he arrived a few minutes after them. We live on a dead end street so we don't get a lot of traffic. Like I said that officer usually stops by during the eleven o'clock news but this was much earlier."

Detective Rolland began to have the call traced. As much as this woman sounded delusional, he knew the rumors that swirled at the station about a few guys. The trace showed the address matched that of Liz Dalker, a retired clinical social worker for the state. Her address exposed what Detective Rolland didn't want to see.

Liz was neighbors to Sergeant Scott McKylie's mistress, Viki Mallard. He rolled his eyes. He knew Viki had been a bartender at Buckley's while she was in nursing school. Rumors never confirmed her affair with Scott but cops talk.

"Ma'am, does anyone else live in that house?" Detective Rolland knew Viki had a roommate so he fished for some confirmation from Liz.

"Yes, two girls in their twenties. One has a baby and I think she is a nurse."

Liz began to speak faster. "And if that was Jessica, I can tell you that they talked for a little while but didn't look happy. Like I said, that girl was on the couch. She seemed to be in pain, clutching her stomach. The police officer brought a bag when he returned to the house. After he handed the bag to his girlfriend or whatever she is to him. I couldn't see anything else after he gave her the bag, because he closed the curtain. When the curtain closed, the view of the living room was gone but not from my mind. They hardly ever close their curtains, but that night they did."

Detective Rolland quickly opened Jessica's file to Kathy's statement. Kathy had told him she dropped off a change of clothes to Jessica; a green skirt.

"Ma'am, I doubt this has anything to do with the case but we appreciate your call. Are there any other details of the truck or the girl that you can recall?"

"No Sir, both vehicles left soon after the curtain closed but I never saw the girl leave with them."

"What time was that?' asked Detective Rolland, as he wondered when he would ask Scott about these details.

"Oh it all was pretty quick, I would say long before ten at the latest. The house was quiet until three am when her roommate came home. I always hear her car and wake for a few seconds."

"Ma'am, would you consider coming to the station to write a statement for the file?" Rolland asked.

"As a former mandated reporter, I don't need to. I have informed you and that is all I am required to do; but I will tell you if that girl across the street gets hurt, I will personally press charges against that cop."

"Ma'am, I assure you, I will look into the information you gave me. May I ask for your contact information so I can follow up with you?"

"I will give it to you, provided it does not go into the file." She gave her contact and he shared his private number telling her that if she saw any signs of abuse again, to call immediately and they would respond.

~~~

Thank you for being here.
As creepy as he is, he can help.
The pain is real. The blood is too.

Can he keep a secret?
Can you?

Please don't make the call,
I just want a little help. I need a little help.
His voice grows faint.

The grass is so soft but I wonder how
I still feel the coldness of the floor.
Shivers run over me.

I wish I had a blanket.
I hear the words, "I'll be right back."
And you arrived.

You shared compassion. You held my hand.
You swore to keep my secret.
Now I need to lay my head.

I trust you. I trust God. Everything will be alright.
I am so sorry.
In your hands I place my trust.

I must trust her too...
Please Lord, let me trust them all.

Please stay with me awhile.
Pray with me awhile.
I am so sorry. I am so thankful.
~~~~~~

AM Grout

~8~ BUCKLEY'S

Officer Mike Piccard stopped at Buckley's Bar after his shift Wednesday night. He showed up with blood on his uniform telling tales of a domestic dispute he came from. The woman had a bloody nose but she refused to press charges against her husband. Mike had to walk away without a report.

Buckley's Bar & Grill was a simple neighborhood bar sitting on the ground floor of the apartment building at 26 Market Street. Mike McKylie purchased the building twenty-six years ago and opened Buckley's ten years after. He moved to Florida two years ago making him an absentee owner. His brother, Scott McKylie maintained the property.

The second floor was Mike's old apartment. Scott kept it for his own use and allowed the living room to be used for private consultations with the precinct's Medical Examiner. Officers could be evaluated and examined there, as well as any concerns their families may have. Having this private office space saved time and paperwork for minor injuries needing tetanus shots and stitches. There was never any trouble at Buckley's unless secrets shared on the second floor made their way out.

The bartender, Ken Levine, kept eyes on everything and kept quiet to everyone except Sergeant Scott McKylie. They graduated high school together and when Ken finished his tour in Panama, Scott recommended him to his brother to run the bar.

Ken heard the rumors that Scott was having an affair with one of the bartenders. He never confirmed any affair but he saw Scott signal Viki many times and she would disappear up the back stairs.

Victoria was in her last semester of her nursing program, and she worked at the Hinsdale Planned Parenthood Center during the day, which was one of the reasons she was hired to work at Buckley's. Dr. LaVallee called on her to assist with an officer's superficial injury, or monitor an IV line of saline to cure one of the cops from a hangover before they had to report for duty. Ken did not believe that all the nights Scott requested her assistance was for those purposes.

Victoria had started working at the Hinsdale Planned Parenthood Center (HPPC) a few years after high school as a receptionist. She appreciated the opportunity to help educate and prevent unwanted pregnancies. Obtaining birth control was as simple as making an appointment at the center, but so many were afraid to walk in because they feared being judged. Victoria didn't judge them, she admired that they were protecting themselves.

After a year at HPPC, Victoria applied to nursing school where she did a clinical program in midwifery with Dr. Dianna LaVallee. Dianna liked her and helped to get her a job at Buckley's with some off duty hours at the precinct's clinic. The cops liked her. She was discreet and always available, especially when Dr. LaVallee was out of town.

Victoria knew the basics and under Dr. LaVallee she could be of great assistance. She rented a small ranch on Clifton Place. Soon after that she began an affair with Sergeant Scott McKylie and he turned to her for private medical attention.

After a few months, he often brought first time drug users and drunk kids to Victoria's house for private attention. Victoria would sober the kids up, nurse them back to health and they would get a second chance without charges being pressed nor their parents knowing. Scott preferred not to be the cop to arrest his neighbor's kid. The kids were thankful and often scared straight to never get in that situation again.

One night, Scott dropped off a fifteen year old kid who was overdosing. He wanted Victoria to help detox him but he needed more help than Victoria could offer. She called for an ambulance. Officer Mike Piccard arrived with the ambulance.

Scott screamed at her the next day. "You can't call an ambulance to your house, it gets the whole neighborhood thinking you are a druggie or a drug dealer. We can't have rumors like that. It will get back to the club and to the Chief. Next time just call me!"

The next time Victoria did call him. Scott came over with Mike Piccard, who carried the comatosed patient to their truck. They dropped him at the corner store and made an anonymous 911 call. By the time the ambulance arrived, the kid died.

A few days after the incident, Mike was at Buckley's drinking with some friends. Victoria was bartending. Mike got her attention and held up three fingers. She expertly filled three glasses with beer as he made small talk. "Hey beautiful, any more trouble at your place lately?"

Victoria winked as she handed him the beers. "Never again." She said.

Mike removed his hat and placed it on the bar. His hair effortlessly feathered on each side. She imagined if he had a mullet he could pass for a girl, especially with mascara on those lashes.

"You got a special arrangement with Sarge, don't you?" he asked her.

Victoria flirted back while looking at the other end of the large oval shaped bar. "Actually, I have arrangements with a lot of men."

"Maybe I could tempt you to make an arrangement with me?" Mike asked.

She pointed to his ring finger and said, "I think there is something in the way."

"I just wear this for a cover. I am single." He winked at her.

She looked at Scott and said, "Yea. I hear a lot of you do that."

Scott chugged his beer and slid his empty glass towards Victoria. "Hey Rookie!" he yelled across the bar to Mike.

Mike ignored him, Mike had been on the force for three years now. He was no rookie.

"I said, Rookie!" Scott walked over to Mike and whispered, "Stay on your own territory. I marked mine."

Victoria ignored Scott as she wiped down the bar.

"Whoa." Mike said, smirking. He lifted both hands and said, "I gotcha."

"Good, and I'll get you later." Scott said pointing to Victoria and walked out of the bar.

Victoria continued to wipe the bar ignoring the conversation about her. She hated when Scott claimed her like property, and she certainly didn't need anyone knowing about their relationship.

Scott left the bar but not before winking at her. Victoria rolled her eyes. Mike watched from under his cap.

When Scott was gone, Mike ordered another beer and said, "Isn't he just a little old for you?"

Victoria smiled and said, "I don't discriminate."

Mike drank his beer undressing Victoria with his eyes. After her shift, Mike caught her in the parking lot. "Would you like a police escort home?" he asked.

Victoria shook her head. "No thank you. I have an escort waiting for me."

Mike whispered in her ear, "That old bastard can't do half the things I would do to you."

Victoria smiled politely and instantly felt like she needed a shower. She ignored him as she started her car and drove away. Mike waved flirtatiously as she drove away. Victoria mumbled to herself, "Creep."

When Viki got pregnant, she hid it from everyone. She only told Dr. LaVallee. Dr. LaVallee recommended her for a job at Country Light, a small nursing home in Tymingsly.

A few weeks before Tori was born, Kristina Legrand moved in. The two knew each other briefly from Buckley's when Kristina and her friends would come in after work. One night Kristina was telling Viki she was losing her job. She was a live in nanny for a family that was moving away. Kristina was bummed about having to move back home with her folks.

Viki struck up a conversation about being pregnant and needing someone to watch her baby after it was born. Kristina jumped at the opportunity to help her. They made a deal that Kristina would be her nanny during the day when she worked the nursing home in exchange for a room in the house Viki was renting.

Viki also was able to talk with Ken and get him to hire Kristina to take her night shifts at Buckley's. Viki was a few years older than Kristina so they didn't hang out socially but they both showered Tori with love.

~~~

Everyone makes mistakes.
It's a human trait.
He didn't mean to hurt me.
I didn't hurt me.
But I hurt you.
...and I am sorry.

There is no excuse.
For anyone being abused.
I cannot watch him do this to her.
She needs to get somewhere safe.
Hear me. Please hear me. Come here with me.
Follow me.

The blue lady calls me.
Soon I am safe in her arms but not for very long.
This was my secret.
No secret is worth the pain that this has caused.
I am so sorry.
Even a pill wouldn't have hid this secret.

Secrets cause pain.
I want to heal you.
My pain was healed when the Blue lady held me.
I am free...but not free to be me.
Everyone needs to be set free.
Hear me. Follow me.
~~~~~

AM Grout

~9~ DR. LAVALLEE

I've worked for the town of Tymingsly for fourteen years. Chief Robinson's predecessor hired me as the Medical Examiner for the town. Doing everything from routine physicals for the officers to autopsies. I wanted to become an internist, but fell in love with gynecology during my clinical years. That is my specialty, however as the town's chief Medical Examiner, my specialties have focused more on general wellbeing and minor trauma care.

Chief Robinson called me when they found her body. I did the preliminary observation and examination of Jessica at Stonewood Extension. The circumstances involved with the condition her body was found in were out of the norm to say the least.

My experience with decomposing bodies was only from my clinical days at Syracuse University in Dr. Malcom Zoma's forensic sciences. It was a class non-pathology students didn't want to take, however the dissection of the cadavers provided hands-on learning for medical students.

My cadaver was a fifty eight year old woman. My lab partners were two guys studying physiology and another studying criminal law. They hadn't planned on me taking the lead on the dissection but I did. We were all stunned to have to cut through several layers of yellow tissue to find the woman's muscle in her thigh. I made a mental note that day to be thinner than her when my body is donated to science; and I have to say, I've done pretty good with that promise to myself. My fifty-three year old body may not be in its prime, but I can still rock a bathing suit and run a nine minute mile.

The moment I saw the condition of her body, I thought of Dr. Zoma and that class. Calculating Post-mortem intervals (PMI) or time of death was going to be important for this case. In class we were never given any information about our cadavers. I already knew this girl had been missing for four days so the PMI had a window of four days.

A few years ago, I read in the Journal of American Medical Association (JAMA): Dr. Zoma was head of PMI advanced studies at a lab in Tennessee. The article shared that he was given a Fellowship Award for his research identifying decomposing bodies after soft tissues were no longer available. Now, I found myself searching for the details of that report.

His contact information was in the report, so I reached out to him. I was hopeful he would remember me because I was one of the ten students he asked to write a letter of recommendation when he was applying for an associate professorship. He was more than interested to assist with a follow-up autopsy.

Jack Sullivan, the District Attorney, had already called Dr. Jared Thomas, the Medical Examiner from Hinsdale. Dr. Jared Thomas was originally from Ohio. He had been with the District Attorney's office for thirty years, transferring to Hinsdale fourteen years ago. When I first met him, he told me he transferred because he was getting burned out in Ohio. He averaged fifty autopsies a year there due to gang murders. Hinsdale was a large city but half the size where he was from.

All twenty-one autopsies in Tymingsly were to rule out suspicious suicides. This would be only the third murder case. The first one was over ten years ago. It was the case of Mrs. Medalis. Dr. Thomas did her autopsy and his opinion was that her husband pushed her down those stairs with the intent to kill her. Dr. Thomas was ready to testify but the case never made it to court.

The second murder investigation was death of Jamie Santucci. Jamie had been shot in the back at close range. The shooter was sentenced to ten years.

Dr. Thomas was out of town Easter weekend. He arrived at the lab on Monday morning. He was impressed I reached out to Dr. Zoma. He knew how important an exact PMI would be for the case.

The news was reporting she was found in a shallow grave, others were speculating she had been kidnapped, tortured and dumped at that site, and still other reports lingered that she was involved in a love triangle gone bad. No matter what those details were, her body held some secrets we were about to discover.

The three of us scrubbed up as I gave Dr. Zoma some of the details of the crime scene. "There is substantial lividity." I said. He nodded and began to take the sheet covering her body off.

We took photos a few hours after her body arrived at the lab. I removed her from the body bag and covered her with a clean sheet when Jessica's father came into identify her. The Chief and I watched as his forehead cringed. I only exposed her to her chin, leaving the sheet to cover the slit to her throat.

The damage to her eyes and face had been caused from the animals in the woods. Her coloring wasn't clean but Walter knew it was his daughter. He closed his eyes, bowed his head and put his hand over the mask covering his mouth, then he quickly turned and lowered his head below his waist. The foul smell was enough to make anyone weak. He began to breath heavy and repeated, "oh my God." The Chief escorted him to a chair outside the room where the air was much cleaner.

With security at the door, we removed the entire sheet so we could view her. Dr. Thomas began to cut off the remaining articles of clothing she had on. The blood stains discolored the shirt, leaving the resemblance of faded stripes. The weather and the animals had also stained her clothing. We used litmus testing for specific areas of the fabric.

After removing all her clothing, we exposed more of her skin's purplish red color, postmortem lividity. Blackened bruises were visible on her right hip and thigh, multiple stab wounds on her torso, a clean slit across her throat, and her stomach opened exposing her insides.

"She was found like this?" Dr. Zoma asked, staring at her abdomen. This was no ordinary murder, animals had

had their way with her. Larvae and maggots crawled within all the open cavities.

I replied, "She was naked from the waist down, laying on a mound of snow under a tree. Looked like the body was dumped. Whoever did this, didn't do this in those woods." Dr. Zoma agreed. "The laceration here," He pointed to her abdomen. "has extensive contamination from the insects and the elements of the crime scene."

Dr. Zoma had reviewed the preliminary report and my field notebook before we scrubbed. The report had a checklist of injuries that could be identified through visual observations for any suspicious death. "Trauma" "Murder" and "Rape" had been checked off. I drew a detailed diagram indicating the positioning of her body. The tree her body was found near provided a structure to begin the sketch with.

After hours of photographing the scene and her body, the forensic team helped to transfer her body properly to the morgue. Before leaving the scene, I gathered soil samples, removed some of the bark which her body had been leaning on, and drew blood from her. This would later confirm what trauma she may have received from laying on that cold ground.

Dr. Zoma confirmed she had been found lying on her left side. The capillaries had been compressed long enough to indicate she had been dead for well over twelve hours. This much loose rigor mortis is found days after a death.

As we examined her, Dr. Thomas shared a story of a guy he examined in Ohio in the late seventies, he had been dead in his home for nearly a week. The neighbors called it in. Most of the officers thought he had just died because his body was slumped over and limp. They expected him to be stiff as a board when they moved him but his body had begun to decompose. After examination, Thomas found the man not only died a week earlier but died from being poisoned. He didn't know it was the ex-wife but the investigators put the pieces together after linking the poison to be chemical found in her home. Plus she apparently cashed in on a huge life insurance policy that he had never took out of her name.

Dr. Zoma stood at the crown of her head. His latex covered hands pushed gently on her scalp. He noticed a slight indentation to the scalp. There was no bruise indicating it was post mortem. "Bruises appear before the system shuts down. She was dead before receiving this blow to the head."

That reminded me of the Medalis case. Dr. Thomas was positive her husband kicked her in the head after she died, however because it was moments after she died, she still bruised. No matter, that case is closed.

I prepped more sterile Cryovials as Dr. Zoma drew more blood and took tissue samples from all the trauma locations as well as her organs, her hair, and under her nails. With the discovery of her naked from the waist down and the sight of dried blood covered with traces of larvae in that area, we knew she had been violated.

Dr. Thomas placed the rape kit on the prepared surface as Dr. Zoma reached for a box marked Adjustable Keplerian Lupos and handed me a pair of glasses which made me look like a bug. I adjusted the lens dial to 6.0x and fixed them snugly on my head. Dr. Zoma retrieved his own pair from the box. He then adjusted his gloves and poked his fingers at the wound to her stomach.

"She bled a lot." He said. He then readjusted her legs into the stirrups and aligned the laparoscope.

"The vaginal walls are damaged, I can't get the scope in far enough to see her uterus but I can tell you that the trauma on the anterior wall is from the exterior. It is more than just a stab wound." He reached up and poked his fingers into the dried blood on her stomach. "I don't believe this is simply a random attack or rape."

"Perhaps, the epidermis was more traumatized by the animals? From what we know of the case, her body may have been in those woods for four days." He leaned in over her abdomen and began to poke his gloved covered hands within the laceration.

Dr. Zoma adjusted the laparoscope. "I can't get a clear view, let's take measurements and then open her abdomen."

Dr. Thomas began to measure the laceration on the abdomen and take photos. Dr. Zoma reached for saline and cleaned the brittled blood to reveal her flesh tone skin. Adjusting the scope, he said, "What is this? Her uterus is gone. It's been cut out."

"That can't be, she is twenty-three. She couldn't have had a hysterectomy." I said. Dr. Zoma stepped back, Dr. Thomas probed around and said, "What the hell?"

Above his mask, his eyes gestured to me to have a look. I took the scope and realized the laceration on her abdomen was an incision. Someone cut her uterus out, it was gone.   Dr. Zoma closed his eyes to listen to his own thoughts. "Someone gave her a botched hysterectomy."

He reached for one of the plastic bottles on the counter. A dozen or so clear plastic bottles were systemically sorted with their labels facing forward. Their leak proof spouts molded on the side had plastic caps on the end. The red caps were on the far right, the yellow and black ones in the middle, and the white ones on the end. Dr. Thomas reached for a large white one with a twist top. He removed the cap off the needle nose spout. With one hand he held the bottle labeled NaOCl-H2O upright, and squeezed enough pressure to dispense the liquid into her abdomen until the dried blood that congested the area loosened enough to slide off her body.

Dr. Zoma adjusted the scope. After a few minutes of silence, he said, "Her right fallopian tube is grossly enlarged. She would have been in a lot of pain." He proceeded to extract more tissue samples and place them in the vials. Then he took a sharp instrument off the metal table and began to cut more of her abdomen.

"There is a tumor there. Or perhaps an embryo stuck in that tube. I want to remove it. Take some photos first." He backed away slightly so that Dr. Thomas could take some photos before we opened her any more. "If an embryo is intact, it certainly wouldn't have been a viable pregnancy. Who knew she was pregnant?"

He made a few incisions and placed some tissue on the petri dish. "Someone may have been trying to save her. The cause of death is from this."   There it was, her right fallopian tube was rupturing." he pointed to the reddish black colored tissue.

I recognized it right away. There it was, a four to six week embryo fully intact. "An ectopic pregnancy." I said quietly.

"The lacerations within her vaginal walls are from a vacuum extraction. When the embryo wasn't exiting, someone removed her uterus. Whoever performed this emergency abortion didn't know she was having a tubal pregnancy. The rupture to her tube put her at death's door." Zoma said.

My eyes burned with tears. "She didn't even know."

Dr. Thomas added, "Not about this. Between the Demerol in her system, she was numb and with the amount of Baclofen in her bloodstream, she would have been hallucinating if she survived the abortion. The real question to ask is why such a violent post mortem attack like this? He pointed to the slice across her neck.

Four hours later, the autopsy was done. A lab technician came in the room and Dr. Thomas handed him the four cryoboxes marked Nalgene. Each of the storage boxes held fifty vials color coded with plastic discs that I labeled APR with chronological numbers and cross referenced them to the report.

Dr. Zoma had wanted me to put the embryo in a Cryo Freezing container, but we didn't have any, so I took a 100mm polypropylene screw top container. He opened it, poured 40mm of isopropyl alcohol inside. Then put the embryo into the specimen container making sure the blue top was screwed tightly. Just as I added the label marked

APR-1L to the container, Chief Robinson and Jack Sullivan the District Attorney came in. "Update me." Sullivan said.

Dr. Thomas was cleaning trays in the sink and Dr. Zoma was starting to close the incision. Dr. Zoma began with the stats of Jessica's age and overall health, then he said "We have determined that 90% of the trauma was obtained post mortem. She sustained four stab wounds consistent with a sharp edged weapon, a contusion to the right side of her skull, and multiple bruising on her hip and leg most likely caused from the position her body was found."

"You say the trauma was caused post mortem?" Sully asked.

"Yes, those bruises are post mortem. The epidermis sustained severe environmental damage which contaminated many of the lacerations. Those stab wounds are two inches deep but definitely post mortem. We could not measure the width as animals caused extensive contamination."

Sully interrupted, "Was she raped?"

Dr. Zoma looked at Dr. Thomas; then at me, I replied, "We can confirm she was sexually assaulted."

"The lab report indicated the blood on the underwear found by the dumpster was hers, as well as the evidence we found in the trash barrel. We did lift some fingerprints that didn't match hers off the water bottle on the floor. Perhaps they belong to the sneaker print on the door," said the Chief.

Dr. Thomas interrupted him and said, "But there is one big matter to share."

"What is that?" asked the Chief.

Dr. Zoma picked up the report from the lab. He flipped past the toxicology page and was about to point at something when the Chief said, "Drugs are involved aren't they? Is this a drug deal gone bad or an overdose like our poor victim at Cumby's?"

Dr. Zoma shook his head no. He spread all the pages of the report on the counter so we all could see it. I pointed to where the letters hCG appeared. 1880 IU/L was written on the line corresponding.

The DA ignored my finger and pointed to the lines which listed Baclofen and Methotrexate. And said, "Drug overdose?"

Dr. Zoma shook his head. "No, these drugs were not the cause of death. She died of hypovolemic shock caused by an ectopic pregnancy."

Chief Robinson and Sullivan both mumbled, "What?"

Chief Robinson and Sully turned to me and said, "Did you find this in your report?"

"The lab test showed a higher level of hCG but I couldn't confirm until we performed the autopsy. Her levels indicated she may have suffered from hypovolemic shock. That alone would have killed her. But finding the embryo intact, confirms she was pregnant."

Dr. Zoma added, "Yes, I found the embryo intact in her fallopian tube. Her tube was ruptured and surviving a ruptured tubal pregnancy in her condition is highly unlikely but it is not fathomable to have a ruptured uterus. And in her case it isn't ruptured, it is missing."

The Chief furrowed his eyebrows and scratched his forehead. "What are you saying?"

Dr. Thomas stood straight and nodded to Dr. Zoma. "I'm saying, someone removed evidence. That evidence being her uterus containing the pregnancy but what they failed to know was that the embryo was stuck in the tube, causing her tube to rupture and most likely causing her to die before the uterus was removed."

"So did she have a miscarriage and then get murdered or did the murder cause the miscarriage?" Sullivan demanded.

I looked at my colleagues and said, "We believe she was having a miscarriage, went to someone for help and died. Whoever was helping her, didn't know she was having an ectopic pregnancy, and when she died, they disposed of her to hide their involvement. There are multiple traumas to her vaginal walls."

"Was she raped?" Said the Chief.

"Not consistent with rape." said Dr. Zoma. "Consistent with a D & C. Without the uterus, we cannot say if it was removed post mortem or not but our guess is PM."

"And that is an incision, not, a stab wound." He put on a pair of gloves and opened the wound.

Sullivan walked towards the body, carrying the file containing my initial notes. He opened the file. Dr. Zoma had put his initials next to all my original findings. His hand written details included the word "sharp object" next to weapon with four tick marks next to it. The report listed two lateral lacerations, multiple bruising, and special circumstances. I had used a blue pen to indicate the points of trauma on the diagram on the paper. A laceration on the throat, four stab wounds to the upper torso, multiple lacerations to the abdomen and neck areas, bruises on the left hip, thigh and arm, and trauma to her vagina.

"But why all these stab wounds?" Sullivan asked pointing to the neck and the other lacerations.

"Those may just be a cover-up. Hitting her in the head, stabbing her to hide the fact that this was a botched abortion."

"I want to know who knew she was pregnant." Sullivan demanded.

Dr. Zoma walked around the body to the counter where the specimen jar was. He held up the specimen jar and said, "Maybe the father?"

Sullivan looked at Chief Robinson, then back at Dr. Zoma. "Can we get DNA from an embryo?"

Dr. Zoma replied, "Yes, but I don't know how reliable it will be."

Sullivan said, "Do it."

AM Grout

~~~

Is this what dying feels like?
Hopeless, lost, missing, alone?

I didn't want to die.
I didn't plan this.

I have a future.
Even if it's not with him.

One night changed so much,
Life can change so instantly.

Struggling to keep the pace,
I lost it all.

The voices in my heart echo their suffering.
Can you hear me? You are not alone.

I am here with you but they cannot hear.
Your blue wings embody me.

I want to be peace.
As I am pieces of you. But there is a missing piece of me.
~~~~~~

~10~ MENSTRUAL EXTRACTION

One of the private procedures Victoria assisted with at the clinic Dr. LaVallee was what she called menstrual extractions. Dr. LaVallee called her the hand holder. At the Hinsdale Planned Parenthood Center, she was more than just the hand holder, as she had to prep the instruments.

Discreet affairs required confidential medical advice. Dr. LaVallee provided that for all the officers. So when they brought a friend needing help, they would wait in the bar as the girl got her menstrual extraction. It didn't happen often but there was one police officer that had waited twice in the past six months. Victoria didn't want to remember or notice that.

Victoria preferred the hand holding role as she knew these girls were scared. She admired Dr. LaVallee's meticulous movements, as she knew that one wrong suction could cause a fatal infection.

Dr. LaVallee always prescribed the girls antibiotics and antidepressants before they left the office. Viki told Dr. LaVallee the girls should be offered counseling before the procedure. Dr. LaVallee said, "It is not for us to judge, nor advise, it is our job to perform the medical procedure they need."

"What if they didn't want it?" Victoria asked.

"They signed the consent form, which is all we need. Consent and confidentiality."

Victoria didn't agree with the procedure but she did remain confidential to the oath of a nurse; and true to her own belief when a year and a half later, she found herself pregnant with Scott's baby.

She knew he would want her to abort the pregnancy but she couldn't. She wouldn't. This was her baby, and she knew the complications abortions caused. She told him he wasn't the father. He demanded to know who but she wouldn't tell him.

Scott started rumors at the bar that Victoria was a slut. He teased her incessantly about being with other men. She allowed the public teasing at the bar because it was much easier to keep the father's identity secret when she started showing.

Dr. LaVallee didn't like having her behind the bar pregnant, and she didn't want a pregnant assistance when she was performing abortions. It would just give the girls on the table mixed feelings, so she recommended Victoria for a job at a local nursing home. Victoria was thrilled.

"I don't know what is going on with you and Scott, and it is none of my business who the father is, but you need to move on and get settled so you can be a good mom," she advised.

Victoria was thankful for Dr. LaVallee's blessing. When she told Kristina about her new job, and the pregnancy, Kristina was so happy for her.

"Will you still bartend?" Kristina asked.

"I don't know how I can, I won't have anyone to watch the baby." Victoria replied. "You can probably take my nights."

Kristina had been looking for an apartment but couldn't afford to move out of her parents' house. "What if I offered to babysit on your nights at the bar in exchange to rent a room in the house?"

Victoria thought about it, it would be perfect. The house had three bedrooms. She agreed. After the baby was born, Victoria returned to the bar on the weekends.

Victoria was happy to have Kristina as a roommate, although Kristina didn't like knowing the rumor that Victoria had an affair with Scott. She knew his wife. She was a nice lady, three years older than him and totally unsuspecting. It would kill her to know. Victoria told her they only flirted with each other.

Kristina hoped Victoria was telling the truth. She needed to believe the baby had another father. She often suspected Scott visited on nights when he didn't stop by the bar for a drink after his shift. A few of those nights, Kristina would find the side door to their house closed but unlocked.

Victoria always locked the doors when she was home. She never knew when someone would be stopping in. Scott always called first, two rings then two minutes later two more rings. She would unlock the door and open it a little. He never locked the door when he arrived, nor when he left; most times he only closed the screen door.

Scott always called, but one day she arrived home from the grocery store and he was inside waiting for her. She had a big fight with him that day. She didn't like him in her space when she wasn't there. She thought about the fact that he could easily plant drugs in her house. Before she got pregnant with Tori, he threatened her and said if she ever told his wife he was fucking her, he would plant a kilo of coke in her house and have her arrested. Told her she would be known as a coke whore.

Whenever she walked in and saw him lying on her couch with the television on, she was irate. She told him she wanted him to call first and he had no business busting in and making himself at home. He ignored her as he stared at Frank Gifford holding an ABC microphone. She walked over to the TV and turned it off. "Did you hear me?" she demanded.

That was the first time he began to get violent with her since she was pregnant. He pushed her up against the wall and started choking her calling her a coke whore. She grabbed his hands and wiggled her finger nails to dig into his hands. He released his hold but not before slapping her across the face.

She quickly got away from him and went to her bedroom. A few minutes later he knocked on her door and handed her an ice pack. "I'm sorry." He said. "You turned off the TV and I over reacted. I was just trying to catch the pregame."

He sat on the bed next to her and touched her stomach. "You are going to be a beautiful mother. I'm sorry I scared you and lost my temper." He looked at Viki and kissed her gently on the cheek. His radio went off and he listened to the dispatcher. "Forgive me?" he asked quietly. She shook her head yes knowing whatever the call was, he had to go. He kissed her on the head, walked out to catch the score of the game and left.

As she laid on her bed she felt the baby move. She closed her eyes and smiled as she traced her hands along her little bump. The words "This is a Very Serious Message" echoed from the TV in the living room. She realized she had left it on since Scott left. She had ignored it while she was putting the groceries away and finishing the laundry.

The announcement was part of a song. New Kids on the Block was singing the song This One's for the Children. It lulled the baby to sleep and brought tears to Viki as the words touched her soul. She gently made circular motions with her hands on her belly and whispered, "For you, I promise to show you there is a better way."

Scott's visits weren't so routine after Victoria was seven months pregnant. She knew their relationship was a hopeless cause. He was married, he was never going to leave his wife, and he certainly would never admit the baby was his. However, the night she went into labor, she called him and he came over.

Dr. LaVallee was already at her house, she wanted a home birth. Scott walked in after the baby girl was born. Dr. LaVallee handed him the baby and said, "I can't be sure, but maybe you want to hold her?" Scott took the baby in his arms and walked over to Victoria. He kissed her softly and asked, "What are you going to name her?"

Victoria whispered, "I was thinking Tori?"

Scott smiled and kissed the baby.

AM Grout

~~~

What is wrong with me?
I am so embarrassed.

She only wants to help.
He brought me a flower.

I tell her the story.
She wishes me the best.

My head is aching.
Fear pounds in my gut.

I pray it will be over quickly.

Dear Lord, Please help me.
Please forgive me.

Mother Mary holds my hand.

Is my heart bleeding?
What blood is this that is shed?

Oh my God, I am so very sorry,
I will never tell this secret.

Of how I love someone I barely know.
Yet here it is, love rushing out of me.
~~~~~~

~11~ JOE DYER

Joe Dyer traveled four hours to Winslow on Monday for an excavation job. His employer, Witkem's Paving, put the entire crew in a hotel for three nights to finish a job for the state. Joe was exhausted when he got home and quickly showered. He was disappointed there wasn't a message on the machine from Jessica. He wanted to call her but it was after eleven.

When she called him Sunday, she said she needed time to think this week. She said she'd call him Friday and told him to have a safe trip. Thursday night, he replayed the answering machine, there were no messages. She was either home asleep or possibly at Buckley's visiting Kristina.

Jessica often stopped by to see Kristina after she got out of work at Greenways. The two have been friends since sixth grade. Visiting at Buckley's during Kristina's shift was about the only time they really saw each other since school started. They were considering getting an apartment together but Jessica still had a year left on the apartment she shared with Kathy.

Jessica and Kathy went to Hinsdale University together. Kathy graduated last year and her roommate moved out, allowing Jessica to pick up the remainder of the lease. Joe wanted Jessica to move in with him but she wasn't ready. She had twelve credits left at Hinsdale University before she would have her Masters in Behavioral Science so she just wanted to focus on school.

Joe didn't attend college, he graduated high school then went right to work for the local paving company. After work, he helped at his uncle's garage fixing motors for race cars. He rented an apartment with his childhood friend Ted Teggotta. Their mothers had been best friends since high school.

Joe recalled when he last saw Jessica. It was Saturday night. Teddy didn't have work at the Theatre that night so they headed over to Buckley's. It was almost 10:30 when they arrived. Jess was sitting at the bar talking to Kristina. It wasn't Kristina's regular night to work but her roommate's baby was sick so they switched shifts.

When she saw Joe, she rolled her eyes. "Are you following me?"

"I'm not following you, I just wanted to talk to you. You haven't returned my phone calls all week." Joe said, shaking his head to Kristina as she pointed to the Budweiser tap.

"I told you I was sorry, I know you don't have anything going on with Mike. It just makes me so mad to see you get worked up when you see him."

Jessica looked at Kristina and took a deep breath. "I am sick of your insecurities, I told you I just need a break."

"Jess, please. We have a good thing. It's been five years. I need you."

"Joe, I need a break."

"Can't we talk about this?" Joe turned to Kristina, and said, "What is she doing?"

Kristina tried to ignore their conversation by moving to the other end of the bar but she knew what was going on. Joe always accused Jessica of flirting with others when she was just being nice. Jessica was sick of it. They got in a huge fight a few weeks ago. She had been drinking, a little too much and she started dancing on the dance floor alone. Joe grabbed her and told her she was making a spectacle of herself. She didn't care and pushed him away.

Officer Mike Piccard saw Jessica pushing him away. He pulled Joe away from her and said, "Dude, back off!" Joe then pushed Mike and told him to back off. If Mike hadn't been in uniform, he might have punched him but instead he forcefully walked him outside saying, "You are out of here."

A few of people followed them outside knowing there could be more words. Mike pushed Joe up against a tree and said, "Face it buddy, she don't want you anymore! A real man treats his lady the way she should be treated, he doesn't stalk her." Joe swung a punch at him and missed. Mike grabbed his arm. Teddy came racing over, "Calm down guys!" he yelled.

Mike forcefully let go of Joe's arm, pushing him back to stumble onto the ground. "You are an asshole." Joe yelled.

Mike walked back toward the crowd that had begun to assemble at the door and said, "Nothing to see here." He walked back into the bar.

Teddy helped Joe up. "He is a hard ass but he is harmless," he said, pointing to Mike.

"I don't trust him. He is just waiting for me and Jess to be done so he can go after her!"

"No he isn't. Come on, let's go to Hinsdale tonight and forget all this." Teddy reached for the keys to his truck.

"No, I think I'll just walk home" Joe said.

"Let me give you a ride, it's already starting to snow and its cold," said Teddy.

"No I need the walk. But you know what, you should go back in there. Make sure Jess gets home safe without Mike moving in on her."

"He won't" said Teddy.

"Just promise me she gets home safe." Joe said, and Teddy promised he would.

The next day, Teddy told Joe that he gave her a ride home. She said she had too much to drink and was happy to have the ride. Joe called her and left her a message. "Jessica, sorry about last night. If you want me to give you a ride to get your car, let me know." She called back and said Kristina gave her a ride.

That next day, Joe called Jessica. "Can we get together for dinner or something tonight?" He asked. He didn't want to leave on his work trip until he knew everything was okay with them. Jessica said, "I can't, I have some stuff to do tonight." Joe was disappointed and sarcastically said, "Plans with Piccard?"

Jessica hung up the phone. He called her back only to get her answering machine. "Jess, I'm sorry. It was a joke. I'm really sorry. Call me back." He tried calling a few more times but each time the answering machine picked up so he decided to drive to her apartment.

She didn't want to answer the door. "Jess, I'm sorry, can we just talk?" he said through the door. She opened the door and came outside onto the steps. "Jess, what is going on?" He asked. They sat on the stairs and she shared that she wasn't feeling like herself. She told him she needed to evaluate her life to see where she was headed. She understood his jealousy and didn't want to end their relationship but she was just feeling confused. She assured him nothing was going on with Mike Piccard and he kept apologizing. Kathy poked her head outside to tell Jessica her mother was on the phone.

She hugged Joe and apologized for hurting him. "You didn't hurt me." he said, then reassured her that everything would be okay. "I'll call you when I get settled tomorrow night at the hotel." She shook her head no and said, "No, give me some time. I'll call you Thursday when I get out of work."

By the time Joe got back home, Jess had left him a message. She said, Greenways was going to be busy because of the holiday and she would call him Friday morning.

Thursday night he wanted to call her or go to Buckley's to see her but he reminded himself that she said she would call Friday, so he flicked on the TV. The Dennis Miller Show was on. He listened to Shelley Duvall talk about her new Bedtime Stories and it lulled him to sleep.

AM Grout

~~~

Friends and family wrapped around the building.
The air thicker than the mist that drenches everything.

I just wanted to stay dry. I couldn't go inside.
The casket was closed. Fear paralyzed my grief.

The blue lady sits on the chair behind the family.
My arms wrap around them yet they do not feel me.

I am in their heart. I am in their mind.
But there is no peace in their soul.

As sore as my soul is, I can soar.
Flying over the rainbow, into the warmth of the sun.

The blue lady carries me.
I dream of a life beyond the tree...

Waiting to explain.
Needing to be heard.

But how?
When?

Who will listen?
With the ocean's tide, I come to the shore for a moment of peace.

I see the fear keeping silent at the wake.
And again, I drift away.
~~~~~~

~12~ DRIVE BY

Kim Cloutier drove by the funeral home not once, not twice but three times before she could gather the courage to enter the parking lot. She circled the building, there weren't any parking spots. She wanted to pay her respects. Not just to her family, but to Jess. She didn't even know Jessica, but she needed to say she was sorry to someone. She felt so guilty not helping her.

Bryant, Colby, Mark and Wyatt were standing in line together. She was glad they didn't see her pull into the parking lot. She sat frozen in her car staring at them thinking about how they might be waiting for her to go in to pay her respects with them. But she couldn't. She shook with fear and anger. She wanted to shout to them. How could they just stand there like they knew nothing? They didn't even know Jessica. Why were they there? Why was she there?

Kim drove away, only to circle the parking lot and see a white four door Chrysler was pulling out of the spot across from the entrance. Knots in her stomach grew. A police cruiser sat idle at the entrance of the parking lot. "Tell him!" a voice in her head cried. The officer was directing traffic. Kim parked her Toyota Celica and looked out the rearview mirror.

Another officer stood at the entrance of the funeral home. Bryant and Colby adjust their hoods, while the others stood hunching their shoulders to avoid the drops of April rain that lingered. She reached for her umbrella in the back seat, then placed it on the passenger seat and said to the mirror, "I'm sorry, I can't do this."

Bryant knew she couldn't do this. She told him she wasn't going to meet them at the wake, but here she was. The cheerleader voice in her head was telling her to just go and pay her respects. Everyone in town was there, and they didn't know Jessica either. Kim wanted to go in and hug the family, but she couldn't face them.

She imagined Jessica's parents standing next to what she assumed was a closed casket. After four nights in the woods, there would be no way an open casket could be an option.

Then again maybe Jessica wasn't in the woods all four nights but Kim knew for sure Jessica was there Friday night because she saw her. Kim wanted to tell someone, anyone, but she couldn't. She shifted the car into reverse and slowly drove out the back entrance of the parking lot.

Friday night was just awful. The weather was milder than past nights as she and Wyatt headed to the hangout near the airport. Colby, Mark and Wyatt found the place, setting up camp last summer. The town had abandoned plans to make a housing development. Maybe they hadn't abandoned them but they stopped.

Wyatt and Kim went parking there a few times. One time, they almost got Mark in trouble. They had rocked the car into the mud and had to get a tow out. Wyatt and Kim walked over to the plaza down the street and met Sergeant Scott McKylie, who helped tow it out.

Sergeant McKylie noticed the make shift fort near where Wyatt's car was stuck in the mud. Wyatt and Kim pretended they had never seen it before. McKylie looked in the doorless refrigerator that lay on its side. On the rusted bottom were a few empty coffee cans that the guys used to store stuff inside; they were empty now. There was also a couple empty cans of beer, and a few crumpled empty bags of Lays potato chips. He lifted the tarp covering the couch and tossed a few of the cushions into the woods. Thankfully, he didn't look under the couch, where Mark buried the cooler under some brush.

McKylie used the winch on his cruiser to free Wyatt's car out of the muck. It didn't cost Wyatt anything except embarrassment. McKylie laughed and told Wyatt and Kim to go parking on a paved street next time.

Kim couldn't get Friday night out of her mind. It was awful. She was hanging out with the guys at the regular spot in the woods, when they all saw headlights coming up the path. Colby said to hide the beer. They figured it was Officer Piccard coming up the path because he regularly patrolled the area and often came through to tell them to keep the music down. All he knew was that they were a bunch of underage kids drinking beers. He didn't know that these guys were distributing Mark's dime bags, although Kim suspected Officer Piccard knew they all smoked.

It wasn't him patrolling then, but Kim wish it had been. The lights of the car simply backed away.

She had to pee so Wyatt walked with her away from the guys to help her find a place to squat. As she was peeing, they both noticed a weird smell. Wyatt used the flashlight to illuminate the area around the tree and that is when he saw the eyes of a raccoon. It didn't run from him, its eyes just looked his way. Wyatt walked towards it and Kim hung onto his arm. The smell grew stronger. Wyatt shined the flashlight on the raccoon and it ran past them. Kim let out a scream.

The guys heard it and headed towards them asking if everything was okay. Wyatt said he saw something. They all moved closer to where the raccoon had been. Kim had to pull her turtleneck over her mouth and nose to stop the smell from being so potent.

"Holy Shit." Wyatt said. Kim was shaking and turned her back towards the guys. The guys came over to see what the fuss was. The girl was covered in a blanket but they could see her hair. Mark used his flashlight to light her face like a spotlight. Her neck was sliced open. Bryant said, "Guess she couldn't yell for help."

Colby punched him in the arm, knocking the joint out of his hand. "You are an ass. We gotta get out of here." He turned to head back to where their trucks were parked. "No!" Kim said, "We have to go tell the police."

Colby stopped and looked at Bryant, then at Mark. Then he and Bryant started running back to the trucks. Mark turned to Kim and Wyatt and said, "They are right. If we report this, we will be suspects in her death. We can't tell anyone we saw her. Let someone else find her."

Wyatt put his arm around Kim and forced her to walk back to the truck. Mark ran ahead. He moved the couch and loaded the cooler into his truck.

When Kim heard the news the body was found, she was so relieved but told Wyatt that they should still report it. "We could make an anonymous call. They have those tip lines setup," Kim said. Wyatt shook his head no and said, "And what are you going to say, I stepped on her when I went to pee in the woods where I was smoking pot and drinking beer underage?" He was right, Kim didn't have any more information than that.

"But what if we told them she wasn't there on Thursday. Maybe that would help them." Wyatt looked at her like she was being sarcastic. "Seriously, it could help them to know when she died."

Wyatt said, "Just because McKylie saw us in the woods Thursday doesn't mean he would believe that we weren't involved. We have to keep quiet." McKylie did see them in the woods Thursday night. It was around midnight. They don't usually hang out there that late but it was a little warmer than usual for early April. McKylie came through in the police cruiser. Bryant and Wyatt were smoking a joint and talking while Kim sat in the truck with the heater on.

McKylie didn't even get out of his truck, he only stopped for a few minutes and left. Wyatt told Kim that McKylie was asking where Mark was. "Aren't you boys missing the rest of your crew?" He asked. Wyatt ignored him. McKylie then said, "Well tell him I'm looking for him. Then again, don't tell him. Let's just say, I was never here. And if you leave now, I'll forget you guys were here too before I check out what might be stashed in your trucks." He had threatened to search Colby's truck a few months ago when he pulled him over for speeding but let it go. Wyatt and Bryant agreed to call it a night.

Bryant dropped Wyatt and Kim off at her house that night. Kim drove Wyatt home around 2:00AM, because her mom hates when he is there in the morning. They drove by Buckley's and saw McKylie's cruiser pulling out. Kim carefully kept her distance. McKylie pulled into Stonewood Extension, probably checking to make sure they were gone. Kim turned down the street past Stonewood Way to bring Wyatt home.

"McKylie knows we were there Thursday night. But he knows we wouldn't be involved in the murder of that girl. We need to stay out of it and out of those woods," said Wyatt. Bryant cleared his throat and said, "What if they find the stash under the couch?" Wyatt let out a sigh and said, "It ain't ours, its Mark's; but Mark grabbed it all Friday night so it ain't there anymore."

Wyatt was right, the police knew that was their hangout. Kim was scared she said, "But Wyatt, if we are questioned about Jessica's murder, I can't lie. I know we don't really know anything but if someone asks, I might say I was there. And we were. We saw her!"

Wyatt calmed her down, "Listen honey, they aren't coming after us. They know who did this. They know we wouldn't slice someone's throat for not paying for weed. Mark doesn't work like that. McKylie knows that."

Kim didn't go to the wake. As she drove out of the parking lot, she headed to the entrance of the path at

Stonewood Extension. She looked at the trees and said, "Jessica, what happened?" She prayed Jessica forgave her for not helping. Kim thought, 'How could I have helped. You were already dead!" Her mind replayed the image of Jessica lying on the ground as she stared at the police tape still wrapped at the entrance. She cried. She had no tissues in her car so the tears soaked her sleeves.

Later that night, Wyatt called her. He was high and hanging out in his house alone. He said, "Officer McKylie told me they have my DNA from the crime scene at Stonewood Ext." Wyatt babbled about McKylie pinning this murder to him just because they hung out there. He said, "McKylie is an ass and he is out to get me." Kim reassured him he was being paranoid. She hated it when he drank and smoked at the same time.

The next morning, Wyatt's parents called her and asked if she had seen him the night before. She said, "We talked last night on the phone around eleven." Kim figured they were just looking for him but then they told her he hung himself in the garage overnight.

The following week was a blur. After Wyatt's funeral, his dad asked Kim if she knew if Wyatt was involved with Jessica Briggs. He told Kim the police suggested Wyatt took his life out of guilt. Kim wanted to tell him about the night they saw Jessica but she felt just as guilty. Wyatt's voice echoed in her ear, "We didn't do anything."

Wyatt's father told her the police requested Wyatt's DNA in response to a tip that Wyatt may have been involved in Jessica's murder. Kim was stunned. She said, "Wyatt and I have been in those woods and McKylie knows it but I swear if he said Wyatt did this, and the DNA matched, it will be a lie. Wyatt called me and told me he was threatened by McKylie."

Kim wanted to tell him that they saw Jessica in the woods and she was already dead but she couldn't. She just said, "I promise you, Wyatt had nothing to do with her murder."

Wyatt's father told her not to worry, they had just got the results and the DNA didn't match.

~~~

I never saw his face before he smiled at me.
Defending my honor, he made me blush.

One more drink, I forgot the fight.
It felt so good to laugh and smile.

There really are nice souls in this world.
If only I could break free from the old.

Comfortable relationships don't like change.
But I am growing, I am needing something to change.

We shared some laughs and perhaps too many drinks.
Mistakes were made but no one was wrong.

Gentlemen shouldn't talk.
He apologized.

My actions didn't prove worthy of the flower.
That showed his true colors.

He could have been the blue ribbon I needed.
Instead I am the blue ribbon flowing in the breeze hoping to be seen.
~~~~~~

AM Grout

~13~ STRANGER FATE

Pam Dolenson walked into the police station on her own accord. She said she had some information that she wanted to share regarding Jessica's death. "It's probably not relevant, but I need to clear my mind," she said.

The dispatcher dialed Detective Rolland's extension. He had just arrived back to headquarters less than an hour ago. Sitting at his desk, he starred at the wall in the hopes that his memory could sort this mess out.

"Detective, there is a Ms. Dolenson here to see you regarding the case."

Detective Rolland jumped up, put his hat on and quickly walked into the dispatcher's office. "May I help you?" he asked.

Pam replied, "I have some information about Jessica that may or may not be relevant."

Detective Rolland opened the door and invited her in. In his office she nervously sat across from him.

"I was at Buckley's on Saturday night when Jessica was there. She doesn't know me but I saw her at the bar. I recognized her photo from the paper. I also saw her there sometime after Valentine's Day. I don't know if this is relevant, but the news keeps saying if you have any information to come forward. So here I am"

Detective Rolland opened his notebook and dated it Friday, April 17. He began to take notes on what she was saying. He nodded his head and said, "Thank you for coming forward, any information is helpful."

He looked in his drawer at his recorder. He wanted to record whatever she was going to say, but first he would have to see if this was relevant.

"Jessica was sitting at the bar. I was at a table in the corner with my friends. They don't know I am here. We talked about it and they said I should stay out of it, but I need to say something."

"Okay, take your time. What is it exactly that you think is relevant to her case?" Detective Rolland asked.

"Well, Saturday night she was at the bar. Her boyfriend came in. I didn't know it was her boyfriend but one of the guys I was with knew he was her boyfriend. Anyways he got in a fight with some cop at the bar. Well, not in the bar but the cop escorted him outside and they kind of fought there. I didn't see the whole thing but I did go to the doorway and heard her boyfriend call the cop an asshole."

Detective Rolland took out a report form. "We know all about the fight. We don't think that has anything to do with her disappearance or murder. But if you wouldn't mind writing everything you just told me down, then I will put it in the file." He took out a pen and placed it on the table.

"Well, I don't want to cause any trouble with that officer. Besides, he did come back into the bar and didn't even go near Jessica for the rest of the night. Jessica just sat there talking to the bartender and the guy next to her."

"Did you see her leave that night?" Detective Rolland asked.

"No, I left before her. She was having a good time laughing. I did see her flirting with the tall good looking guy around Valentine's Day. I only remember because that was another night I saw her and her boyfriend fighting. I'm not saying she was cheating on her boyfriend but it looked like he is the jealous type."

"Would you be able to recognize this guy she was talking to if we asked you to come in for a line up?" Pam stared at him and said, "Her boyfriend, sure. The cop, I know him. But the other guy. I don't think I would recognize him. I will just say he was tall, that's all I remember. Tall and lanky with a big smile and brown eyes. He looked about her age, but he could have been my age. I don't know. I just thought maybe there was something with her and that guy."

Detective Rolland thanked her for the information and took down her information in case he had any questions. He reassured her their meeting was confidential.

Pam walked out of the police station relieved. She did the right thing. They had to catch the guy that did this. What if he did this to someone else? What if it was her? Her sense of relief was being over taken with fear. She drove to her friend Barbara's house.

Barbara was unloading her car of groceries. She was curious to see Pam park her car behind her in the driveway. She grabbed a few bags out of the trunk. Pam walked over and grabbed the rest. "Hey there. Do you have a minute?" Pam asked following her into the house.

Barbara was with her that night. She reassured Pam that no one was after her for reporting the truth to the police. "You told them all you know, and that is all you can do."

"But what if that cop is involved? I don't want any trouble from him. You've seen how mean he can be." Barbara handed her a glass of ice water and said, "Calm down, the police know how to find the guy that did this. Did you tell them about the guy she was flirting with?"

"Yes. I gave them a description but he looked harmless." Barbara stood at the open refrigerator and put her groceries away. "Who knows who is harmless?"

"What do you think? Who would do this to her? I heard she was raped and stabbed and wrapped in barbed wire. Someone at the pool hall was talking about how they probably did it at the dry cleaners and then cleaned up so no one would know."

Barbara closed the refrigerator. She had been thinking about the night Jessica went missing a lot. She had been next door to Greenways. It was her Wednesday night pool league at The Korner Pocket.

Around 8:30, a few minutes after Barbara and her partner Jana had started their second game, a police officer walked in the pool hall patrolling. There wasn't any unusual activity so he walked back out. Barbara assumed he checked in all the opened businesses that night.

Just as Barbara and Jana finished their game, they saw the cruiser's lights go on and take off headed down Market Street towards Lakeview.

Jana asked the bartender, "What time is the pharmacy next door open until?" The bartender told her Gallo's Pharmacy was open until nine. Jana asked Barbara if she wanted to go for a quick walk. She needed to get a birthday card for her nephew. They got to Gallo's just as they were closing. The sales clerk held the register closing until Jana got her card. When they headed back to The Corner Pocket, they walked past Greenways again.

Pool league usually end by eleven but that night they ended a little before then. She and Jana noticed the lights were still on at the dry cleaners. She mentioned it to Jana. "It says they close at 9." She checked the door, and it was unlocked. Jana yelled, "Hello?" into the store. Barbara grabbed her and said, "Come on nosey, let's go."

She hadn't told anyone that. Jana had called her the next day after the news reported the girl had gone missing at Greenways. Jana she told Barbara she called the tip line and told them she saw the lights on. She debated to tell Pam.

Pam was still talking about all the rumors she heard. "I don't think it is a serial killer, we haven't heard of any other missing girls. Plus, I heard from one of the bartenders at Buckley's that her father has friends in the Italian mafia."

Barbara had finished putting all the groceries away and reached to answer the phone. She told Jana, "If her father has friends in the mafia, then they will find her."

AM Grout

~~~

I cannot fathom the grief left behind.
On bended knee, so many hold their beads.

I want to keep them all so near.
Yet thoughts of me only stir more fear.

Words of the Lady shine some light.
On earth as it is in heaven is so right.

Tear soaked petals may dry with this breeze
As the blue lady comforts me.

There is no words, no story to share the news.
There are so many scared to explore any truth.

Whispering in the breeze and floating on the clouds;
Thoughts emerge with the words I want to say.

"Any story is better than no story."
For when a dreamer awakes, was not the dream real?
~~~~~~

~14~ DETECTIVE DREAMS

There are two Catholic Churches in Tymingsly. St. Anthony's and The Rolland's church, Sacred Heart of the Child Jesus, which was also the Brigg's family church. The Catholic Women's Group organized a prayer service for Jessica after the standard Good Friday service. Jessica had been missing for two full days and everyone was scared and concerned.

Suzanne Rolland volunteered to tidy the pews after the service. She got home after ten. Her husband was sitting in his recliner listening to a tribute of the Doors, on the radio. The dinner plate she left for him was empty and in the sink. She was glad he ate.

"I went to the prayer service this evening. The Briggs weren't there." She said.

"I know, I was with them. Mariam said she just couldn't go, wondering if someone at the service had something to do with Jessica's disappearance. I can't blame her. Everywhere I look, I wonder. It's making me question even members of my own circle."

Suzanne sat across from Dave and picked up her knitting. "My own imagination is running wild. If she just ran away with some guy, then couldn't she have left a note?"

"She didn't run away." Said Dave, knowing the circumstances that have been unfolding, he knew there was someone involved in this. "We just want to find her alive. The longer this goes, the chances aren't in our favor." He got up from his recliner and went into the kitchen. He took his beeper off the charger. It showed it was charged at 100%. Turning off the kitchen light, he said, "I'm headed up to bed."

Suzanne knitted for another half hour thinking about the prayer service. The bare altar reflected not only the tone of the holy day but the somber thoughts of everyone in attendance. After the traditional Good Friday service all the candles were extinguished. Tears welled in many of the people's eyes, including her own. Remembering Jesus's suffering and death was a very sorrowful event but she reminded herself of the Easter message, there was hope for what his death signified.

Over two hundred people stayed after the service to pray for Jessica's safe return. No one spoke of her after the service, but the somber dismissal didn't bring any peace to Suzanne. She wondered what the meaning of Jessica's disappearance was. Where could she be? Why would anyone take her? And she prayed no one was hurting her.

Suzanne put her knitting away and silently found herself saying the prayer to St. Anthony that her mother had taught her to say. "Tony, Tony turn around something is lost and must be found." Over and over she substituted Jessica's name for the word something.

She was grateful to see Dave sleeping when she got into bed. His eyes fluttered as he slept dreaming. He was walking in the woods. He looked for a path, but he couldn't see any clearings. He pushed his way through the high weeds and ducked his head to avoid hitting a tree limb. A bird caught his eye.

A mother bird was sitting in her nest on the tree limb. He picked up the mother bird and saw three eggs in the nest. One of the eggs began to shake. He quickly put the mother bird back on the nest, and found himself standing beside a campfire where the ashes were glowing. Suddenly the glow disappeared.

The shadow of the moon illuminated the area. Its rays were shining on a trash barrel. He walked over to the trash barrel slowly listening for sounds other than those found in the natural habitat of the woods. The barrel was empty except for a single gum wrapper. The shiny foil glistened, beckoning him to pick it up. When he did, a hole appeared in the bottom of the barrel.

He fell in head first and landed standing upright within the barrel. He looked up out of the barrel into the moonlight. The snow on the trees gently melted and dripped on him. He reached his hand out to catch the water and it formed into a baseball with writing on it.

The words, "Find me" appeared written on the ball. As soon as he read the words, the entire ball melted into his hand. He reached up and grabbed the side of the barrel and climbed out. Running towards a truck, he tripped on a branch and sent his shoe flying off his foot, landing in the muddy ground. While he was looking for his shoe, he found another ball. This time it said, "I'm sorry." Again the ball melted leaving his hand empty and his foot shoeless.

Lying in bed, he wrestled with finding his foot. His wife nudged him and said, "Honey, what are you doing?"

Detective Rolland replied, "Putting my shoe on." He looked at his wife, shook his head and said, "I was having a dream."

"Well, go write it down," she said, knowing he worked this way. Often waking up in the middle of the night to jot random thoughts, dreams and words onto papers. Most times the scribbles were illegible so he threw them away, but his wife always retrieved them and put them in a dated file just in case he ever needed them.

Detective Rolland walked into the kitchen and opened a door into his private office. He had converted the pantry years ago. The original counter and shelves remained on one wall holding all his notebooks and folders, along with a few cookbooks as well. Across from the shelves was a desk he made from the old cabinet. Dave had removed the first two shelves above that counter to make more head space and hung a corkboard when he remodeled this room.

Notes, reminders and phone numbers were tacked along with the certificate he received when he became a detective eighteen years ago.

He reached for a yellow pad and began to write his dream. Underlining the words "missing', "find me" and "I'm sorry.". He began to make a list titled the Woods, A Waterfall, and A Baseball field. Then he wrote ask Kathy about a hunter or if anyone Jessica knows plays ball.

He thought about the size of a baseball bat and if that could have caused the bruises on Jessica. It was hard to know what trauma was sustained from an attack and what happened in those woods.

The clock in the kitchen ticked. He glanced at the digital clock on his desk. It was 3:36 am. He yawned and headed back to bed. He just wanted to get the image if Jessica's battered body out of his head. His wife rubbed his arm and he fell asleep.

In the morning he called the Chief and told him he wanted all the woods and baseball fields searched. The Chief asked, "Why?"

Dave simply said, "I got a hunch, but then again I also had a dream about a waterfall and Tymingsly doesn't have a waterfall so my hunch could be wrong."

At this point of the investigation, no hunch would be overlooked. Dave told the Chief he was planning to go talk with Jessica's roommate Kathy again. The Chief said, "Sounds good. Meet me at my office at noon. The DA is sending a Special officer from Hinsdale to assist us so let's talk then so they will be informed too."

Dave got dressed, called Kathy and headed over to the apartment she shared with Jessica.

AM Grout

~~~

You ask what I would do to protect my son.
The blue lady holds my hand and says, I will show you.

As you are my daughter, I will protect you,
In a rush of energy we are merged with the universe.

I see sadness on those who see the truth.
Yet there will be relief when they hear the truth.

The situation was out of control,
True love is unconditional.

Come with me, my child and dream the miracle.
For giving is only two words away.

Some receive truths, others must forgive the pain.
All live with the goal to forgive what they do not understand.
~~~~~~

~15~ APARTMENT SHARING SECRET

Detective Rolland hadn't worked a Saturday morning in months. He parked his unmarked cruiser outside Kathy and Jessica's apartment. Kathy was in the living room looking out the window when he arrived. She opened the front door as he walked up the three cement stairs. "Good morning Detective." She said. She was curious about the message he left the night before on her answering machine and eagerly wanted to help find Jessica.

"Good Morning Kathy. Thank you for meeting me this morning."

"Of course. Does this visit mean no new news yet?" she asked.

"Afraid not." He said gently shaking his head no.

Kathy led him into the kitchen and he took out his notebook. They sat at the small kitchen table for two that was nestled under a pot rack. "Can you tell me about Jess's relationship with Joe?"

Kathy rolled her eyes and said, "Joe and her weren't in the best relationship. They fought, broke up, made up and then the cycle began all over again."

"When was their last fight?" he asked, scribbling the words, 'volatile relationship with Joe'.

"Saturday night. Teddy drove her home. I heard them come in. Jess was drunk and babbling about ending it with Joe. In the morning I heard the phone ringing. Neither of us answered it. It was Joe apologizing for making a scene at Buckley's. When Jess woke up, I told her about the messages because I erased them. She told me about the fight. She said, Joe was causing a scene and Mike Piccard tossed him out of the bar. It sounded like repeat of a few weeks ago. Joe was always jealous if she was talking to someone else. And truth is that she was contemplating seeing someone else but she wasn't. I started thinking she took off with someone, but she would have called me and taken her purse. Joe says he didn't see her that night, I hope that is the truth. Is it?"

"We are checking out all possibilities at this time. May I ask where you were the last few nights?" Kathy's eyelashes opened wide as she said, "I didn't have anything to do with her disappearance. I told you I brought her the clothes she asked for, and met my friends for a drink in Hinsdale. Thursday night and last night I slept at my boyfriends because I am a little freaked to be here."

"Relax, I just have to ask." Said Detective Rolland. "Now, tell me again about the phone call she made to you on Wednesday afternoon."

"She left a message on the machine so when I got home I called her. She asked me to do her a huge favor. She said needed a change of clothes. She told me which skirt to grab from her closet and a pair of underwear, and a few pads. I joked with her about being twelve and getting her period for the first time. She laughed. I told her I was headed to McDonald's and asked her if she wanted something. She said a burger and a sprite. I brought it all to her and that is the last time I saw her."

"Did she say anything or did anything look unusual when you were there?"

"No, she was waiting on a customer and I waited until the customer left. Then I handed her the plastic bag with her clothes and the McDonalds bag. She asked if I would stay while she changed quickly. She went to the bathroom as I stood at the front counter. No customers came in. When she was returned from the bathroom, she joked that at least she could wash her clothes while she worked, then I left."

"And this was around six o'clock?"

"It was a little before six. I got home from work at 5:15, listened to the message and called her right away. I grabbed her stuff and drove to McDonalds. The drive-up surprisingly had no line so I ordered and drove straight to Greenways. I didn't stay long at Greenways because my boyfriend was meeting me at the apartment at seven. I was back here by twenty after six."

"You mentioned she was interested in someone else. Do you know who this other person is? Is it Teddy?"

"Uh, not Teddy and I don't think he is into her that way but I can't stop thinking how he was the last to see her." Kathy thought about it for a minute and then looked at him and said, "Teddy is a mess over this whole thing. He said she was fine when he left. I just don't get it."

Kathy dabbed her eyes. "You know, Mike Piccard often stopped in on his patrol. Did he say anything?"

"He wasn't patrolling that area Wednesday." Detective Rolland said.

"Well, I know he creeped her out. She told me how she almost didn't go to Buckley's Saturday night because he was going to be there."

"How did she know he would be there?" Rolland asked.

"She ran into him at the coffee house on Main Street and he asked her if she was going. That is what she and Joe were fighting about. Joe accused her of liking him. He was jealous of everyone."

Detective Rolland scribbled in his notebook the words, 'talk with Mike'. Dave knew Mike's reputation with hooking up with women. "Are you sure she didn't have anything going on with Mike?"

"Definitely not." She said firmly. "Like I said, he creeps her out. Jess can't stand him. Teddy says he is harmless but I think he's cousins with Mike or something. He definitely flirts inappropriately especially for a married guy."

Mike was married, not faithful and certainly not the best character on the force but Dave knew Kathy was telling the truth. No way would Jessica date a guy like Mike. Dave knew Mike had been written up once for indecent conduct for a routine traffic stop but he didn't want to imagine a fellow brother would be involved in this. He dismissed it from his mind except to write 'talk with Mike' on his notepad.

"Every time Jess broke up with Joe, he would get so jealous of whoever she was talking with. I think that is why she kept taking him back. They have been together for over four years."

"Does Joe have a temper?" Rolland asked.

"I wouldn't call it a temper, just jealousy, but I don't think he would ever hurt her if that is what you are implying. He probably wants to hurt Mike but seeing he is a cop, I'm sure Joe wouldn't think to fight him."

"Tell me about the guy she was contemplating leaving Joe for?" Dave asked watching her fidget with the napkins.

Kathy took a deep breath. "Jessica has been confused the past few weeks. She had an impromptu date with some guy. She met him at Buckley's. She was honest with him and told him she was in a relationship. She hasn't seen him as far as I know. But I know she keeps thinking of him. I started to think that maybe they ran away together but she wouldn't do that. I know her pretty well. I don't understand where she could be."

She started to cry. Dave handed her a napkin from the stack on the table. "I know this is scary, but I need to know who that guy is. I have to talk with him."

Kathy leaned forward in her chair and rested her forehead on her hand. "I never met him. She met him at Buckley's the night she broke up with Joe, well one of those nights. Kristina might know. Jessica only goes there on the nights Kristina is working so I'm sure she was there."

Rolland took out his notepad and made more notes as he continued to listen to Kathy. "All I know is she said the guy was really nice. It was kind of a one night thing. She felt guilty because she and Joe weren't done yet. She felt guilty but I told her to let it go. I told her it was probably a sign that she was ready to move on from Joe. Jessica is honest to a fault so I wasn't sure if she would tell Joe but I knew she was ready to be done with him. She just didn't want to hurt him so she decided she wasn't going to date for at least a month after she broke it off with him. I was just never sure when that month was starting."

"Tell me more about that night." Said Rolland.

"Well I wasn't there but Jess told me they had a fight. It was the night she met that guy. She hadn't slept here that night and in the morning when she got home I asked her what was going on because Joe called several times. I ended up taking the phone off the hook that night just so I wouldn't have to hear him leave another message."

Kathy continued. "Jess told me what happened. She said Joe came into the bar and they got into a fight. About her ignoring him. She told him she thought it was time for a break. He got all loud and stuff. Accused her of cheating. She told him to get a life and went to the bathroom until he left. When she got back to the bar, some guy bought her a drink. She enjoyed talking with him. Said he was nice."

Kathy heard a car door close outside, she looked out the window. It was her neighbor's daughter. She waved to her. The Meals on Wheels program brought food to her elderly neighbor on Monday, Wednesday and Friday between 10:30 and eleven. Once when her neighbor had a doctor's appointments, she took the food for him. She had a key to his apartment. His daughter gave it to her, just to check on him in case of an emergency.

"Sorry, where was I. Oh yeah, Jessica said they struck up a conversation. She said he was really cute and made her laugh, helping her to not think about Joe. At the end of the night, the guy offered to drive her home because she had a lot to drink. Jess agreed. When they got in the parking lot, Joe was in his car and followed them. The guy somehow lost Joe and drove Jess back to his place in Hinsdale."

Detective Rolland asked, "Did she tell you this guy's name or did she say where in Hinsdale he lived?"

Kathy put her hand on her head and rubbed her temple. Her eyes searched the corner of the ceiling for his name. "No. She just said she stayed at his place in Hinsdale. I don't remember if she told me his name. Wait, it ended with a 'y'. Maybe Jimmy?"

Her eyes continued to search the room, stopping to stare at the tree branches outside the kitchen window. "Jess regretted going over to his house." She bit her lower lip.

"Did she sleep with him?" asked Rolland.

"Oh my, I don't think so. I think she would have told me that. She was just embarrassed by the situation. She isn't that type of girl. She said that he was a really nice guy and they talked all night. She told me it was really over with Joe. She was determined to make this break up final. But I know the next week they were going back out again."

"Did Jessica tell you what this guy looked like?" Dave took his notebook back out and began to make more notes.

"No, just that he was really cute."

"And she didn't she see him again as far as you can remember?"

AM Grout

"Not like that. Like not as a date. He stopped at Greenways the following week. She told him she was back with Joe. She said he looked like a rejected puppy when he left."

"When was that?"

"I don't know, maybe three weeks ago. It was around St. Patrick's day."

"Can you think of anything else about this guy?"

"No." Kathy covered her mouth, "Oh my God, do you think he was jealous she rejected him and kidnapped her?" Rolland shrugged his shoulders.

"You should ask Kristina, maybe she knows more."

Detective Rolland had already written 'ask Kristina about one night stand.' "I plan to."

The phone rang again. "Hello." She said, "No, no news. But listen do you remember her talking about meeting some guy at Buckley's?" Detective Rolland looked up. Kathy shook her head no to him. "Ok. It's probably nothing. I am just trying to find anyone that might know something. Listen, can I call you back."

"I don't know what else to tell you. I totally feel like a gossip queen. Jessica is going to kill me for letting all this stuff out but it helps right?" she said.

"Yes." said Detective Rolland. He headed for the door and said, "You have my number, call me if you hear anything."

"I will," she said.

The phone rang again and Kathy got up to answer it. Detective Rolland motioned his head towards Jessica's room. Kathy shook her head yes. Yesterday he had searched

136

through her drawers looking for any clue. She was very organized, her makeup brushes lined up, her clothes folded neatly and her nightstand containing a set of rosary beads, a bible and some prayer cards. A glass of water was on the nightstand next to a Danielle Steel novel, dog-eared at page 124.

Kathy was still on the phone so Dave made more notes. He could hear her answering questions that there was no sightings of Jessica with the caller. Dave looked in the bathroom again. The closet held the normal toiletries for women. Toothpaste, Tylenol, nail polish, face wash, hair spray, etc. Kathy had pointed out which were hers and which were Jessica's. Admitting the box of contraceptive sponges were hers. There weren't any prescription drugs and nothing looked suspicious.

The room looked exactly the same. It was obvious Kathy hadn't used it. The towels hung neatly and the pink shower curtain was pushed to the side revealing the assortment of shampoo and conditioners that lined the tub shelf.

He could hear Kathy sniffling when he entered the kitchen. "People are saying she is dead. Do you think she is dead?" she asked, wiping her eyes with tissue she grabbed from the box on the counter.

"We have to find her first to determine anything; and I am doing my best to find out all the information I can to find her." Dave said tucking his notebook into his breast pocket. "Is there anything else you can remember about Wednesday night?"

AM Grout

"No. It was really a quick visit." She dabbed her eyes. "What if that is the last time I ever see her?" her eyes began to burst with more tears.

"Don't think like that. We will find her. I am talking to everyone that knows her, and we will find out what is going on." He spoke with authority.

When Dave got back to the station, the Chief was briefing Amy Ashlyn, the special officer from Hinsdale.

Chief Robinson needed to make sure all the officers were handling this case professionally. Personally interrogating suspects was not his job and avoiding an internal affairs investigation was top priority. He put a call into Hinsdale for help with the interviews. Tymingsly was a small town. Chief knew the Briggs family not only from church but he also had went to high school with Mariam. This murder was a little personal for him as well.

Detective Rolland had the most experience on the force but he couldn't interview all the leads coming in. The D.A recommended Amy Ashlyn to assist. Amy became an Internal Affairs agent after graduation from the police academy. She had been an airman with 82nd Airborne Division flying a Sikorsky SH-60 Seahawk helicopter.

In August of 1988, she was deployed to Panama to be part of Task Force Green, a Special Joint Operation that organized specialized missions. During Operation Just Cause, her AH-64 Apache helicopter carried Team Gold of the 75th Ranger Regiment. The Rangers successfully parachuted into the water in front of Panamanian ruler Manuel Noriega's beach house, quietly they made their way onto his property. When Noriega surrendered, Amy's helicopter transported Noriega to Howard's Air Force Base.

The very next day, she learned her father had been killed in a motor vehicle accident. She returned to Hinsdale for his funeral. At her father's military service, she was told that she would not be allowed to return to Panama due to the Sole Survivor Policy.

Forcefully being discharged from the military prompted her to pursue a career in law enforcement. With her military experience and substantial training in forensic science, the Hinsdale Police Department offered her a civilian position with their Division of Criminal Investigation (DCI).

As a woman, Amy was very concerned about the abduction of Jessica Briggs. As a Special Force Officer, she was honored to be assigned to the investigation.

Amy arrived at the Tymingsly Police Headquarters and introduced herself to Chief Robinson. Chief Robinson was careful not to apply too much pressure to his handshake. Her delicate frame forced him to think she should have been denied combat missions but her handshake and her eyes shared her confidence and intelligence.

Teddy Teggotta, Jessica's friend and the last to see her before she disappeared was in Dave's office. The Chief called him and asked if he would come down to help with the investigation. Teddy eagerly agreed and headed straight over. He had been sitting for almost a half hour when Dave arrived. Dave said hello before entering the Chief's office.

Chief Robinson introduced Amy and Dave. Her Irish complexion could not be mistaken. If she wasn't in uniform, Dave thought she could have been a college friend of Jessica's here to make a statement.

The Chief nodded his head and motioned for them to head to another room. It was a small conference room where the officers had their daily meetings. The walls were lined with marker boards. A poster for getting the proper counseling for officers was one wall and the other had a map of Tymingsly. The marker boards had the timeline of Jessica's last whereabouts.

She left Helping Hands with a stop at the bank. Then off to Dunkin Donuts where she got a large coffee. She arrived at Greenways a few seconds after five and was alone except when she rang up someone at the register. Officer Mike Piccard and Sergeant Scott McKylie were assigned to research who those customers were. Their names were written next to the list.

Dave headed to a desk in the corner which had two phones on the table. The one with the fax machine was beginning to beep indicating a paper would soon be coming through. On the desk were yellow papers embossed with the stations logo. The ones written on had the word TIPS written in black sharpie at the top. Each paper was filled out with information from callers, some anonymous and others with names to follow up with.

Dave picked up one of the papers and read it. The Chief said, "Amy can help with checking those leads too."

Dave nodded to the Chief and said, "Ok, well I'll go get Teddy. He is in my office." The Chief stopped him and said, "No, Amy you get him."

Dave raised an eyebrow. Robinson ignored the look of Dave questioning his authority on who would interview Teddy. Robinson was well aware of Amy's credentials. The DA said, "I'm sending Special Officer Amy Ashlyn. She was an information advocate during Desert Storm and when you see her work, you will understand why I am sending her."

Amy asked, "Who am I interviewing?"

Chief Robinson replied, "Teddy Teggotta, he was the last of her friends to see her alive. He stopped at Greenways the night she went missing."

Teddy was sitting in the small conference room. There was no mirrored glass like the movies, but there was a camera mounted in the corner and a recorder on the table. Chief Robinson and Amy Ashlyn entered.

Chief held his hand out to Teddy and said, "Thanks for coming by Ted. I know this is a difficult situation for you. This here is Special Officer Ashlyn from Hinsdale, she will be asking you some more questions pertaining to the night Jessica went missing. I sent Detective Rolland to follow up on some leads."

Amy shook Ted's hand and turned on the recorder.

"Am I a suspect?" asked Ted wide eyed.

"At this time, everyone is a suspect." said the Chief.

Teddy put his head in his hands. "I can't believe she is missing. I just stopped in to pick up the chair covers that were getting fixed..."

"Do you stop by often when she is working?" asked Amy.

"Uh, no." said Ted.

"What did you talk about at Greenways while you were picking up your dry cleaning order?"

Teddy wanted to tell her more but he promised Jess he wouldn't tell anyone. He squirmed in his chair. "Uh, we talked about Saturday night a little, she apologized for drinking too much."

"Oh, yea, we heard about you giving her a ride home from Buckley's. Can you tell me what happened that night?"

"I met Joe at Buckley's, we were playing a game of pool when Jessica came in. Joe talked with her for a little while then told me he was leaving. He asked me to make sure she got home safe."

"Did he often ask you to do that?"

"Uh, no, but he was suspicious that she was cheating on him. And well," Teddy looked toward the doorway, "Mike Piccard was there. Mike is a cop here in town, and well, Joe doesn't really like him. Mike can be a flirt. And Joe knows he flirted with Jessica. Joe just didn't want Jessica to get a ride from him."

"Has she gotten a ride from him in the past?" Amy asked, writing Mike's name down on her notepad.

"No. Jessica doesn't like him. She has told me that he creeps her out. I think Joe was just paranoid that Jessica was seeing someone and his first thought was Mike."

"What would have given Joe that impression?"

"About a month ago, Joe and Jessica got in a fight at Buckley's. Mike came over and forced Joe to leave the bar.

Joe tried to start a fight with Mike outside the bar. Mike made some comment that Jessica didn't want a guy like him. I took Joe home. Later that week Mike started some trouble telling Joe he saw her leave with another guy. Joe thought it was him."

"Was it?"

"No, Jessica went home with Kristina and stayed at her place."

Amy made some notes then poured herself a cup of coffee from the pot brewing on the side table.

"So you said, you gave her a ride home Saturday night?"

"Yes, we went home. I mean, I dropped her off at home. And I went home."

The ride home was crazy. Jessica was drunker than Ted thought. When he pulled up to her apartment, she fell out of his Jeep, scraping her hand on the sidewalk. Ted practically carried her to the front door as she fumbled to get her keys.

Once inside, she fell onto the couch. Teddy retrieved a Band-Aid in the bathroom and cleaned her hand up. Then he got her a glass of water and made her drink it so she wouldn't have a hangover in the morning. Kathy heard the commotion and woke up. "What's going on?" Jessica smiled and said, "I had a personal escort home tonight, and Teddy is fixing my boo-boos."

"What the heck happened?" Kathy asked. Teddy explained how she fell out of the Jeep. Then he told her how Joe and Jessica broke up again; and that Mike tossed Joe out of the bar. Kathy rolled her eyes and said to Jessica, "Good.

143

You keep saying you are going to end it. You should have never taken that insecure ass back last month." She went back to bed and Teddy helped Jessica to her room.

~~~

Tears stream everywhere.

I cannot wipe them.
I cannot stop them.

Forgiveness is not needed.

Accidents happen.
Mistakes are made.

Lives are forever changed with a single action.

In a single moment.
It wasn't mine. Well it was.

I called for help. Help with a secret.

Friends protect.
Friends never forget.

I want to forget.

Blue skies appear in the distance.
There is so much love, and kindness, and compassion.

There is an embrace that needs no forgiveness.
~~~~~~

AM Grout

~16~ KRISTINA and A COURTEOUS RIDE

"Usually I'm babysitting Tori on Saturday nights, but last Saturday and today, I took Victoria's shifts so she could stay with Tori." said Kristina as she came around the bar to sit next to Detective Rolland.

"I needed to work today, I can't sit home and watch the news. I'm hoping she will just walk in here tonight. I can't believe she is missing. I really want this to be some big joke but this isn't like her at all. It doesn't make any sense. She is far too responsible to just take off!" Kristina wiped the tear forming in her right eye.

"We have been friends since third grade, she has no enemies. I drove all around last night after the prayer service looking for her but I don't even know where to look. If she wasn't at school or work, then she is usually with me or Joe."

Detective Rolland unbuttoned his jacket and took out his notebook. Gesturing to it, he said, "I need to ask you some questions, and I want to take notes. We are trying to find out everything about where and who she has been with in the past month."

Kristina's eyes looked at his notepad and she shook her head. "Yea, that's fine. I really don't think Joe had

147

anything to do with this. He is so distraught. He and Teddy were at the service last night and he knows everyone is looking at him."

"We are looking at everyone," said Rolland. "Now, can you tell me about the guy she met here last month?"

Kristina's eyes drew wide and her chin dropped. "Gerry? Oh my God. You think she is with him?" She shook her head and covered her mouth. "I don't know. She was avoiding him."

"Why was she avoiding him?" Rolland asked.

"Uh, she went out with him just that one time and well, was embarrassed that she kind of cheated on Joe."

The door to the bar opened, Kristina turned around. A group of four bikers entered. They chose a round table near the door and motioned for her to get a round. She got up and began pouring four waters.

"I'll be right back." she said to Detective Rolland as she carried the tray over to the table. After she took their order and dropped it at the kitchen window, she said, "Gerry had stopped in at the dry cleaners a week or so after they met. She told him she had a boyfriend."

"Did she say how he took that news?" asked Rolland.

"Jess said he looked like a sad puppy dog leaving Greenways, but he said he understood. He told her Joe was a lucky guy." Kristina took a sip of the water she had poured herself. "She liked Gerry but she knew it was too soon to get involved with anyone. Joe and she had been together for over four years, she wasn't sure if she wanted to move on."

"What about Mike Piccard? Did she have anything going on with him?"

"Ugh, no!" Kristina said then pierced her eyes through Rolland, "He is a creep. Some say he is a harmless creep but I've seen him creep on some of the girls here. Feeds them a drink or two and then somehow works his way to giving them a ride home. I don't want to talk bad about a cop but he seriously needs a better role model than Scott."

"Scott?"

"Yea, Scott McKylie. Please don't put this in your little notebook but I can't stand either of them. They both wear those wedding rings just for show. I can't believe their wives never ask me any questions. It makes me sick when I see them flirting and even sicker that they actually walk out of here with a girl."

She poured a glass of water and handed it to Rolland. The guys at the table didn't notice her being upset. She quietly took a deep breath and said, "What about the rumor I heard last night about a van that was seen at the pool hall?" Kristina's mind swirled with thoughts. Rolland pushed the water back towards her, she drank it all in one swallow.

"We found that van, it didn't have anything to do with her disappearance. I'd like to talk with this Gerry guy. Do you know his last name or where he lives? Rolland quickly asked.

"No. The night him and Jessica met was the first time I ever saw him in here and the only other time was Saturday night, he was with some friends at the back table."

Detective Rolland underlined Gerry from Hinsdale on his pad. "Can you remember any details about him?"

"He was probably six feet and had nice brown hair that feathered like John Stamos."

"Who is that?" Rolland asked.

"That actor on the soap opera General Hospital. Well he isn't on GH anymore but when I was in high school he was. Jess and I watched the show every day. Gerry reminded me of him but taller."

Kristina pointed to the stools across from them. "They were sitting right there."

Kristina thought back to that night. Jess hadn't planned to break up with Joe at the bar but she also didn't plan to see him that night. He and Teddy said they weren't coming down. Jess stopped and planned to have one drink.

She was perplexed and that was the word she used to figure out how to break it off with Joe; and still remain friends with everyone. Kristina, Joe, Teddy and Jess have hung out since sophomore year in high school.

When Teddy and Joe walked in, Jess spotted them instantly. "Oh my God, of course he would be here." She said, putting her head down with her fingers still looped in her hair.

Jess had the habit of constantly scrunching the curls of her hair. She had beautiful curly long hair but always complained that it was frizzy. She twirled her curls in an effort to keep the strands less frizzy.

Joe quickly made his way over to the stool next to her and said, "Jess, I just want to talk. You haven't returned any of my calls."

I walked to the other side of the bar and said to Teddy. "This isn't going to be good. She isn't ready to talk to him." It ended fast. Jess shook her head no then she got up and headed to the bathroom. The whole bar probably heard her when she pushed her stool out and said, "It's over. Leave me alone."

Joe asked me to go get her but I refused and told him, "She will call you when she is ready. Let it be and let her be." Joe and Teddy left after Joe realized I wasn't going to get her and she wasn't coming out of the bathroom until he was gone.

"Coast is clear." Kristina poked her head in the bathroom. Jess was standing against the wall and saw Kristina's face in the mirror. "Thanks" she said. Kristina opened the door and Jess came out. "What did he say?" Jess asked.

Kristina said, "Nothing, I told him you would call him when you were ready." Jess let out a deep breath and sat back at her stool. That is when the guy next to her, this Gerry guy offered to buy her a drink.

He pointed to her drink and said, "Welcome back. Looks like you need your drink refreshed. Can I buy you another?" I laughed as he motioned for me to pour her a new drink.

Jess laughed and accepted the drink. "I thought you were escaping out the bathroom window to get away from that guy." He laughed.

"I didn't even think of that." Jess said smiling and thanking him for the drink.

"Usually girls come to a bar to meet guys, you seem to hide from them?" he said winking.

"Long story. I'm just running from him tonight. Well at least wanting to avoid him for the moment. I'll forgive him another day for being an ass, but not tonight." said Jessica. Kristina gave her the thumbs up from across the bar.

He smiled, "How forgiving of you." They both laughed. Saving The Best for Last was skipping on the jukebox so Ken went to fix it as Kristina slid Jessica's drink down the bar into Gerry's hand.

There were a couple of guys at the other end of the bar sharing loud stories of their hunting adventures. Jessica asked Gerry if he was a hunter. He proceeded to share the only hunting story he had. He was fifteen, his uncle took him hunting in New Hampshire.

They sat in a tree stand for hours listening to nothing. His uncle took him to breakfast an hour after the sun came up. At the local diner his uncle asked the waitress how hunting season was going. The waitress told him that hunting season didn't start for another week yet. His uncle quickly told him to not say a word. Apparently if they had caught anything, they would have been arrested or fined. Gerry decided then that hunting wasn't for him.

Maybe it was the liquor that made the story so funny but it was nice to see Jess smiling and laughing. Gerry continued to share stories of his uncle's hunting adventures. He never went on any others but he sure remembered them as they were told to him.

After I served drink number five to her, I said, "Hey, you are not driving home tonight." I told her that I would give her a ride after I closed the bar. Jessica agreed but then at closing time, she said she wanted to get something from her car. Gerry offered to walk her out, and a few minutes later she popped her head in and said, "Gerry's going to give me a ride. I'll explain tomorrow."

"Did Gerry give her a ride home?" Rolland asked, remembering that Kathy said she didn't sleep there that night.

"I assume so. We never talked about it more, except that she said he was really nice and well, she wished she and Joe were officially over because she thought Gerry was the kind of guy she would like to be with."

Kristina bit her lip silently as her stomach did a flip. She was never a good liar. She knew if Mike Piccard's wife or any of the cheaters that frequented the bar ever asked her if she saw anything, she wouldn't lie. She didn't want to hurt them or anyone else but remaining silent was far different than just giving information when not wanted. She remained silent with them but now, for the sake of Jessica she wanted to share all the details. But what if Jessica had just run away with him?

Ken walked over and asked Kristina if she could hand him a bottle of Peachtree. She did as she thought about what she didn't want to share with Detective Rolland. At least not until she talked to Jessica.

Kristina didn't want to give too much information about that morning. Jess trusted her. She knew Gerry dropped her off at her car that day, then Jess headed straight to Kristina's. She was freaking out saying she said she made a huge mistake. I calmed her down. Jess told me about Gerry walking her to her car and seeing Joe stalking her.

Gerry said he would go say something to Joe, but Jessica declined the offer, instead asking him to give her a ride home. Gerry agreed and flirted with her saying, "That will make him jealous for sure." Before they got in Gerry's truck, she went back inside and told me that Gerry was giving her a ride.

Kristina evaluated if she should tell Rolland that information. And she did, she just didn't say where Gerry drove her.

"I assume he dropped her off at home. She told me Joe followed them and Gerry offered to lose him. He drove down all these side streets and then into Hinsdale. They lost Joe and then I guess he dropped her off."

What Kristina couldn't tell Rolland was that she knew Jessica stayed at Gerry's house. She wished she knew where he lived but she didn't. Maybe Jessica was there now. Panic swept over Kristina as she considered sharing that intimate detail but she knew Jessica would be furious and Joe would be crushed.

Jessica told Kristina that she didn't want to go back to her apartment. She knew Joe would show up and she was too tired to fight. Gerry asked her where she wanted to go and offered to let her sleep on his couch. She planned to sleep there but then as they cuddled, she did something she had never done before. She said, "I don't know what happened, he smelled so good and well, we just did it."

Jess began to pace the kitchen saying, "What did I do? He was such a nice a guy. He kept apologizing. He said he wants to see me again. I said no. I feel like such a slut. I haven't been with anyone besides Joe and now even if I wanted to start something with Gerry, I ruined it. He thinks I'm easy." She started crying. I gave her a tissue and sat her down on the couch.

"Listen, you are not easy; and no one thinks you are a slut. Maybe this is a sign that you need to move on from Joe. I saw the way you were smiling last night. I don't remember seeing you smile like that with Joe." said Kristina.

"That was all the alcohol you served me!" Jess bit her lip. "Sorry. I know it's not your fault." Jess blew her nose and said, "He really was a nice guy and funny. This morning he told me I was beautiful then he said he understood why Joe was so jealous. What am I going to do?"

"You don't have to do anything." Kristina said.

"But Mike saw me leave with him and I am sure Joe knows I didn't sleep home last night."

"Relax, just tell him you slept here. Besides you don't owe him any explanation."

Victoria came into the kitchen. "Hi. Sorry, I didn't mean to eavesdrop but the walls are thin. Kristina is right, you don't owe Joe any explanation." Victoria began to mix a bottle of baby formula and shook in their direction. "But I hope you used protection."

Jessica stopped twirling her ponytail and stared at the wall. "Shit, I screwed my pills up this week. Do you think I have to worry?"

Victoria shrugged her shoulders and said, "Probably not, if you doubled up the next day but just make sure you track it. If you go to the Planned Parenthood Center in Hinsdale, they might give you the morning after pill if you want to be extra cautious." Viki pulled a pamphlet out of her kitchen drawer and handed it to her.

"What is that?" asked Kristina.

"It's technically RU-486. It's not an over the counter pill, but a doctor can give it to you. It prevents fertilization if taken within seventy-two hours of intercourse. It's better than having an abortion if you opt to not have a child." Victoria had retrieved Tori from her crib and was giving her the bottle.

"I can't have a kid now." Jessica said. "And I certainly can't have this guy's kid, he'd really think I was a slut. I, I can't be pregnant."

"Then go to the center and take precautions," said Victoria.

Jess looked at Kristina, "What have I done?"

Kristina responded. "You're not pregnant, relax. Just double up your pills." Jess shook her head yes. "See, nothing to worry about."

Detective Rolland adjusted himself on the barstool and scratched his head. Kristina finished filling the pitchers and offered him a glass. He took it. "Is there any possibility she might have stayed at Gerry's so that Joe couldn't find her?"

Kristina didn't want to answer but she looked around the bar and moved closer to Dave. "Listen, I don't want Joe to find out and I told her if Joe asked, I would say she was at my place. But truth is, she did stay at Gerry's. Please don't tell anyone I said that."

"I appreciate your honesty and I understand your reluctance to share that kind of information. We will keep it confidential. Can you tell me anything more about what was going on in Jessica's life?"

Kristina got a piercing headache. She was prone to headaches but this was different. She considered maybe she was coming down with the flu but the truth was she wanted to share more details, but she didn't know more. She told him as much as she felt Jessica would want anyone to know. She didn't want to tell him that exactly one week ago Jessica was freaking out that she was late for her period. That wasn't any of his business and thankfully, she got her period on Monday but Detective Rolland didn't need to know that either.

Kristina said, "All I know was she wasn't feeling good. She told me she thought she was coming down with the flu. That is why I wasn't surprised when she didn't stop by Buckley's when Greenways closed. She didn't come by the night before either. I figured she went home to get some rest. It had been a long week for her."

Kristina told her to take a pregnancy test because she said she was almost a week late. She took it and it was negative. They were both relieved. That night they celebrated, which is why she had too much to drink and Teddy drove her home. Anyway, on Sunday, she told Kristina she had bad cramps so that was a good sign. Then Monday, she called Kristina at lunchtime and said, "Code Red arrived." We both laughed as we both breathed in the relief.

The kitchen alerted Kristina that food was ready. It was the order for the Bikers. Kristina excused herself to serve them. Detective Rolland put away his notepad and knocked on the bar. "Kristina, thanks for the info. If you

AM Grout

think of anything else regarding this Gerry guy, call me." He placed his card on the counter.

"Ok." She said, putting the plates of nachos, ribs and fries on the table where the bikers sat. "I'll be here. And if you find her, please call me."

Detective Rolland adjusted his jacket and nodded at the bikers. "Ride safely guys." He said and left out the front door.

~~~

This is scary but real.

Those who know will step up.

Those that have been punished will be free.

Fear had chained too many for too long.

Legends are remembered.

Truths are forgotten.

People will believe what they want.

We cannot change that.

All are royalty but true loyalty never quits.
~~~~~~

AM Grout

~17~ TEDDY'S WORRY

Teddy stared at the recorder on the table next to Officer Ashlyn ignoring her questions. He didn't want to say anything until he talked with Scott, and Jessica. He wanted to help without breaking a promise.

When Mrs. Briggs called him and told him that the door was unlocked at Greenways, Ted had knots in his stomach. Granted not the knots that Jessica had when he got to Greenways on Wednesday night but he was just trying to help her. He was so mad at himself for not thinking to lock Greenways and take her purse. Of course it looked suspicious, and it was, but it wasn't his responsibility to say what really happened.

Amy repeated, "Ted, Ted," he snapped back to reality, "Can you think of anyone she might have left the shop with?"

Ted rubbed his temples and repeated, "I don't know. Maybe she went for a ride with a friend. I don't know. It doesn't make sense. When I saw her she was okay."

He wanted her to be okay. She wasn't when he arrived at Greenways at 8:15. She had been in the bathroom when he got there. She was relieved to see him but he could tell she wasn't feeling well.

"You okay?" Teddy asked.

"Uh, I am so sick. I think I have the flu."

"Why don't you just go home?"

She readjusted her hair in her ponytail and said, "Carol had to teach her class tonight so I didn't want to let her down. I have less than an hour left. I'll be fine."

Jessica doubled over in pain and tried to catch herself on the counter. Before collapsing to the floor. Teddy ran around the counter. "Jessica, Jess. Are you okay? Can you hear me?" She was unresponsive. He reached for the phone and dialed 911.

Jessica grabbed the phone cord out of his hand and said, "No, please."

The phone dangled from the counter with the 911 operator saying, "911 please state your emergency." Teddy hung up the phone and attempted to take her hand to help her up.

"Jess you are burning up and you just passed out! What is going on?"

Her body trembled from the fever and her eyes swelled with tears. Teddy sat next to her. "Jess, what is going on?"

Jessica took a deep breath and held her stomach. "I don't, I don't have the flu. Well, maybe I do, but truth is I think I am having a miscarriage."

Teddy looked at her stunned. "What? You are pregnant?"

"No, well, maybe, I don't know."

"Did you take something?" Ted remembered hearing about a pill called RU-486 a few years ago. His mother was watching a show on TV about birth control options. Mom was talking to her girlfriend on the phone, "are you watching 60 minutes?"

The show was featuring the controversy around the Roe vs. Wade case. They do that every year around the anniversary.

"A pill can't just get rid of a baby. That doesn't seem right. They better have some strict laws in place so that girls don't just use this for birth control. I understand the birth control pill but a pill to abort a baby is just wrong. Pregnancy is a gift from God." She said.

He had no idea what was being said on the other end of the phone but his Dad chimed in to her conversation by saying, "What about when a girl gets raped. I think it's a great thing!" Ted's Mom rolled her eyes at him.

"Yeah, well what if the Virgin Mary got an abortion? Or took this pill? Then none of us would know Jesus!" she shouted back to him.

Ted ignored the conversation from his bedroom after hearing his father shout, "Son, make sure you wrap it up!"

Jessica reached for the trash barrel and threw up. He handed her a paper towels and bottle of water. She put the water bottle on the back of her neck. Trembling and crying she began to cough hard.

"I think you need to see a doctor."

"No!" she said. "I am not going to the hospital. I don't want anyone to know about this. I'll save you the gory details but it has been happening for two days now. And the fact that I also have the flu isn't helping. Please, Teddy please don't say anything."

"Does Joe know?"

"No. and I have to keep it that way. He is a good guy and would have supported me having his baby, but…"

Locking eyes with her, Teddy thought about New Year's Eve. About an hour before the ball dropped Jessica asked him for a ride home. Teddy was the only one with a car. They were all at Buckley's earlier that night when Victoria reminded them that Kathy was babysitting her daughter. They all hopped in Teddy's Jeep and went to visit her.

Joe was being an ass and Jessica wanted to leave. On the ride home Jessica asked Ted if he was going to make any new year's resolutions. He said probably not.

Then Jessica said, "Well, I am. I'm going to break up with Joe."

"When?" Ted replied.

"I don't know. I just know its time. I can't stand his insecurities, and well I just don't love him anymore."

"Well high school relationships aren't meant to be forever." He said. "If you had gone away to college, it would have been over long before now."

"I agree."

She gave him a hug and walked up the sidewalk to her apartment. As Teddy drove back towards Kathy's, he noticed Jessica had left her purse on the floor of the Jeep. He turned around and went to her door. Her neighbor had their TV blaring. Shannen Doherty was introducing Boys II

Men at Dick Clark's New Year's Rockin Eve Party. Ted rang Jessica's door bell and she let him in.

He just planned to give her the purse but then when she hugged him goodbye, the hug was a little too long. He pulled back and started to walk to the door saying, "Everything will be okay." Jessica grabbed his hand and said, "Ted, stop."

He looked back at her and she said, "What if the reason I want to end things with Joe is because I have feelings for you?"

She walked closer to him and kissed him. She then said, "I've been wanting to do that for a very long time." He kissed her back and said, "me too." Soon they were naked in her room as the neighbors were celebrating the New Years. After a few minutes, Ted stopped and said, "Jessica, we shouldn't be doing this. You are still Joe's girl and well I can't do this."

"I won't be his girl for long, and I just want you. Come on, I know you feel it. If you didn't then you wouldn't be lying on top of me."

When they were done, Jessica said, "What are you going to tell everyone? How are you going to explain why you were gone for so long?"

"I'll tell them I stopped for gas and ran into a friend and chatted."

They did chat New Year's Eve and Saturday night, and that is the only part of the story Teddy told Amy. He said, "Yes, she has been wanting to end it with Joe. Not because she was seeing anyone else but because she felt they had grown apart. I will admit I have feelings for her, but not like that. I love her like a sister."

And that was the truth. Even if he wanted more, they agreed it wouldn't happen again. Jessica told him "I've been wanting to get away from Joe so bad that turning to you felt safe. If Joe ever found out about what happened between us, he would never forgive you or me. And I know breaking up with him could end our friendship too, and I don't want that." Tears formed in her eyes, and she said, "Please don't tell him about us. He is going to hate me enough. I don't want him to hate you too."

Teddy put his arm around her as she shivered. "I just need to let this pass. Whether I was pregnant or not is not my biggest issue right now." She reached for the barrel and threw up again. Then she leaned into him and he held her. Sitting on the floor at Greenways, he couldn't ask if this was his baby.

Amy shuffled through the file that contained Dave's notes from his initial meeting with Teddy. "So, let me get this straight. You stopped in around 8pm to pick up something for Rosewood's. She was fine then?"

Teddy cleared his throat; "Yes. Well, she mentioned that she felt she was coming down with a cold. She was coughing a little but other than that she was normal."

"Where was she when you walked in?" Amy asked.

Teddy said, "Behind the counter organizing some slips or something."

"Are you aware that a 911 call was received here from Greenways around 8:00? Were there you then?"

~~~

Every friend
Every mother
Every healer
Every teacher

Even Me.
Look upon my name with wonder.

Pondering not only the whys but
The would haves, and could haves, and should haves.

He was good enough for me.
He dared to take a risk. And I let him.

Silence caused his suffering.
The truth will be heard.

We both were worthy of more.
Threads bind more than just the fabric.
Secrets stitches on the linen long to be shared.
Unraveling mystery that created the fear.
~~~~~~

AM Grout

~18~ NORMAL NIGHTS

Sergeant Scott McKylie's wife, Lara, left for work when the phone started ringing. Groggily, Scott answered the phone. "Hello."

"Hey it's me, Ted. Jessica's mom just called me. She said the owner of Greenways just called the cops. We left the shop unlocked; and Jessica's car is still there, she is real worried. She asked me when I saw her last. I told her I was there last night. Where is she? Can you call Victoria and tell her to tell Jessica to just meet me at the dry cleaners. Tell her to say she slept at Kristina's and forgot to lock the door."

Scott sat up in bed, "No, don't say anything. I'll be over in a little while. I repeat, don't say anything!" Scott silently mouth a few swear words, "And don't tell them I was there, I will cover my own ass. But you need to worry about yours! Shit. Why didn't you lock the door?"

"I didn't even think of it. I'm sorry," said Ted.

"Keep your fucking mouth shut. Jessica will come up with something about the door. Just don't say anything except she was fine when you left her."

Teddy was Scott's second cousin. Teddy's father had lived with Scott and his family for a while when his parents and sister died, but after a year of mourning, he proposed to his girlfriend and moved back to run the Theatre.

Scott was on duty last night when he got the call that a 911 hang up came from Greenways. When he walked into Greenways, he saw a yellow sunflower on the counter which reminded him that next week was his anniversary. Teddy was hugging Jessica on the floor behind the counter.

Scott looked down and was confused seeing them on the floor. With his deep raspy voice which had more shares of nicotine than a small tobacco shed, he said, "Hey cuz." Teddy nodded. "Everything okay? We got a 911 hang up call from here a little while ago. "

Teddy shrugged his shoulder and helped Jessica up. She started laughing. Scott raised his eyebrow and said, "Catching you two off guard?"

Jessica clutched her stomach and kept laughing, she said, "Uh, yeah, everything is fine. I heard a noise so I started to call 911 and that is when Teddy jumped up from behind the counter." She pointed to the front of the counter. "He was just being Ted but it freaked me out. It's all good." She hit Ted in the arm. "You seriously scared the shit out of me."

Scott leaned on the counter and said, "Ok. Well Teddy tell your Dad I said hi. I'm sorry I didn't make it to Teggotta's this month. How have the shows been doing?"

"There are good. We had the Legally Wed Dinner Show last week, it was sold out. Mom is thinking of bringing it back. Dad hired a new chef and the new menu is awesome. You really need to try the Bacon Meatloaf."

Jessica put her hand to her mouth and ran to the bathroom. Before she go to the doorway, she passed out. Scott reached for his radio, Ted stopped him. "No, please don't call anyone. I promised her I wouldn't take her to the hospital."

Scott knelt down next to Jessica and began taking her pulse. "She is burning up, what is going on? Is she on something?"

Teddy put a wet paper towel on her forehead and began to say no but Scott interrupted him, "What the hell is going on?"

Jessica opened her eyes and said, "He didn't do anything." She began to rock on the floor holding her stomach. Scott looked at Ted and said, "You better tell me what you didn't do."

Teddy pleaded with Jess, "Just tell him, he can help."

Jessica said, "No." Then she threw up in the trash barrel again.

Scott grabbed Teddy and said, "What did she take?"

Teddy pushed him off and said, "She didn't take anything. She is pregnant. Well she was, and she is miscarrying. No one knows except me, and now you. She doesn't want to go to the hospital, she doesn't want anyone to know."

Scott looked at Jessica and said, "Is this true?"

Jessica tried to hit Teddy but her stomach pains forced her to clench her belly even tighter. Chills ran over her body as she shook her head yes, then she said, "And I have the flu."

Scott reached for the phone, "Let me make a phone call, I might know someone that can help."

Teddy continued to hand Jessica paper towels so she could wipe her face and put some on her forehead.

Jessica looked up at Scott and said, "Please don't call anyone."

Scott said, "It will be fine. Let me just see if I can get you some help."

Scott let the phone ring twice then he hung up and dialed again, he adjusted the receiver and said, "Hey, it's me. I need a favor. Now. Listen, I'm with a friend who needs help. She says she has the flu and she is having a possible miscarriage. She doesn't want anyone to know so can you just check her out? "

He winked at Ted. "Yes, she has a fever. No, I promise this is not like that time. That kid overdosed. She isn't on drugs, she needs help. Let me just get her over to you. You've worked with pregnant women, just help her out. No, I'll send my cousin Ted. I'll be over after my shift. I will. Just help her out. It's my cousin's girlfriend."

Teddy looked at him and said, "She isn't my girlfriend."

Jessica asked, "Who is he talking to?"

Scott hung up the phone and wrote an address on a piece of paper. Ted recognized the address right away, "Victoria's?"

"She's a friend, a nurse. She used to work at Hinsdale Planned Parenthood Center. Just take her there. She can help, trust me. She helped your brother when he got alcohol poisoning and your parents never knew. It will be fine."

Jessica repeated, "Victoria?   Viki?   Kathy's roommate?"

Scott's radio went off, "Need an officer to respond for a domestic at 583 Eastward Street. Over." Scott clicked the button on his receiver and responded, "In route." Then he turned to Jessica, and said, "I'll be over after my shift. If Victoria needs anything she will call me."

Jessica smiled weakly at him and said, "Thank you for not making a big deal of this. Viki will be able to help. I know her. Thanks"

Scott got in his cruiser and left. Teddy helped Jessica into his Jeep and drove in the opposite direction heading to Victoria's.

AM Grout

~~~

I see a farmer watching his garden grow.
Tending to every seed.

He nurtures it daily.
With water, prayer and working hands.

He sees no change until
He looks away.

It may have looked the same
But something changed.

The farmer knows the girl and forgives the mistake.
She rejoices until she realizes the forgiveness was fake.

Assuming the best, ignoring the truths.
She questions why she planted that way.

Shockwaves sent her seeking a hand.
Not understanding the reality of the plan.

A farmer cannot force a root to blossom.
Some roots that spread tend to be the ones he wanted dead.
~~~~~~

~19~ PROCEDURAL CARE

Viki knew it was Scott calling, he always rang twice then called back. It was their signal. Right after Tori was born he stopped calling, but after she helped the Chief's nephew, he came by more often for a late night quickie. That was two months after she had Tori. She didn't know it was the Chief's nephew, but Scott brought over a nineteen year old kid who was too drunk for his own good. Scott got an IV from the medical office above Buckley's and Viki was able to hydrate him back to health. Scott later told her the Chief was grateful that she could help.

A month later, Scott brought her a kid who clearly had overdosed. The kid was convulsing and choking on the couch. Viki called Scott and told him he had to get him to the hospital. She had wanted to call 911 but knew she couldn't. She could never explain what the kid was doing at her house. Scott had Mike Piccard come by and pick up the kid. Scott ordered Mike to drop the kid off at the local Cumberland Farms down the street.

The next day, the news reported a kid overdosed and died there. Viki was devastated. She called Scott, his wife answered his phone. She told her she was a friend of Sergeant McKylie and he told her she could call if she ever needed help. Scott's wife was suspicious. Victoria was a little slow to speak and Mrs. McKylie often had hang-ups. She told Scott about the call.

"What was her name?" Scott asked.

"She said you would know. How many whores do you have working for you now?" Scott ignored his wife's inquiry. She knew he operated with some shady clients. They have had many nights of jealous arguments but he always denied cheating. She didn't trust him but for the sake of their three kids she wouldn't leave him. Plus the issues some of the other police officer's wives had when they divorced wasn't worth it to her.

Scott went to Viki's later that day and screamed at her for calling his house. The fight got physical and Viki almost fell down the stairs. She yelled, "What did Mike just dump him off at the convenience store hoping for someone there to help? That is ridiculous."

Scott smacked her hard, knocking her into the stairwell to the basement. He said, "Listen, how we handle situations is up to us. I was trying to protect you too, the ER would have known someone was helping. You want me to report what really happened? I'll tell them you sold him the drugs he overdosed on."

He helped her regain her balance as she wiped the tears from her face and said, "I was only trying to help." He moved closer to her and grabbed her arm. "Listen, you know it was better for him to die there than here." He pointed to the couch.

Now Jessica was on the couch. Her body was shaking as she moaned with pain. Victoria asked her how long she had been bleeding.

"Since Monday but today it got really bad and I started throwing up a few hours ago." Viki pushed on her stomach, Jessica shrieked with pain. "Jessica, I think you should go a hospital. They can do an ultrasound and confirm everything."

Jessica cried, "No, Please. Scott said you had experience with pregnant women, you even told Kristina many girls get a false positive. I have to believe this is the flu."

Viki held her hand to calm her down and said, "But hun, this could be more than the flu."

Jessica shook her head, "Won't it just pass? Bleeding is good, right?"

Victoria knew it was a sign but she also knew some pregnancies didn't pass as quickly. Jess moaned loud, and Victoria turned to Ted, "Can you get Scott? Ask him to bring me the supplies from the Aspirator cabinet at Buckley's."

"Why don't we bring Jess there?" Ted asked.

Jessica moaned and rolled herself off the couch and began to rock on her knees. "No, I don't want Kristina to know anything right now. I told her the test was negative, and well, I don't want her to know anything. Come on seriously, why do I have to be the one with this side effect. I just wanted it to be over. "

She held her breath and then looked at Viki and Ted and said "I can't think right now, I trust you guys, please just promise me you won't tell Kristina or anyone."

Ted held her hand and said, "I won't. I promise. Just let Victoria help you. I just want you better." He leaned down and kissed her forehead. She let go of his hand and moaned.

Victoria jerked her head to the door and said, "Just go. Tell Scott to bring me the bag. I got this. I'll have her call you in the morning."

Victoria gave Jessica a few pills from a bottle marked Baclofen. They were for some back pain that Victoria had a few months ago after Scott practically tossed her down the stairs during a fight. She told the doctors she pulled a muscle weeding.

Jessica swallowed them then followed her directions to go to the bathroom and change. Jessica used the toilet, then took off her sweater and hung it on the back of the door. She removed her skirt and underwear; and put Kristina's bathrobe on. Viki grabbed a few towels and sheets from the linen closet. The phone rang, she didn't wait for the signal, and she just picked it up. It was Scott confirming what she needed.

Viki laid several sheets on the couch and went into Tori's room to get some disposable crib pads. She filled a bucket with water and placed it next to a stack of towels on the coffee table. Jessica came out of the bathroom, "Whatever you gave me is definitely helping a little. I am so sorry about all this. I really didn't want anyone to know. This is so embarrassing."

"It's not embarrassing, it's sad. You are losing a baby, and if you don't have it extracted, you could seriously die."

Jessica started to cry. "What did I do?"

Viki said, "You didn't do anything, your body just can't expel it on its own. If you want me to do it, I can but you also can go to the hospital and maybe they can save it."

"Do what you have to do."

Viki avoided eye contact and said, "I understand."

"Do you?" Jessica whispered. "I know you tell everyone that you don't know who Tori's father is, but we all know."

Viki ignored her just as the backdoor opened in the kitchen. Scott handed a bag to Victoria as he walked swiftly to the front window to close the curtains. "I've told you a million times, this house is a fishbowl with the curtains open."

Victoria ignored him and opened the bag on the coffee table, fishing out a white tube of lidocaine and Prilocaine ointment. She squeezed the white cream on Jessica's arm and gave her an injection of Demerol.

Scott looked at Jessica and asked, "How are you doing?"

Her vision was blurry but she smiled and said, "Thank you for not making a big deal out of this."

He replied, "You are in good hands with Victoria." He winked at Viki and said, "I'll be back after my shift." Then he whispered in her ear, "You are one amazing woman."

That was the good side of Scott that she loved but she questioned if she loved herself at that moment. Helping Jessica was the right thing to do but performing this extraction was not something she wanted to do.

She washed her hands, slid them into the latex gloves from the kit. Then adjusted her lampstand to imitate a spotlight. She wished she could be at the clinic but it was too risky, her living room would have to do. She adjusted Jessica to be situated on top of the towels. She used a few trash bags to cover the mattress and towels. In all the abortions she assisted at, there was never enough padding on the table to absorb all the blood.

She reminded herself she wasn't performing an abortion. She vowed she wouldn't even assist again in one after she got pregnant with Tori. Menstrual extractions were common at the Planned Parenthood Center where she had worked prior to coming to Tymingsly. It allowed the girls to feel they were simply forcing their body to expel any potential implantation.

Protestors often formed barriers for those girls to get to the clinic making it dangerous some days to go to work. One morning, she was threatened when she entered the parking lot. Dr. LaVallee reminded her of the good they did at the clinic that the protestors never mentioned. The receptionist at the time ended up quitting after only a few weeks working because she couldn't handle the threats.

Working at the clinic was rewarding for her. She enjoyed helping the girls learn about safe sex and preventing pregnancy. She didn't counsel any of the girls requesting abortions that was the job of the doctors; however she did inform many of them of the RU-486 pill. The doctors at the clinic didn't allow the nurses to distribute the pills but she certainly would recommend it.

When she got pregnant with Tori, everyone at the clinic assumed she would have taken the RU-486 but after seeing so many discarded embryos in the vacuum chambers, she knew what she would be doing.

She lied to Scott, she told him she was seeing someone else, he was upset but he believed it wasn't his. She loved being pregnant, and she loved Tori with all her heart. She had made the right decision, Scott would never be a real father to her. He would never admit Tori was his, he couldn't.

Jessica moaned slightly and drifted to sleep as Viki inserted the speculum. Once the instrument was in place, Viki attached the vacuum aspirator. Blood came pouring out. She reached for a towel and placed it around Jessica's bottom.

She wished she had an assistant, not just to hold Jess's hand but to guide her through the procedure. She took a deep breath and inserted the tube of the Bel Em instrument, repeating the steps made easy with the letters of the instrument. B for Being calm, E for Easy in, L for Leaving room for the pump handle, E for Eyeballing the tube's distance, and M for Making swift progress. She did it. She exhaled a little as she attached the hand pump and began squeezing the handle.

The blood slowly stopped spilling onto the towel and entered the tube. She pumped the vacuum gauge counting to ten then stopped to drain it into the water. Then she would began again.

On the third time, the tube slipped out. She began the mantra to put it back in, but Jessica began to convulse. "It's okay, Jess, only another minute, hang on" she said, moving the towels to soak the new batch of blood seeping.

Her heart was racing as she tried to balance the extractor, the tube and the pressure she needed to complete the procedure.

Jessica started to choke. Viki immediately began a Heimlich procedure to stop her from choking. Jessica was gasping for air. Blood began to spurt out of her mouth. Viki tried to clear her airway. She reached for Tori's nasal aspirator in the drawer of the coffee table. She put it in Jessica's mouth to suction her airway, then she began pushing on her chest. She put her ear to Jessica's mouth then repeated the process. After almost three minutes, she stopped to readjust Jessica. She began the suction again but Jessica was limp.

Viki continued for another six minutes, then she had to stop, she was exhausted. She looked around at all the blood soaked towels. She placed a new one between Jessica's legs and then grabbed a stethoscope from the bag. Sobbing she said, "Jessica, please, please wake up."

She placed her hand on Jessica's heart, then listened through the scope. She pumped her chest a few times, and then just buried her head in Kristina's robe and cried. The time on the microwave in the kitchen was 10:48.

~~~

Who am I without a body?

My Child, when the body is healed we shall return.
What if it can't be healed?

The weakness settled in. I have no trouble breathing.
I have nothing wrong.

Accidents happen, even medical ones...I am fine.
I am in good hands. I trust.

Until now, when I do not see my body.
Did someone take it?
Does someone else need it?

Take parts of me but not all of me I beg.
My soul hears these words, "My child, it is yours forever."
The lady opens the curtain, I see my body.

The blood, the panic. I understand what is happening.
I am dying. I have died.
I want to save it, I want to cry.

Dry your eyes, she says. It is done.
She holds me in her loving arms.

Questions swirl, anger builds and then...the chatter ends.
Only love, and sadness, and confusion remain.

I hid the answer. You await the truth.
When it happens will you recognize me?

Will you trust me? I didn't mean to hurt you.
I didn't mean to hurt me.
~~~~~~

AM Grout

~20~ THE CALL OF DUTY

Ted hesitantly left Jessica at Victoria's. He had been gone from Rosewood for over an hour. His mother asked where he had been. He said he had to run out to get more olives for the bar because they were running low. "Where are the olives?" she asked. He replied, "Everywhere was sold out."

He headed back to the office area. Mrs. Teggotta knew he was lying but she let it go. She figured the truth was he might have been out back with Marina, the new girl that had a crush on him. She didn't want to know.

Teddy wanted to go back to Victoria's after work but he stuck to his Thursday night routine and went to Buckley's. Kristina was bartending and it was busy as usual. She nodded to him and began to pour him a beer. "Hey is Joe back in town?" she asked handing him his usual.

"Not sure." He said hoping she wouldn't ask if he had talked to Jessica. He didn't want to lie to her but until he talked with Jessica, he didn't want to say anything.

Kristina said, "Good, then we won't have any disturbances here tonight. I hope he hasn't bothered Jessica. She isn't feeling well so she probably won't come by tonight either."

"How do you know she isn't feeling good?" asked Teddy, concerned Jessica had called her.

"She called me yesterday and told me she felt she was coming down with a cold. She didn't stop here last night after work because she wanted to curl up alone in bed she said. I'll see her Friday at my place, we planned on a movie and cheese pizza night. Maybe you and Joe will get an invite" She said sarcastically.

"What is that supposed to mean?" Ted asked suspiciously. He couldn't help but wonder if she knew about the pregnancy. Kristina is her best friend but he couldn't ask. He promised Jessica to remain silent.

"Just saying, I know she and Joe are working things out, but I'm not too sure she is ready for things to go back to normal." Kristina noticed the guys on the other end of the bar getting her attention for another round. She poured their beers. Ted finished his and began to search to put his jacket on. "Leaving so early or are you cold?" she said to Ted.

"Yea, I'm going to catch the end of the Late Night show." He told her as he fished his keys out of his pocket. "See ya tomorrow." He said. She winked at him as she continued to make drink orders.

In the parking lot, Mike Piccard was standing with the driver's side back door of his pick-up truck open. He had already changed out of his uniform but still had his police jacket on. He removed his jacket and tossed it on the seat. Ted's Jeep Sahara was hidden behind the roof rack of Mike's silver pick-up. "Just getting off duty?" Ted asked.

"Oh hey, yea late night. I had a domestic call at the Terrkale Glen Condos ten minutes before my shift ended.

Waste of time going there because no one wanted to talk, you know the routine, the neighbors called in the disturbance and the paperwork takes longer than the call."

Ted patted him on the back and said, "Tough job buddy."

Mike reached for Ted's other hand and shook it. "Why are you headed home so early? Come have a drink with me."

Ted reluctantly agreed and the two headed back into the bar. Kristina said, "Back so soon?"

Ted laughed and said, "He twisted my arm."

The two grabbed bar stools and shared a few more beers. Kristina announced last call at 1:30. Scott McKylie walked in at that time. He poured another round for Mike and Teddy as Kristina turned the lights on. Everyone headed out the door. Kristina cleaned up, while Scott, Mike and Teddy had a second round.

At 2:20, she said, "Guys, after I wash these last glasses, I'm closing up, so finish up."

They agreed to her demands and by 2:30 were in the parking lot. Ted drove away. Mike watched Kristina drive away, high beaming her as she turned onto the main road. He then spotted Scott in the police blazer high beaming him. He pulled next to Mike and rolled his window down next to Mike's truck.

Scott said, "Park your car and get in, I'll give you a ride home."

"Naw, I'm okay." He said.

Scott repeated, "It wasn't an option."

Mike pulled his car into a spot and locked it. He wasn't about to argue with a Sergeant, even if they were friends. He opens the door to Scott's vehicle. "You got a hunting knife in your truck?"

Mike says, "Yeah, why?"

"Get it, I want to see it."

Mike opened his driver's door and reached under the seat. The wooden handle was fastened under a leather strap in its ornate leather holster. Mike's father had handed it down to him after he shot his first deer. It was the knife that he used to gut his first deer. Mike usually kept the knife in his hunting shed locked up but turkey season was approaching so he packed it under his seat.

Handing it to Scott, he said, "What's up?"

Scott nodded for him to hold the knife and said, "Just hold it and let's go for a ride."

Mike took back the knife and closed the door. Scott then took a left.

"Why you still got this vehicle?" Mike asked, knowing Scott usually parks the cruiser at the station and drives his own car after hours.

Scott looked in his rear view mirror and said, "I had a little issue I had to take care of personally. And not writing you up for OUI is one of them."

"Uh, thanks." Mike said, noticing Scott wasn't driving in the direction of his house.

"I don't think you could pass a sobriety test at the moment, especially finding you in a parking lot trying to shoot your gun at a tree."

"What are you talking about?" Mike knew he had a few too many beers to drive but he wasn't drunk, and he certainly wasn't shooting his gun.

"I need you to take the call of duty test tonight. If you pass, then I won't have to write you up for OUI or public endangerment."

"Is this a joke?" Mike chuckled to himself, as he turned to look out the back window to see what Scott kept looking at in the rear view mirror, but nothing was there but the blackened streets illuminated by the street lights.

"What's so funny?" Scott asked.

Mike said, "I'm imagining what it would be like to have a horse's head in my bed."

Scott said, "Well, then I guess you are understanding my vibe."

AM Grout

Running my fingers over the frame.
Together we were one, and now it's just not the same.
Reflections behind the glass never can be changed, but I have.

The engraving in bronze had the words I know
An oath. A promise. A love to uphold.
Chosen to protect and serve, not just to die.

Now I set my gaze upon your eyes.
Energy surges as I touch the sky.
Limited wisdom comes with truth.

In books and looks a guide comes through.
And I see that color is a language of its own.
Together it is black but alone colors stand true.

Who protected me? Did they try?
Remember the oath that so many walk by.
Embossed in bronzed it stares back at you.

Now I forget who was protecting who.
With faithful allegiance I gave you my love.
For you simply knew me but couldn't come through me.

When the bullet in the night passed in silence.
You shook with fear; now a guiding hand stains with black ink.
So the truth may be exposed in full color.
~~~~~~

~21~ MORNING CALLS

"Hello." Kristina answered the phone and sipped a cup of coffee. "No, Jessica isn't here. No, I didn't see her last night. Ok. I will." Kristina hung up the phone. Viki came into the kitchen carrying Tori on her hip. "Who was that?"

"Jessica's mother, she wanted to know if Jessica was here. I don't want to even know where she stayed last night." Kristina rolled her eyes. "How are you feeling this morning?"

She gives Tori a kiss on her forehead. "You feeling better sweetie?" she asks Tori. Viki tries to smile and says, "She is much better. Must have been something she ate. By the way, I am calling out today. I told work Tori was sick. But now that she is feeling better, I am going to run some errands."

"That's fine. I didn't have any other plans. By the way, I changed the wash, did she throw up on all those sheets?"

"Uh, yeah. She was in my bed so I changed my sheets and then took a shower after she went to bed so I just washed it all."

"Well the laundry is done and folded."

"Thanks." Viki said.

"Hey, have you seen my bathrobe?" Kristina poured herself a cup of coffee.

"Uh, it might be in my room. Sorry. I meant to put it in the wash." Viki put Tori in her highchair and headed to the bathroom.

The phone rang, after two rings, it stopped. A few seconds later, it rang again. Kristina answered, it was a hang up. Victoria stared at herself in the mirror and held back tears. She wanted last night to be a dream, a really bad dream.

Scott showed up at 11:25. She sat frozen on the coffee table holding Jessica's hand. Scott walked in and said, "How's it going?" She couldn't look at him.

"You okay?" he asked.

"Okay?" she said quietly, then she yelled, "No, I am not Okay. Nothing is okay."

Walking closer to her he said, "I'm sure everything will be fine after she recovers." Tears streamed down her face. She frantically began to shout at him. "She won't recover. She's dead! I couldn't help her. And now I'm going to lose my license and probably my kid and my life and go to jail!" She sobbed uncontrollably.

"What do you mean she is dead?"

Viki squeezed her red eyes shut and shouted, "I was just trying to help her. I tried, I really tried. I think her uterus ruptured or maybe she had an appendicitis I don't know, but clearly my medical practice in my living room wasn't enough to help her, she needed more help!"

She stood up and headed towards the kitchen, "And don't fucking say this is my fault! You should have never brought her here!" She lunged at Scott with her blood stained gloves. He grabbed her arms stopping her from touching him. "Stop it, I know you were just trying to help. It's going to be okay."

"How?" She removed her gloves and tossed them in the kitchen trash barrel. Scott paced the living room repeating the word shit.

She turned the sink on and washed her hands. "What are we going to do? You can't drop her off at Cumberland Farms! How do we explain why she was here?"

Scott grabbed the bloody instruments on the coffee table and carried them to the sink and began washing them. Viki started to shake, "Kristina will be home within the next few hours. This is her friend. What are we going to do? What do I tell her?"

She stood up and grabbed Scott by the arm and said, "How are you going to fix this? Who is going to protect me?"

He shoved her into the wall and said, "Shut up, and let me think." He quickly wrapped the sheet around Jessica and said, "Open the door, let me get her into my truck."

"What are you going to do?" she asked.

"I don't know right now, but you don't need to know. All you need to remember is she wasn't here tonight and neither was I." Scott carried Jessica's body to his truck and laid her on the tarp he had in the back.

He quickly came back in the house and finished cleaning everything. He put the bloody towels in a trash bag and carried the rest of the towels and sheets from the couch to the washer. Viki started the washer. Tori began to cry.

She went to check on her while Scott quickly wiped down the table and dried the instruments in the sink.

Carrying Tori back to the kitchen, she asked, "What exactly are you going to do?"

"The less you know the better. You need to just take care of her and trust me." He walked over and hugged them both. "I promise, no one will know she was here."

Tori was drifting back to sleep in Viki's arms. "Take her back to her room and get some rest yourself." Scott said, "I have business to take care of." She squeezed her lips tightly together as she stuttered, "Where are you going to put her?"

"Even if I knew right now, I wouldn't tell you. You have to trust me." He moved his face close to hers and said, "And I have to trust you too. If you speak about this to anyone, I'll leave you next to wherever I leave her."

He walked out the door. Viki slowly sat on the kitchen floor and rocked Tori. What had she done?

Kristina knocked on the bathroom door, "Victoria you okay in there?"

"Yea, I think I have what Tori had last night."

~~~

I will miss the kids.
I will miss my family.

I will miss the laughter and the dancing and the chatter.
I made plans; I had lunch; I needed a real friend.

Friends are loyal, the lady in blue proves that to me.
Angels surround even those that have to frown.

I was there, now I am gone.
Yet I am still here.

Have you forgot me?
Have you forgiven?

If you have forgotten me, it is alright.
If you have not forgiven me, I pray you are all right.

I will only follow you if I am called.
I will only shine light if you let me.

Push me into darkness if you cannot revisit the past.
My goodness remains and that is that.

We all make mistakes.
What I would have done, could have done, and should have
done, echoes lightly.

I did as I did. Never meaning to hurt anyone.
Always meaning to make the best of time.
~~~~~~

AM Grout

~22~ SHIFT CHANGE

A few days after Jessica's body was found, Viki left a message for Scott to call her. She used her code name that they had setup when she was working at Buckley's. "Would you please have Sergeant McKylie call Whitney." The first time she ever did that she was nervous but he reassured her that all the officers had code names for their informants; so the message would be seen as just that.

Viki didn't answer her phone so Scott drove by her place. Her car wasn't in the driveway so he sat at the end of her street and waited for her to drive by. He pretended to do paperwork in his SUV cruiser that he had run through the car wash the day after visiting Stonewood Extension.

The street wasn't as quiet as it had been the last night he was there. That had been a long night. Scott left a little after 1am, with Jessica in the back of the cruiser. He started driving toward the park but then he thought of Stonewood Extension. With all the kids hanging in those woods, he would have plenty of heads to point at.

He pulled in and started to walk around to the back of the cruiser. A pricker bush caught his leg. He kicked it free and walked to the back of his truck. Before opening the tailgate, he heard music in the distance. Wyatt's crew was partying in the woods. He had busted them a few times for drinking when they were underage, now they are legal but still hang here smoking their weed and talking motors.

Scott quickly got back in the cruiser and drove away. Again, he headed towards the park but decided to drive by Buckley's. Teddy's Jeep and Mike Piccard's truck were there so he pulled in.

The guys were sitting at the bar having a beer. He nodded to them. Teddy raised his eyebrows at him. Scott nodded and told Kristina to get the boys another round. He wasn't about to tell Teddy that Jessica was in the back of his truck. The less Teddy knew the better. He sat next to him and whispered, "She's good. Home and resting. She made me swear we never tell anyone about this."

Teddy winked at him and said, "Thanks Cuz."

"What you thanking him for?" asked Mike.

"For the next round." said Teddy pushing Scott in the arm. Scott walked around the counter. Kristina had already called last call but since Scott's brother owned the bar, he poured more drinks for Ted and Mike.

Kristina finished closing out the registers. She dropped a pen on the ground near Scott's feet. She bent down to pick it up and spotted a round ball sticking to his pant leg. It resembled a miniature porcupine. She was tempted to pick if off but instead she said, "You got some furry creature clinging on your pants." Scott looked down and picked it off, tossing it in the trash.

By the time they closed the place it was after 2:30, which Scott knew gave Viki plenty of time to calm herself down. Hopefully Kristina would tiptoe to bed and not notice anything out of place.

Scott spotted Viki's car about to turn onto her street. He put his lights on and forced her to drive straight. He followed her to the end of the road and parked behind her. She got out of her car and met him in between their bumpers.

"What the fuck are you calling me for?" He threw his cigarette on the ground and snuffed it out.

"Teddy came by and wanted to know what happened."

He lit another cigarette and said, "What did you tell him?"

"I told him I helped her as best as I could. I told him Jessica just had the flu and she wanted to go home. He asked why you drove her. I told him I couldn't leave Tori, so you came and got her and brought her home." The cold air forced her to cross her arms and hold her jacket tightly.

"He told me you said you dropped her off at the entrance of her apartment building and some guy was stalking her." Scott nodded.

"And that is what happened." He said firmly.

"But the news said she was stabbed." Victoria looked at his badge. "Why? Why did you do that?"

"Listen, I didn't do anything. And you didn't do anything. Teddy was lucky that she was stabbed. It most likely got rid of any evidence that she was pregnant because if he was the father, there was no match because of that."

Viki whispered, "Teddy wasn't the father."

"How would you know?"

"Kristina has been talking about some guy Jessica met one night. I think it's him."

"Have you been talking about this with Kristina?"

"We live together, Jessica was her best friend. I am just trying to help her but it is so hard looking at her knowing what I did." Viki starts crying and shouting at him. "I hate you, I hate that you forced me to help her."

Scott grabbed her scarf and twisted it tight. "You didn't do anything. No one did anything. And you say anything, this whole mess will be out of control. Trust me, no one knows anything. Remember, Jessica didn't want help, she wanted to keep all this a secret. And that is what we will do. Honor that for her. For you. For Tori."

She looked at him in disbelief. "Out of control? You think THAT would have got this situation out of control? She's dead and I couldn't help her."

Scott slapped her hard and said, "Calm down. No one knows she was at your house, no one knows you murdered her."

"Murdered?!!" she grabbed her scarf and flung it to the ground. "Is that what you are going to say I did? Am I going to be charged with murder? I didn't kill her." She walked to the side of his truck, her fingers intensely rubbed her temples as she shook her head.

"This can't be happening."

Scott reached for her and said, "Calm down." She avoided his touch but he grabbed her arm. She tried squirming out of his hold and hit him in his arm. "This is all your fault!" He pushed her away, she lost her balance and fell.

"Stop it!" he said.

She was out of breath. He helped her up and said, "You won't be charged with anything. No one knows you saw her or you tried to save her. No one knows she was there except me and I won't say anything. Chill. You have to trust me. They know she was pregnant and I'm going to find the guy that did it and he will have to prove he didn't do any of this."

She held back her tears as she rubbed her elbow. 'But what about Teddy?"

"Let me handle it. He's not going to talk. Trust me. As long as you keep quiet. I will keep my distance, understand?"

He lifted her chin with his hand, "If I so much as hear you chirp, you will be one silenced bird."

AM Grout

~~~

Attracting one like yourself is a gift.
Blood matches a family yet love
brings decisions that no one can question.

Sharing secrets, protecting moments provide a loving hand.
Though decisions change lives when
unplanned events arise.

Giving present to the presence allows the best to emerge.
However even with the best, some things
are just better unheard.
~~~~~~

~23~ SUSPICIOUS THOUGHTS

Chief Robinson dropped a bag marked evidence on Dr. LaVallee's desk. "This was found in the dryer at Greenways. Can you test it? They are Jessica's clothes."

Dr. LaVallee looked puzzled. "I have her clothes in that bag." She pointed to another evidence bag on the counter. "And test it for what?"

"I don't know, to see if Kathy's story checks out. Kathy tells us she brought Jessica a change of clothes because she got her period. Can you test them to see if any blood matches?"

Dr. LaVallee opened the bag, "There isn't any blood on them."

"They were washed." said the Chief.

"Then I don't think I can help you." said Dr. LaVallee. "Do you think Kathy had something to do with this? Did she know Jessica was pregnant?"

"Detective Rolland said no. But it just doesn't make sense, if she was miscarrying, how did she end up in the woods?" the Chief put the clothes back in the evidence bag and zipped it closed.

"Makes perfect sense to me." Dr. LaVallee had all the reports spread on her desk, including several photographs of Jessica. "Look here." She pointed to the word embryo on the autopsy form. "Someone knew she was pregnant and wanted it to be over, perhaps hiding they are the father or stopping her from having the baby. They even went to lengths to perform a botched abortion but they didn't realize that she had an ectopic pregnancy. We have the father's info within that embryo."

"And how exactly do I find him?" Chief asked.

"Start with her boyfriend and anyone that knew she was pregnant but I wouldn't tell anyone she was pregnant. Let them come forward." She said.

Chief Robinson picked up the DNA report. Joe had already volunteered to be tested, it didn't match. He was distraught to know that someone raped her. Chief Robinson couldn't disclose that the rape was not the sexual kind like most think. Aggravated Rape includes violating a person after death, and someone did that.

The report read, "Body was found decomposing in the woods. Epidermis deterioration indicated the weather, animals and the time of death had influenced in the damage. Interior lacerations were post mortem with the uterus unprofessionally removed and discarded. Puncture wounds to the chest, arms, and back indicate entrance from a right handed individual using a sharp object."

The Chief had read this report three times before stopping at the sentence reading, "sharp object." The report stated the entrance wound for each puncture was quick and forceful with the object creating the wound making a round puncture. He considered the options, and thought of his bow and arrow hunting days. He immediately paged Scott on his beeper.

A few minutes later, Scott called, "What's up Chief?" he said.

"I got a hunch that I think you can help me with." He said. "Meet me at the clinic in an hour."

Scott hung up the phone and told his wife he had to leave. He had been leaving a lot lately. Ever since Jessica was found murdered. She knew he was working the case and she couldn't ask questions but the questions she really wanted to ask were related to their relationship.

Lara McKylie knew her husband had cheated in the past, but she never had any proof. And whatever suspicions she had about that night, wasn't that she thought he was involved with Jessica or her murder, but she knew he was hiding something.

The night Jessica went missing, Scott had been on duty. He told his wife he saw Jessica in Greenways but he didn't go in. A drive by. He regretted that he saw the lights on after his shift but he had to get to the station to fill out some paperwork. He told his wife, "I should have stopped in but I figured she was maybe working late."

Maybe she was working late and that is how someone kidnapped her and then did god knows what to her before leaving her in those woods. But Scott worked late that night too. Actually a little too late because even when he goes to Buckley's, he is always home before the kids wake up.

That morning, Lara's alarm sounded at 5am, and she noticed Scott hadn't come to bed yet. She began to panic, what if something happened. She looked out the window and seeing Scott's cruiser in front of the house dissolved her worst fear.

She pushed aside her jealousy to get the kids moving along then went downstairs where she heard the washing machine start. Scott came around the corner in just his boxers.

"Are you just getting home now?" she asked.

"Uh, hi, yea it was a late night. I'll tell you about it later, I got to shower and get some sleep." He made his way up the stairs and greeted his sons good morning.

Under her breath she said, "I'm sure." She knew the rumors of some officers having whores on call after hours. She just tried to ignore them. With a freshman and junior in the house, she had enough worries. She hollered at the boys to get a move on it as she prepared peanut butter toast for them to take.

Once they left, Lara grabbed Scott's jacket on the laundry room door. She sniffed it and then searched his pockets. Nothing but the keys to the cruiser. She hasn't done this in months, but then again he hasn't done wash in months.

The washer swished. She opened the cover and saw his uniform in there. She closed the lid and went to work.

~~~

I am not wounded beyond repair.
No one ever is.

Faith fills my heart with a love so divine.
No one ever can see it but feeling it is possible.

It is here. Glowing brighter every day.
I bow my head with such great sorrow as
She lifts my wings to fly.

I question why I fly when all it does is ignore a lie.
My soul hears truths yet knows no song to sing.

Will the words to be understood?
With hope, I accept and trust.

Learning to fly
For my journey has just begun.
As it is said, thy will be done.
~~~~~~

AM Grout

~24~MISTAKEN LOOKS

Kristina could tell that Scott had been over. It's not that he leaves anything behind but if Victoria is up that late, it usually means he was here. Kristina never asks.

She has heard the rumors at the bar. She only asked Viki once about Tori's dad, asked if he would ever be in Tori's life. Viki told her that he didn't even know she was born. She told her Tori's dad was an old flame she hooked up with one night. He didn't live in the area so it was just as easy to never tell him. She didn't want to wreck his life, not ever give Tori false hope that he would play Daddy to her.

Kristina stopped playing detective. She appreciated the opportunity Viki gave her and she respected Scott as her boss. Even though Ken was her boss, Scott ran the bank deposit for Buckley's so his brother could retire with his wife to Florida. He really did run the place.

Kristina knew that Dr. LaVallee recommended Victoria to bartend at Buckley's so she could afford her nursing school. Scott flirted with her and among many. When Viki got Kristina the job, Kristina said, "Why do you let him talk to you like that?" Viki laughed and said it was just his was of being friendly.

"Uncomfortable is more like it." She said.

AM Grout

As Tori made more eye contact, Kristina couldn't help but think of Scott's eyes. A month after Tori was born, Mike Piccard made a comment to Scott. "Victoria has a cute daughter; too bad she has some of your genes." Scott immediately said, "You've spread enough legs, maybe she's yours."

Kristina was washing a few glasses near where they were sitting and still remembers hearing him lean over and say, "Keep your rumors to yourself, bullets fly pretty fast."

Mike winked, "Well, I don't get half as much skin showing from the speeding broads I pull over."

Jessica told Kristina how uncomfortable Mike made her. She had seen him a few days before at the coffee shop. She ran into pick up her bagel and tea and he was there. Apparently he was sitting at the counter with Scott and another guy. They were teasing Mike for not bagging a deer during hunting season. Jessica heard Scott say to him, "Doe in the headlights." Mike winked at Scott and walked over to get in line behind Jessica.

"Good morning Ms. Briggs" Mike said flirtatiously.

"Good morning." Said Jessica, patiently hoping the cashier could ring her up faster.

"Rumor is you are single again? Can I buy that coffee for you?"

"No, thanks. I'm good." She said, getting her change from the cashier.

"Ok. Well then maybe Saturday night at Buckley's? Will you be there?"

Jessica grabbed the bag with the bagel and thanked the cashier. She walked out mumbling, "Not sure."

210

She was second guessing going. She told Kristina that night. And maybe if she didn't go, she wouldn't have gotten so drunk. Thank goodness she got a ride home.

Kristina's mind swirled with scenarios about what happened. Detective Rolland made her think about the scenario that Joe stopped by Greenways and Jessica broke up with him. She imagined him getting upset but couldn't imagine him killing her then loading her dead body in his car and dumping her in those woods.

"Are you certain she wasn't seeing anyone else besides Joe?" Detective Rolland asked.

Kristina said, "No. She was loyal to him."

Kristina didn't want to share Jessica's secret affairs. When she was just missing, Kristina considered she could have been whisked away for a romantic weekend with that guy she liked. She couldn't tell Detective Rolland that, or Joe. What if she just ran away with some guy for a few days and forgot to tell her.

When Jessica's body was discovered. Kristina didn't know what to think. The days that followed were filled with shock. Kristina spent days at the Briggs house. No one seemed to know anything and everyone was talking about how perfect Jessica was. How no one would have wanted to hurt her.

Kristina knew this was true but she had knots in her stomach thinking about Gerry. She didn't want rumors to spread that she was cheating on Joe. It was only one night and it was something she never had done before. She didn't know anything about the guy except that Jessica wanted to date him.

211

The Thursday after the funeral, Kristina was at Buckley's. Chief Robinson sent Officer Amy Ashlyn in to chat with her.

Amy had caught herself up on the files as quickly as Dave typed them. She walked each crime scene and reviewed the photographs taken at Greenways, Stonewood Extension and Jessica's apartment. Jessica's apartment wasn't considered a crime scene but it provided some information on Jessica that they hoped would help.

Chief Robinson assigned Amy to look into Kathy's statement about the guy Jessica met at Buckley's. Joe suggested that Jessica might have been cheating, he even suggested Mike but as Amy listened to Joe's recording about the night he sat in Buckley's parking lot and had some crazy car chase with Jessica and the mysterious guy. She wasn't so sure that this story was true, as Joe was a prime suspect.

Introducing this random guy along with suggesting a fellow officer was involved certainly caused Dave and the Chief to wonder what story was true.

Kristina had just started her shift when Amy walked in. Amy felt good having her hair down. She straightened it before she decided to pay Kristina a visit, hoping it made her look more like a patron than an investigator. Since her military days, she always wore her hair in a tight bun under her hat but now as a special operations officer she preferred the bun without the hat for most days.

There was an hour left for the happy hour specials and judging by the couple at the far end of the bar, they were fully taking advantage of the buy one get one drinks. Another couple sat in the booth by the back door. Their amorous affections had Amy considering they might be having an affair. The woman wore an oversized sweater and her hair had to have used half a can of hairspray to hold its curls that wide. The guy in the booth had hung his weathered leather jacket over a hook at the end of the booth hiding the petite framed woman sitting next to him.

Amy took the stool at the corner. There were no tables behind her so she could see the entire bar. Vanessa Williams was playing through the speakers, Kristina was singing quietly to herself, "the very thing you're looking for is the one thing you can't see." Kristina smiled and walked over to Amy.

"Hi, what can I get for you?"

Amy smiled at her and said, "Just a ginger ale please with a lime."

Kristina nodded as she added ice to the glass. On the wall behind her was a poster with Jessica's photograph requesting information to be called to Detective Rolland's number.

"Sorry about your friend." she said.

Kristina looked at Amy confused and said, "How do you know we were friends?"

Amy took the drink from Kristina, cleared her throat, and said, "I'm working the case. I'm Officer Amy Ashlyn, special investigative officer. I've been reviewing the files and wanted to talk with you."

Kristina looked around the bar. The couple on the opposite side of the bar were deep in conversation about which ski resort they preferred. "Okay. About what?

"Kristina, I know this is a difficult time but I'd like to ask you about the last times you talked with her."

Kristina told her about Teddy stopping in and planning to leave early to watch the late night show. She also recounted his story of the olives.

"Teddy told me he had a rough night at work. The bar at Rosewood ran out of olives and he went out to find some but no one had any. I told him he should have called me. We laughed at how funny it was that Rosewood would need a jar of olives from Buckley's. Other than the olive conversation, there was nothing weird."

"What time did he leave?"

"Same time as me and Mike and Scott. Around 2:30 I think."

"Did they leave in the same car?"

"No. Teddy had his Jeep and drove away at the same time as me. Mike was behind me. I couldn't see his truck because he parked around front. Mike high beamed me as I left."

Kristina put her hands in her pockets and leaned against the counter. "Did anyone say anything about Mike Piccard? I am not accusing him of doing this to Jessica, I am just saying she found him kind of creepy."

"I really couldn't say but tell me about that." Amy knew this was why she was probably brought on the case. Internal investigations usually mean a fellow officer is involved or too close to the victim. In Jessica's case, Amy knew it could be both.

"Listen, Joe wouldn't hurt her. He protected her. Mike is a creep. Jessica told me how he had showed up at

Greenways and made a pass at her. She said she tries to ignore his flirting but that week, the week of my birthday, he made her really uncomfortable."

Mike often patrolled that area, stopping at the Corner Pocket pool hall and paying quick visits to Jessica often telling her "Young girls working alone at night need special security." Then he would wink at her. He often did that with Kristina too. One night he even smacked her ass. Kristina told Amy about the week before.

"Jessica told me he made some comment about being able to treat her better than Joe. She was upset. She called me after but I was here and it was busy. She stopped by later and told me Mike sat in his cruiser across from the shop for another twenty minutes. She felt he was stalking her."

The couple at the end of the bar wanted another drink so Kristina went over and made it for them. Then she poured herself a water and came back over to Amy. "My mind keeps replaying the conversation I had on Tuesday with her. She told me she wasn't feeling good, period related. She told me she wanted this week to be over. She never came to Buckley's that week but I figured it was because she wasn't feeling good. I didn't think it was because she was going to be dead! I can't believe she is gone."

"Tell me about her and Joe."

"It was complicated. They have been together for a long time, we all hang out together. Jessica didn't know how breaking up could work. She still wanted all of us hang out together. Her and Joe not being a couple kind of makes it uncomfortable for everyone."

Amy took another sip of her ginger ale and said, "Do you think Teddy could have been upset about them breaking up?"

"Are you really looking at Teddy for doing this?" Kristina asked.

"We are looking at everyone."

"Me?" Kristina asked.

"We know it is a man that committed this terrible crime but we haven't ruled out any possibilities."

Kristina ran her hands through her hair. "I dreamt of her a few nights ago. We were at a Valentines dance and there was this girl with short blonde hair and many ear piercings. She was dancing all alone and then this guy dressed as Cupid walked in and shot her several times with a bow and arrow. The girl's hair turned pink and she instantly fell into the arms of the security officer at the door. I woke up thinking Jessica fell in love and ran away but then the reality of the news hit. She really was dead. Stabbed multiple times and not by Cupid's arrow." A tear fell onto the counter. She reached for a napkin.

"I'll be honest with you, Joe's alibi checked out and he voluntarily gave his DNA which didn't match the DNA they found in her, but I need to know if there was anyone else she was involved with."

Kristina hated those words, "in her". As in she was raped and the DNA of some bastard was inside her! Detective Rolland wouldn't give details as to when Jessica was killed but it was obvious it was within the four days she was missing and not the day she was found. Kristina wanted details, and all he could say was that what this person did to her was disgusting. She couldn't even begin to imagine.

Kristina's heart pounded, "I lied." She whispered.

Amy tilted her head, "What about?"

Kristina was shaking, "Jessie had seen someone else."

Amy took a sip of her soda. "Yes, that is what I wanted to talk to you about."

Kristina's eyes widened. "You know?" Amy nodded her head.

"I'm so sorry, I know I should have said something. I lied to Detective Rolland. I didn't know Kathy knew about that date but when Detective Rolland asked I didn't want to share anything Jessica wouldn't want anyone to know."

"It's okay. I understand. You just wanted to protect your friend. What can you tell me about him?"

"His name is Gerry. I don't know his last name. He's only been here twice that I know of. You could ask Ken, he was here at the time."

Amy looked around the bar, there were no cameras to request watching footage of that night, never mind a small establishment like this probably would only keep recordings less than thirty days.

"Tell me about him, what do you remember?"

"Uh, he was kind of tall. Average build. He seemed really polite. Had a nice smile. I don't know. I'm terrible at describing people and obviously if he did this, I am a terrible judge of character."

"Tell me how Jessica ended up leaving with him that night."

"Well I was going to give her a ride home since she had a little too much to drink. Gerry walked her to the parking lot where she was going to get something out of her car, apparently when they got in the parking lot, Joe was there. Gerry offered her a ride, and she took it, was just trying to avoid Joe. However in the car with Gerry she realized Joe was following them and she was afraid he would either fight Gerry or her when they arrived at her apartment."

"Is Joe the fighting kind?" Amy began taking some notes.

"No, but Jessica just wanted to avoid any confrontation. She never liked confrontation, which is why she had a hard time breaking up with Joe. Anyway, she went back to Gerry's place after he lost Joe swirling through the streets."

"Where was that?"

"She never said. She only said how stupid she felt the next morning because Gerry was really nice. She kept saying how nice he was and how stupid she felt for being so easy."

"Did she sleep with him that night?"

Kristina didn't want to say yes, but she knew she did. Jessica was so embarrassed. She nodded

"When was this night?"

"Over a month ago. Gerry had been sitting with some friends in the corner when Jessica and Joe kind of had a fight. Jessica stayed in the bathroom until Joe left. When she came out of the bathroom his friends had left and he wandered over to the bar and bought her a drink. I heard their conversation, he seriously was just making her laugh. She needed to laugh, she had been so upset. They talked and had a few more drinks until around 1:30. That is when he walked her out to her car to get her purse."

"How do you know she left with him and not Joe?"

"She came back in and told me Gerry was going to give her a ride. She said she would explain later. I told her okay. I knew I would be another hour before closing. The next day, she told me about Mike being in the parking lot and going back to Gerry's."

"Did she ever see Gerry again?"

"He stopped in and saw her at Greenways that week. She told him she was in a relationship and needed some time. She and I talked about how she could maybe start a real relationship with him. But she didn't think she should jump into another relationship right after dumping Joe. She figured he would think she dumped him for another guy. Plus she had the issue that she hadn't broken up with him yet."

Amy didn't like the sound of this Gerry guy. She need his last name. "Kristina, you don't remember Jessica ever telling you what Gerry did or where he lived or his last name?"

Kristina thought about it, she felt sick to her stomach, she wanted to tell Amy about the pregnancy scare but no one needed to know that.

"No, she just said he was a really nice guy and she was embarrassed that she put him through the car chase with Joe."

"Do you remember what he looked like?"

"Uh, yea a little, he was tall and thin and had great hair. Brown hair, and he dressed kind of preppy. Well, not like a prep school nerd but just not like the hunters that come in here. Oh yea, he did tell her he was a hunter but he didn't look like one."

"When did he tell her he was a hunter?"

"That night, I heard them laughing and when I came down to get something for some drink I was making someone, I heard him say, 'Yup, that is my hunting story."

"Anything else you can remember about him?"

"He had a big smile. I wish I could remember more. I think he came in a few times before that night, with some friends. They sat in the table back there. Again, not anything unusual. I haven't seen him since." Kristina pointed to the back table then put her hand over her mouth holding back a thought. "Wait, he was here about two weeks before Jessica went missing. I think he was anyways."

"What makes you think that?"

"Well I remember his friends were at that table, they were playing some card game. I didn't pay much attention but yes, I do remember him being here that night."

A few people walked in the front door and sat at the bar. Kristina brought napkins over to their table and took their order. Returning to the bar she said, "I really don't remember anything else. I know Jessica didn't want Joe to know she was having feelings about anyone else. She wouldn't want to hurt him. I hope you find Gerry to ask him questions. If he did something then my radar sucks because he did look like a nice guy and Jessica is usually a good judge of character."

Amy took out her business card and handed it to Kristina. "Listen, if you think of anything else, will you call me?"

"Yes," said Kristina.

"Oh, and if that guy comes in here, call me!"

Kristina nodded.

AM Grout

~~~

Actions speak when words must be shared.
Sharing wisdom isn't always accepted.

Protecting the innocent is hard to do.
You can see the truth looks back at you.

If the truth could justify more pain.
These wounds would remain the same.

The past cannot be undone.
How the why began might shine a piece of the sun.

Fluttering by, hovering by, passing by, I do go.
Sharing the peace of where the wind does blow.

In your heart forever I will stay.
Moving on only when it's the right day.
~~~~~~

~25~ WHO'S YOUR DADDY?

Kristina got home that night and took a hot shower and cried. She reached for her robe on the bathroom door, it wasn't hanging on there; but Jessica's sweater was. She must have borrowed it, along with the necklace she still had. She intended to return it, but it just slipped her mind. Kristina wore the necklace to her funeral.

She forgot about her bathrobe as she inhaled the fibers of the sweater. She remembered the day she went shopping with Jessica at the mall, they each bought one of the Forenza brand sweaters. She had a pink one, but Jessica chose this light green one. It was super soft, and when Kristina wore hers in high school, her father would comment, "Glad you are wearing that backwards because that V is too low for the front." She rolled her eyes and told him, "It's not backwards, its fashion!"

Kristina embraced the fabric and sat on the bed. It smelled like Jessica. Happy Jessica, alive Jessica. Viki knocked on her door. "You home?" she asked.

Kristina opened the door and Viki saw she was crying. "Oh honey, I am so sorry. I wish there was something I could do for you."

"How about having the answer to who did this to her?" Kristina sobbed. "Why would anyone do this to her? I can't understand?"

Viki swallowed hard and hugged her. "I don't know why these things happen."

Kristina pushed her away gently and said, "This isn't some grandmother that passed away on your shift, this is my best friend and she", she paused, "I can't even say the word. She was murdered! How is that possible? I look at everyone that walks into Buckley's and wonder if they did it. And why?"

Viki handed her a tissue from her nightstand. There was only a few left. Kristina blew her nose and tossed the tissue on the floor next to all the ones she cried in the day before. Viki handed her another and said, "I'm freaking out too, I heard someone say this could be a serial killer. It seems like a movie, I just pray no one else gets hurt and her family can find peace. And you. You were such a good friend to her always. She loved you like a sister. I saw that." She rubbed her back.

"I don't think it's a serial killer and unfortunately I withheld some information that maybe could have helped."

"What was that?" Viki's chest tightened.

"The night Jessica slept with Gerry. She met him at the bar. I told Scott tonight about it, he said Joe knew she was cheating but they didn't know with who. I wish I knew Gerry's last name. I pray they find him. The cops think Joe did this or Teddy because he was the last one to see her. I never told them about Gerry because it was one night. I can't believe you don't remember that day. She was freaking out about messing up her pills"

Viki shook her head no.

"Jessica told me she really liked him. I was hoping she ran off with him so when she was missing I kept my mouth shut. Now all I can imagine is that he kidnapped her and tortured her because she rejected him. And truth is if she and Joe were broken up, she wouldn't have rejected Gerry."

Scott had told Viki that the father would have to prove he didn't do this. She felt bad for the guy. "Have the police talked with Gerry?"

"I don't think they found him. I don't know anything about him." She began to cry harder. "And I let her go home with him that night."

Tori was waking from her nap, Viki stood up and said, "Listen, you didn't send her home with any killer. You can't blame yourself for this. You did nothing wrong. Jessica doesn't need all her secrets exposed. So what, she had a one night stand; you were right not saying anything. Some secrets are meant to be silent. Why do you think I don't talk about Tori's father?"

Tori was crying in the next room. Viki left the room and came back with Tori. Kristina took her from her arms. "Hello pretty girl, yes I know I am a mess." Tori's blue eyes stared at her tear soaked faced. Viki began picking up the tissues on the floor and putting them in the trash barrel in the room. Kristina played with Tori.

"Do you want something to eat?" Viki asked.

Kristina shook her head no.

"Well, I am going to get Tori's cereal ready."

A few minutes later, Kristina brought Tori to the kitchen and put her in the bouncy seat. "Viki?"

"Yes?"

"So you do know who the father is?"

"I haven't had that many one night stands. We had only dated for a few weeks, it wasn't anything serious." Viki needed to think fast. She knew Kristina wanted to ask if Scott was the father. "When I found out I was pregnant with Tori, I decided it was best not to say anything. He had a job offer out west. I didn't want to hold him back."

"Did he have blue eyes?"

Viki thought about Scott's eyes. It was the first thing that attracted her and she was so glad Tori had them, she just hoped they would stay. "No. I bet Tori's eyes will change but I do love her eyes."

"Me too." said Kristina.

~~~
I've dreamt of the words that are for you to see.
And the lines shall focus your eye to me.
Searching for truths; exploring the lies.
And understanding the space between that lies.

I have heard the prayers.
Feeling the fear over the years, I have merely hovered here.
Fearing to scare, seeking to share, and
Not willing to trust a friend, again.

A stone wasn't there to trip.
The stone in the ground was there to split three ways.
Learning forgiveness is the hardest gift to fall.
For without a word, suffering is all so many hear.

Forgive the pain and feel my love.
See the orb of light that can warm a soul.
It has been me comforting your heart,
But so often the fear pierces through, killing me again.

Unsettled in you I have remained loving you just the same.
Hear the words of the fabric promising things will be better.
Time has not healed you and yet no time shall pass when
Face to face we reunite at last.
~~~~~~

AM Grout

## ~26~ TRUTHS FOR TRUST

Driving down Stafford Street, Viki passed the cruiser. Nausea called her name as the lights pulled up behind her. She cringed at the thought of that night he first played bad cop with her. Scott walked over to her window, leaned in, and flirted, "Need to get out of this speeding ticket?"

He had followed her home from Buckley's and turned his lights on her. She flirted with him by lowering the middle of her shirt. "Why officer, what did I do wrong?" she said in a cute southern accent.

He told her she was making his heart beat too fast and he would need to search her privately. She laughed and he followed her home. That was the night he invented the game of resisting arrest. In the kitchen he forced her to her knees with a gun at her head, then he threw her on the bed and choked her as he fucked her.

She woke up in the morning alone in her bed, realizing what had been done to her. When she went to work the next day, no one commented that she wore a turtleneck because it was the fall.

He summoned her to the office and asked how she felt. Viki showed him the welt. He kissed it and told her that wouldn't happen again. He kissed her neck over and over again, until she needed to kiss him back in return. Then in one swift act he grabbed her hair and pushed her to the floor. She knew what he wanted and that was the first time she did anything with him at Buckley's.

Now with his child, she knew she needed to protect herself. She said, "Kristina told me Teddy is a person of interest. Is he going to say he brought her to my house?"

Scott lit a cigarette and puffed smoke in the air. "Teddy is only a person of interest because he was the last to see her. He won't say a thing. He knows if he so much mentions that I was there, he knows he is going down. And that means you too. He has a loyalty to Jessica and to me. Besides, there have been several guys coming forward saying that they dated her. But unless their DNA matches, there will never be any charges."

"Can you just ask every guy she dated for a sample of DNA?"

"Well, first we have to find out which guy is telling the truth. You can imagine the freaks that call claiming to have something to do with this. Never mind all the girls that accuse their own boyfriends. It's a needle in a haystack, unless this guy volunteers his DNA, he will never be known."

"What if he does give his DNA? He didn't kill her?"

Scott inhaled the remainder of his smoke and said, "They still have to prove it."

He snuffed his cigarette on the ground and said, "If you blab a word you will quickly find that the rumor of the coke whore at Buckley's is true. And the nursing home would be shocked to learn that you've been stealing their drugs too."

"I'm going to quit there. I think I want to move far away and start over." Viki wished she hadn't said that out loud.

Scott pulled another cigarette out and said, "That's a good idea. But if I hear any chirping from you, I will find you." He lit his cigarette and walked back to his car. She stood there watching him drive away hoping she could find a way to get away.

## AM Grout

~~~

The attack was sudden and unprovoked.
The attack was extreme, especially to me.

I wanted to fight, I wanted to run.
I tried to live but I had to die.

A blue cloud lifted me to an angelic place.
Comfort and cures were all over the place.

The memory make me mad.
The truth makes me cringe.

He could have stopped.
He should have confessed.

He could have died, but he feared his fate.
For when he arrives, I will be here.
~~~~~~

~27~ A THREATENING GET AWAY

Viki read the note on the table. "I had to run to the bank before work, meet me at Buckley's." Viki was late getting home. She got back in her car and headed to Buckley's. Kristina was sitting in a booth with Tori feeding her cheerios.

"Hi there" Viki smiled as she walked towards the table. Tori's eyes widened and her feet kicked on Kristina's lap.

"Sorry I had you come here, but I knew I would be late."

"It's okay, it's my fault. I got held over at work."

Viki picked Tori up and gave her mommy kisses. The door opened and startled Tori. Viki continued to feed her the cheerios while she thought about how she would find another job.

A tall guy wearing a white oxford shirt opened the door. Kristina instantly recognized him. He nodded at her and smiled as he grabbed the stool closest to her. She greeted him curiously and calmly. "Hi. How are you?"

He fidgeted with his hair and said, "How are you doing? I mean, well. I guess I want to say, I am so sorry about your friend."

Kristina glared at him thinking about what Amy said, "If he comes in here, call me." She wanted to play cool but she felt so much anger thinking she could be looking at the killer of her friend.

"Thanks. It's been hard. Can I get you a drink?'

"Uh sure, a jack and coke." Kristina headed to the far end of the bar. She reached under the counter for Amy's business card that she placed there the night she came in.

Viki put Tori's jacket on and walked over to the bar. "Hey Kristina, I'm going to get going."

Just then the phone rang. Kristina lifted a finger to the sky and told Viki to wait a minute. She answered the phone. "Buckley's. Please hold." "Viki, wait a minute I need to tell you something."

Viki walked over to the bar where Gerry was sitting. The smell of Old Spice reminded her of her father. She hadn't seen her father since he remarried and moved to Roseland, California seven years ago. Other than gifting her the house when her mother died, he simply seemed to forget he had a daughter. She contacted him before she was pregnant with Tori and learned he had started a new family. She has four brothers, she probably would never meet. When she had Tori, she considered calling him.

Tori wanted her car keys, so she handed them to her. As Tori's grip misjudged their weight, she dropped them on the floor. Gerry smiled, picked them up and handed them back to her.

"Thank you." said Viki.

"You work at Country Light Nursing Home?" he asked. She forgot she still had her badge on.

"Yes. Just got out of work."

"My grandmother was there for a brief time. It's a nice place."

"Thanks. How is your grandmother doing?"

"Oh, she was doing great, moved back to Florida but then died a few months later."

"I'm sorry to hear that. My condolences."

Kristina finished writing down a message for Ken and hung the phone up. As she walked back over to get a glass, she raised her eyebrow and asked, "You guys know each other?"

"Well kind of. My grandmother was at Country Light." He nodded.

Viki watched him move his bangs out of his eye. "Probably before I was there. What was her name?"

He smiled and said, "Maye Williams"

Viki thought for a moment, "Oh, I remember her, I was her discharge nurse."

Kristina quickly made a mental note of the name, Maye Williams. She needed to call Amy. "Hey Viki, Gerry knew Jessica."

Viki wanted to drop her chin when she realized this Gerry might be the Gerry that Jessica mentioned to her. "Uh, how did you know her?"

Gerry looked at Kristina and said, "We kind of had a date."

Kristina had tucked the bottle of Jack under the counter and said, "Hey I have to run in the back to check something. Be right back."

Viki swallowed hard. Tori dropped the keys again and Gerry got off the stool to retrieve them.

"Uh Gerry, I have to talk with you privately. Like it's really important." Viki said.

Gerry's eyes looked around the bar curious of how much more private they needed to be. There wasn't anyone in the place except Ken who had went into the back office when Kristina went behind the bar.

"Ok. Is it about if I plan to join the class action lawsuit against Country Light for patient negligence?"

Country Light had a class action lawsuit for negligence on patients. With the laws changing, there was plenty of reports that Country Light was not staffed properly. An investigation that patients were intentionally ignored was front page headlines. Viki knew patients weren't intentionally being ignored, but being short staffed certainly caused longer wait times for patients needing attention.

The lawsuit was brought to the public's attention after an elderly man was found dead, trapped in his bedrails and obviously not check on for hours. His red button had been pushed but no one came to help. He was strangled by his bedsheets. People approached Gerry often when it made the news knowing his Grandmother was there. But he never saw any neglect toward her.

"No." Viki said, then she whispered. "It's about Jessica."

He raised his eyebrows and leaned into listen.

"You cannot tell anyone what I am about to tell you. And I mean anyone. But you need to know something." She looked towards the back room where Kristina disappeared to. "I know you slept with Jessica, she told me. And well; I. Well," She stopped herself because Tori dropped the keys again.

"Well, what? The cops know all about our date. It wasn't a big deal. I have nothing to hide."

"They know?" She froze as she began to pick up the keys. He got them for her.

"Yes, I told them a week after her funeral. I couldn't sleep thinking that maybe her boyfriend found out about our date and did this to her."

"Did you give them a DNA sample?"

"No."

"You can't give them one. If you do, they are going to get you for her murder."

Gerry stared into her eyes, "What? You are nuts. I didn't kill her. I have nothing to hide."

"But, you do." Viki said leaning closer to him. "She liked you. She told me. And she was embarrassed that she slept with you that night. She wanted to get to know you more but then this happened, and she, well, she didn't want you to know she might have been pregnant."

"What?" Gerry looked speechless. No wonder Jessica was pushing him away. He could tell she had feelings for him, they seemed valid but if she was pregnant, that really complicated life for her.

"She was. She didn't want to tell you. And you would probably never know because she wouldn't have had the baby. She miscarried; and well it got complicated."

"Did her boyfriend know she was pregnant?"

Viki again looked towards the backroom to see if Kristina was on her way back. "Listen, promise me you won't tell a soul but you have to trust me. You cannot give your DNA to the police. Don't do it."

Kristina came back with the Jack in hand and apologized, "I am so sorry, there was a problem with the keg line." She began to refill his drink.

"Listen, I feel terrible that Jessica died and I totally want the person responsible to be caught, but it's not me. I told the police everything I knew."

Kristina looked at Viki and said, "What is going on?"

Gerry picks up the keys on the floor and tossed them on the counter, "Nothing." He looked Kristina in the eyes. "Cancel the drink."

Kristina hoped Amy would get there soon. She said she was on her way. "Keep him at the bar. I'll be right there."

Gerry reached in his pocket and pulled out some cash. He threw a $10 on the bar.

Kristina raced around the counter and grabbed him by the arm. "Gerry wait, I want to know more about you seeing her at Greenways. I miss her so much. I need to know more about what she was doing that night."

He reached for her hand and held it. "Kristina, I am so sorry about everything that happened to her. I really am. I am just sick over it. She seemed like a sweet girl. We only talked briefly that day. She told me things were still complicated with Joe at the moment and she wasn't feeling good. I wish I had more I could tell you."

"How long did you stay?'

"Maybe ten minutes, not long. She was on the phone when I walked in. We talked only for a few minutes, then a customer came in so I left." He hung his head and said, "That was the last time I saw her."

Kristina didn't want to believe she was looking at the killer of her best friend. "What time did you see her?" Kristina asked, knowing Teddy had stopped by at 8.

"It was a little before six. I had to be at work for seven. And I was at work all night." He looked at Viki and said, "And the cops verified it."

Agent Amy Ashlyn opened the door. She wasn't in uniform. Her eyes told Kristina to meet her at the other side of the bar. Kristina took her drink order.

Viki whispers, "I'm serious, I know that Jessica was pregnant, and it was your baby. She told me."

Gerry turned around and headed for the door saying, "You are fucking crazy!"

Amy quickly rose and headed out the door. "Sir, Sir, Wait."

Gerry ignored her and headed towards the parking lot. Amy tried to stop him as he put the key in his door. "I have to ask you some questions."

Gerry opened the rusted door of the Oldsmobile that his father had given him for high school graduation. It was beat up but it got him where he needed to go. He slammed the door and drove away.

Amy reached for her keys and quickly threw a police light in her window. He pulled over one block over from Buckley's.

"License and Registration please." She asked when she got to his window.

"What for? What was I doing?"

"Sir are you drunk? I saw you leaving Buckley's parking lot without a signal and well over the speed limit."

Gerry rolled his eyes. "What is going on? I told the police about my date with Jessica. There isn't any more to tell. I'm not getting framed for her murder."

"Why would you think you were being framed?"

"That nurse told me Jessica was pregnant with my baby. That is ludicrous!"

"Would you be willing to provide a DNA sample?"

Gerry felt nausea. "Was she really pregnant?'

Amy asked him to get out of the car. She looked in his car. There wasn't anything noteworthy to arrest him on. No drugs, no open alcohol, no weapons. She wanted something, anything to bring him down to the station but she also played by the rules. Nothing is nothing.

Gerry stood next to his car as she searched it looking for anything to arrest him on. She wanted to bring him down to the station. "I didn't kill her. I have an alibi, check the reports."

"I will." Amy handed him back his license and registration.

~~~

So many deaths.
So much loss.

The lady says to me it is now time to talk.
Silently she guides my hand.

Together I don't want to understand.
Yet in the deep of the night...
There is still so much to fright.

All the colors of the light are coming towards me.
Gentle are her words flowing like a cape in flight.

Relief from a super hero can bring peace.
From the air to the garden the blue sash flutters in the wind.

The white ribbon knots a tree for innocent ones to be seen.
Oh, Mother Mary, you have always been real to me.
~~~~~~

AM Grout

~28~ PROFILING PROOFS

"Well Dr. LaVallee could have told her, they did work together for years. Maybe she slipped and mentioned it." Said Amy reviewing the bio she had on Victoria. "Or Jessica may have confided that to Kristina."

The Chief looked at Rolland as Rolland began flipping through one of the blue binders on his desk. He finally came to the page he was looking for. "Here, you have to see this."

Amy and Robinson looked over his shoulder and read the yellow document marked TIPS. It was the phone call from Liz Dalker. "Shit." said Robinson. "I want someone to talk with Victoria now! And without Scott knowing."

Obviously missing some facts, Amy stated. "Scott?"

Rolland walked over to the Jessica's timeline board and pointed to Scott's name. "Scott McKylie. The one who was supposed to have checked on Jessica after that 911 call. And rumor is he had an affair with the Victoria Mallard listed from this call. He pointed to the yellow TIP paper.

Amy stared at the report. "So this neighbor saw McKylie go into Victoria's house with a girl wearing a green skirt. He closed the curtains and then what they just killed her? Why?" She paced the room. "What if he did respond to the 911 call? It says here the girl was clutching her stomach. And ..."

"And, Victoria is a nurse." Added Robinson.

243

Chief Robinson turned to Dave, "Have you followed up with this?"

Dave said yes. The Chief said, "I assume it was nothing to you."

Dave wanted it to be nothing. "I talked with Scott. It was nothing."

He shared the conversation he had with Scott. "Hey buddy, listen we got a tip that said someone saw a cop visiting a house on Clifton Place that night." Scott smirked, "What I do with who is no one's business after hours." Dave told him he just wanted to follow up on the tip. "I can assure you it had nothing to do with Jessica. More to do with a Whitney." He winked. Whitney was a code name the officers used for their informants. Dave let it go, even though he had a pretty good idea that Viki was more than a Whitney.

"The pregnancy." said Robinson. "Shit, what if McKylie gave Jessica his business? Is this his baby?"

Amy looked up. "Could that have been possible?"

Chief said, "I won't rule anything out regarding who he may have spent his time with. Chat with her roommate again. Someone knows something. She didn't get pregnant alone."

"No she didn't get pregnant alone." Amy said, "I want to know if Scott was having an affair with her;" she paused, "what if he raped her?" Amy felt sick thinking of the possibilities that linked Scott and Jessica. "What if Jessica's call to 911 was for help, she obviously would had been in pain. Did Scott stop her from calling so he wouldn't be exposed?"

Amy looked at the map, the drive from Greenways to Stonewood Ext. wasn't that far. Her mind raced with visuals of Jessica's gutted body lying there. With the uterus removed, and the violent force she sustained, it didn't make sense.

"Why don't the two of you go talk with Liz Dalker? Find out more details about that cruiser on her street. And maybe while you are there, one of those girls across the street will be home."

Amy drove to Buckley's taking the route past Greenways. She timed the drive from Greenways to Buckley's, tracing the road Jessica drove many nights when she went to visit her friend. It was four minutes including hitting the red light at the intersection.

She popped her head in at Buckley's. Kristina wasn't working. Amy drove the four miles to Clifton Place. It was a residential area of all ranch style homes, the four houses in the cul-de-sac all had attached garages, whereas the remaining two dozen houses either had detached garages or the old fashion carports. The neighborhood was built in the fifties, however it was obvious the houses in the cul-de-sac were built in the late seventies.

Amy drove by Kristina and Viki's house slowly checking out the full size picture window which definitely was in direct viewing for the neighbor across the street. Dave's cruiser was already parked in her driveway.

Amy was happy to have an unmarked cruiser so that she could pay Viki a visit. As she climbed the porch stairs, she noticed the uncared for plants that had died long before the winter snow came. The doormat had hardly been used.

Its bright yellow flowers surrounded the paw print of cats. The word "Wipe Your Paws" made Amy's lips curl upwards remembering a childhood memory.

The curtains in the picture window were open exposing a simple small living room. She could see a couch, a chair, a large square coffee table with magazines and a vase of fresh flowers on it, at least they looked fresh from where she was peeking in.

To the right of the screen door, a ladder shaped bookshelf decorated the space with painted terracotta pots on each shelf. The pot on the top shelf had a yellow mum plant in the pot, as well as the smaller pots on the third shelf. The bottom shelf had stacks of empty plain pots nestled within each other. Amy didn't see the doorbell as it was hidden behind the bunch of artificial mums that were stacked on the second shelf. She knocked twice.

Viki was changing Tori's diaper. Curious to hear a knock from the front door, she gathered Tori in her arms. As she opened the door, her heart skipped a beat when she saw the cruiser in Mrs. Dalker's front yard. Amy stood behind the screen. "Hi, I'm looking for Kristina."

Viki recognized Amy from the bar. Kristina had told Viki who she was when she dashed out the door to follow Gerry. "She is a private investigator looking into Jessica's death. She had asked me to call her if Gerry came by the bar. I'm so lucky you were there so I could sneak off to call her."

They expected Amy to return to the bar after she followed Gerry but only Scott showed up. Ignoring Viki and Tori, he went straight to his office.

Viki held Tori tight and said, "I'm Victoria, Kristina is running errands. Is everything alright across the street?"

Amy pointed at Liz's house and used it to her advantage. "Her car was broken into last night." A cool breeze sent the screen door to flying out of Viki's hand. Amy said, "Would you mind if I come in to ask you a few questions?"

Viki hesitated as she looked at the cruiser and was relieved it wasn't Scotts. "Certainly, come in."

A blue knitted blanket laid neatly across the top of the couch which was adorned with matching pillows. Tori's walker sat under the picture window next to the television stand and was surrounded with stuffed animals.

Amy took a seat on the chair and took out her notebook. "Victoria, may I call you Victoria?"

"Viki is fine." Viki said as she busied Tori with the blocks that had been stored in a small wicker basket next to the flowers. "Was anything taken?"

Mrs. Dalker was really sweet. She knitted a baby's blanket for Tori as a welcome home gift. She had left it on the doorstep with a note. They never socialized but Viki often saw her at her mailbox, which is where she thanked her for the blanket.

Amy shook her head, "I don't know the details of that case. I just heard the call over the radio. I'm actually here to ask you both about Gerry Williams."

Viki's stomach knotted. "Well, to be honest, I don't really know him. I only know of him. I was his grandmother's discharge nurse."

"At Country Light Nursing Home?" Viki shook her head. "Yes, the same one that is all over the paper's because of the death of that elderly man." She added, "I worked on a separate floor."

Viki worked on fourth floor, completely unaware of anything happening until the newspaper article came out. Her supervisor held a meeting and told the nurses to dot their 'i's" and cross their "t's". That was one of the reasons Viki ended up coming home late every night, the paperwork was exhausting. Her floor hadn't had any complaints because her supervisor was a pain in the ass requiring the nurses to keep a summary of daily interactions with each patient.

"I'm not from the area so I am not aware." said Amy.

Every floor except the fourth at Country Light was a long term nursing facility that has been short staffed for years. Incoming nurses always requested transfers to the rehab floor since so that their patient success rate is higher. Rehab was on the fourth floor and really hard to get into.

Amy continued, "Gerry is a person of interest for us at the moment and it is vital that I get to know as much as I can about him"

Viki's stomach was doing flips. All she could think about was Jessica saying how nice he was and how stupid she felt. She mentioned his name only once but Viki was sure it was Gerry. "I really didn't ever talk with him until the other day. He recognized me at Buckley's. I remembered his grandmother once he mentioned her name. Like I said, I was her discharge nurse. She had undergone surgery for breast cancer and stayed on my floor for two weeks before being well enough to go home."

"How long ago was that?"

"Well, I was three months pregnant, so about a year and a half ago. Can I get you something to drink?"

"No, I'm good thank you." Viki headed to the kitchen to get Tori a bottle and the back door opened. Kristina walked in carrying some bags.

"What is going on across the street?' she asked Viki, then noticed Amy sitting on the chair. "Oh, hi. It's Amy right?" Amy nodded. "What is going on?" asked Kristina.

"There was a break in across the street." said Viki.

"And I wanted to ask you both some questions about Gerry Williams."

Kristina sat on the couch and told Amy about how Jessica had one date with him. "She really liked him but she hadn't broken up with Joe so it was complicated."

Viki wanted to leave the room. She prayed Tori would get fussy and need a nap. As Kristina recounted the story, she looked at Viki and said, "Do you remember the morning Jessica came over freaking out that she missed her pill? That was the day after they had their date."

"I don't remember that." Viki said distracted and thankful to hear Tori's cry.

Kristina said, "You told her about that abortion pill."

Viki said, "I did? I don't remember that. Did she take one?" Viki's heart skipped a beat as she considered what the complications would be on an ectopic pregnancy.

Kristina said, "No, she didn't need to. But I just remember that day so vividly now. She was freaking out that day, and now she's" Kristina took a breath, "Dead."

She began to sob. "Jess was so stressed about Joe and confused about how to start a relationship with Gerry. I told her it was just stress and it was. I know Joe didn't do this, and Gerry hadn't seen her in weeks." Kristina got up to get a glass of water. "Jesus, she freaking had her period when she was raped." Kristina looked at Amy and said, "What a sick fuck."

~~~

Decades fall among the beads.
One pink rose preserved in glass.

Shares a color of thankfulness.
As purity makes the white space last.

Send me some real signs.
Tell me nothing fake.

Trust the guidance that protect the innocence.
For the wicked flow low and their branches do break.

The tops of the tree can share how calm the wind blows.
No leaves shall fall but a dream will create a ball.

Find the rock to scatter the petals.
Don't conceal the truth, for innocent lives bear fruit.
~~~~~~

AM Grout

~29~ MAKING A CALL

Leaving the station late, Amy put a box of files in her trunk. Scott parked next to her. He knew the DA sent some women to organize the files on Jessica's case. Since he worked the night shift, he hadn't yet seen these ladies. "Hey there. You see that game the other night?" He nods to her NHL hockey bumper sticker.

"Of course." Amy smiled. "Boring first period but what a game. When Corriveau scored that overtime goal, I could sleep a happy girl."

"Well, it's always good to go to sleep happy." He said with a wink. Chills ran over Amy's spine. She reached her hand out and said, "Sorry we haven't met, I'm Agent Amy Ashlyn."

Scott raised an eyebrow and extended his handshake. "Scott McKylie. Pleasure to meet you. I had no idea agents were this good looking."

Amy often got complements but not as forward as this. 'Hey Scott, I got a question for you."

"OK…I hope it's that you want to grab a beer after my shift and talk more hockey."

"I was thinking that but maybe you can tell me more about Kristina."

"Kristina?" he asked

"Yeah. Kristina Legrand. She works for you at Buckley's right?"

"Yea."

"Well, I am sure you are aware that she is Jessica's best friend. I am just trying to figure out if she is hiding anything from us. We have Jessica's boyfriend saying she may have been dating another guy but Kristina denies it. Do you think she would cover for her? How well do you know her?"

"She's a good kid... And you know friends, they cover for each other. But at this point, I don't know why she would. If she was dating someone else, then I'd think she'd be screaming his name from the rooftops. That girl was destroyed in those woods. I know you didn't see her, but I still have nightmares about what, they did to her."

"They?" Amy asked. "Do you think there was more than one person that did this?"

"I don't know. I say they because well, I personally patrol those woods and I know there are some kids there that I've been looking at but I can't see a connection between Jessica and them."

"Who are they?"

"Wyatt's crew. I wrote the report up the day after we found her body but I seriously can't connect them. Jessica has no record of drug use or any reason to hang with those boys. I've arrested two of them for possession and constantly warn them to stop partying in the woods. I know they were in those woods the days Jessica disappeared."

"How do you know?"

"Saw their smoke butts and beer cans scattered. They admitted to being there. After I talked with them I knew they didn't know anything, they are just delinquents hanging in the woods"

Scott looked at his watch, "Hey, I got to check in. Let's talk later. Maybe after the game." He smirked.

"Yeah sure." Amy said, "Thanks for the info. Good luck tonight. Stay Safe."

"Always." Scott said.

AM Grout

~~~

Life is an incredible journey.
Family is everywhere, not only in blood.

Respect and honor doesn't always give forgiveness.
We must shine radiant power of internal love.

For you are where you are suppose to be.
Possibilities have no distance when love attracts.

Darkness attracts light for those that tremble.
Yet fragments of peace blow like a breeze.

Every turn we move forward.
In the direction for us to meet.

Embrace the wind and feel the warmth of the sun.
It radiates onto the welcoming ones.
~~~~~~

~30~ A RECOGNISABLE FACE

Viki drove to the nursing home, the counter in the lobby was filled with flowers from far away children wanting to wish their mom a happy mother's day. She knew none were for her. She quickly went into the office to look up Gerry Williams' parents address. She stared at the words before Gerry's father's name. Atty. Richard Williams. She had planned to just ask them how to get in touch with Gerry but now she considered that maybe he could help her.

On the drive there she rehearsed what she would say and it sounded so stupid. "Hi Mr. Williams, your son is going to be charged with murder because I know he got Jessica Briggs pregnant."

He would probably think she wanted to be paid off for not saying anything to the police about what she knew. She laughed at the opportunity to blackmail him but then thought maybe she could trade her silence for his representation.

She started to imagine her life with Tori. Moving to some remote island. She could get a job as nurse or a bartender at a beach resort. Far away from Scott McKylie.

The Williams house was beautiful, set back off the road. The driveway was adorned with large statues of lions on each side. She wondered how much a statue of that size would cost. Two of the four garage doors were open. A black BMW, and a white Cadillac Seville.

Walking up the stone sidewalk she took deep breaths like she was in labor. "You can do this. You have to do this." She said to herself. The doorbell chimed echoing through the walls. Mrs. Williams answered the door. "Hello?" she said, not recognizing Victoria.

"Hi Mrs. Williams, I don't know if you remember me. I was the discharge nurse for your mother-in-law at Country Light Nursing Home."

Mrs. Williams looked at her husband sitting on the couch. "Does this have anything to do with that lawsuit I read about in the paper?" she asked.

"Well, no." she stuttered. "This is awkward, but I was hoping to talk with your son."

"Gerry doesn't live here." She said. "I can take your number and have him call you."

"Uh, Okay." Viki said nervously. Mr. Williams had heard the conversation at the door and was now standing behind his wife. "Viki?" he said.

Viki smiled, "Hello Mr. Williams, I wasn't sure if you would remember me."

He smiled, "Of course." "Come on in." He opened the door wider.

"Thank you." She followed Mrs. Williams into the living room.

"On the flight back to Florida, mom talked about how sweet you were. You took her hair out of the curlers without pinching her she said." He said.

Viki sat on the Victorian style couch. The magazines on the coffee table were neatly stacked except for one opened magazine. Mr. Williams had been reading an article titled, Why Law and Letters Shouldn't be Strangers.

"I am so sorry to bother you. I looked up your address at work, which is probably against the law but at this point, I am desperate." she said.

Mrs. Williams made eye contact with her husband. He nodded to her and she left the room. He preferred appointments in the office, however there had been several occasions clients visited his home to obtain a lawyer.

"Are you in need of a lawyer?" he asked her.

"Maybe; but your son definitely will." She said biting her lip.

Mr. Williams tilted his chin as his eyes squinted. "How exactly do you know my son?" he asked. His mother told him Viki was a sweet girl. Said she wanted to fix Viki up with Gerry. Viki was flattered but confided in her that she was pregnant. Mr. Williams wondered if she was going to claim Gerry was the father.

"Gerry is in danger. He was involved with a girl in Tymingsly, the missing girl on the news. I know he is innocent and I can prove it but if I do, I think I will be the next missing girl in Tymingsly." She said with tears in her eyes.

Mr. Williams said, "This is a serious accusation you are making young lady. How exactly are you pointing the finger at Gerry for her murder?"

She started to cry. "I tried to help. You have to believe me. I tried and because she died, he is going to be blamed."

As a perspective client, Mr. Williams wanted to listen to the words behind Viki's tears, but as a father, his concern intensified. "Calm down honey. Tell me what is going on."

"I have a child, a little girl. She is the love of my life. Her father is not. He is a very bad man. He has abused me for years and I should have just left when I found out I was pregnant but it was too hard. I've tried to end it with him, but he still contacts me. As you know I am a nurse. And I am a good nurse."

She dried her eyes and continued. "Tori's dad. That's my daughter's name. He says he will plant drugs in my house or even leave me next to Jessica if I tell a soul what I know."

"How does this involve my son?" Mr. Williams asked, hoping to understand this girl's situation. As calm as she seemed, the fear was real. He was assessing if she was delusional.

"Gerry," she said, "Gerry, uh, dated her. It was only once. And well this is probably something he doesn't want you to know, but you have to know."

"I know he dated her. He told me. It's okay."

"No, it isn't. You see Jessica got pregnant and had a miscarriage. The police have the DNA of the father." She took a deep breath and said, "Its Gerry's baby."

The sound of a diesel truck drove up the driveway and rattled the windows. "I know this all sounds crazy but it's true. I don't know where to turn to and if Gerry gives the police a DNA sample, they will pin this murder to him and truth is it was an accident." She put her head in her hands and sobbed.

"An accident?" Mr. Williams asked.

"Jessica's death. I mean she didn't die, well she did, but she wasn't murdered."

"How do you know this?"

"I was there. I was helping her. She told me she really liked your son and wanted to be with him but felt so stupid for sleeping with him, and well, she didn't think she was pregnant, she thought she was just sick."

Viki sobbed uncontrollably. "She didn't have the flu like everyone said. That was a rumor she started. Well, not rumor, but she didn't know the truth."

Mr. Williams reached for the box of tissues that was in the drawer of the end table next to the couch they were sitting on. Viki blew her nose and stuttered. "Jessica didn't know the truth. No one knew the truth, not even me. I thought I was helping her and she died. She died on my couch." Viki cried harder.

The sound of the door to the garage alerted Mrs. Williams. She poked her head in the living room and said, "Gerry is here."

Mr. Williams gestured to her to have him come into the living room. Gerry saw Viki sitting on the couch, tissues in hand and mascara down her face. "Dad, the girl is crazy. I think we need to call the cops."

Mr. Williams motioned for his son to sit, "Gerry, you know how I have always said to give people the benefit of the doubt, so just hear her out."

Mrs. Williams listened from the doorway. "Viki is worried about you, and herself. She says that girl you dated. The one you told me about."

"Jessica." Said Gerry.

"Yes, Jessica." He looked towards his wife, then back at him, "Viki says she was pregnant with your child. Do you know anything about this?"

Gerry looked at Viki and said, "You are a fucking liar. You are starting rumors to get me framed for her murder."

"No, no, no" Viki said over him. "I am telling you the truth. I told your father. I was there when she died! She told me you were the father." Viki spoke as fast as she could. "I didn't know it was you. I only knew it was some guy named Gerry. When I saw you at the bar, and Kristina introduced us, I seriously put it together."

Gerry thought about their conversation at the bar. Viki hadn't recognized him as Maye's grandson.

Viki continued, "What are you going to do if you give your DNA and it matches?"

Mr. Williams looked at Gerry and said, "Is this possible?"

He nodded.

Viki started to cry, "Listen, I tried my best to help her. I thought I removed the pregnancy but I was told it was an ectopic pregnancy."

"Were you giving her an abortion?" he asked.

Viki told them everything that happened.

"Is this Scott a cop?" asked Mr. Williams.

Viki pulled another tissue out of the box and wiped her eyes. "U-huh" she moaned.

Mrs. Williams sighed. She trusted her instincts and felt Viki was telling the truth. "Viki, you need a lawyer. Richard, can you represent her?"

"I can't afford a lawyer. I just want to get out of here. If he finds out..." She started sobbing again. "I just want Tori to be safe."

"Where is she now?" asked Mrs. Williams.

"Home, with my roommate Kristina."

"Does Kristina know about Scott being abusive to you?"

"No! No one knows anything about our relationship. There were a few rumors once but he squashed them along with threatening me. When Tori was born, I told him he wasn't the father and he flipped on me. He started calling me a coke whore to my face and threatened to prove it." She held back her sniffles and added, "I'm not!"

"Is Tori his?" asked Gerry.

"Yes. She has his eyes. They are beautiful but I pray they fade away as she gets older." Viki blew her nose and took a deep breath.

AM Grout

I want to talk.
I want to scream.

There is an open door for all to see.
Those beads bring light praying in the night.

Colors changes on an angel's wing.
Sorrow and stress doesn't heal grief's time test.

Skyward eyes pause to stare.
For within the blueness, pieces share the path to justice.

My eyes have dried but my heart was pierced.
Forever remembered for a death that was fierce.

I need to cry.
To accept that I died.

I shall hover a light to shine faith and hope
In the black of the space that give me flight.

~31~ CONFESSIONS WITHOUT GRACE

Mike Piccard sat at the breakfast counter at Coffee Currents. He hadn't stopped thinking about Jessica. The Chief questioned if he dated her. Truth is he would have. Heck, he dated anyone he could, and Jessica was as fine as they came. The fact that reports that he was stalking her surfaced, freaked him out. He had stopped in several times. He was on duty. He didn't admit to flirting with her for the record, but he did. Then again he did that with everyone.

The Chief understood when he refused to give his DNA. At the crime scene Mike removed his gloves after hearing the others get scolded for not having any on. With bare hands, he picked up a ski pole, a can of beer and a plastic cup. Carrying them to mark them as evidence, the Chief yelled at him. He apologized and quickly grabbed a new pair of gloves.

The day Jessica's body was found, he acted just as shocked as everyone but truth was when Scott picked him up at Buckley's that night. He was in for the test of his life. He wanted to be a police officer since he was nine. Busting criminals and writing tickets was all he dreamed of. Now less than four years on the job and he wanted to transfer out of Tymingsly.

He thought about approaching the Chief a few times, but the fact he was a person of interest, and a responding officer the day her body was found, made it out of the question to be transferred.

Two days after they found her body, he met Scott here, in these same seats. Teddy sat on the other side of Scott when he raised his coffee towards Mike. "Hey Mike, you been out hunting lately? Teddy smirked, then Scott said, "You still looking to break your cherry?"

The waitress chuckled as she poured Mike's coffee.

"Uh, No. I'm good." Mike winked.

Scott replied, "Good. Let it be. Keep your hunting equipment clean and just let it be. Trust me, it will happen."

Teddy could care less about hunting, his mind raced wondering how Jessica ended up dead in those woods. Scott said he dropped her off at the corner of her apartment building. Teddy believed him but when she turned up dead, he questioned his cousin, "Did you really drop her off at the corner?" Scott barked back at him saying "You're questioning me? Where the fuck did you drop her off?"

Mike didn't even want to look at Scott. It questioned everything in his bones. Ethically he knew he had to report but how was the question. It would be his word against Scott's. Someone had to talk.

Mike came back to his reality and raised a thumb to tell the waitress to bring him another coffee. Scott glanced at him from the side and said, "What's up?"

Mike lowered his chin, "So they think Jessica was cheating on Joe."

Turning toward Mike, Scott said, "What the fuck are you talking about? Whose 'they'?"

Mike lowered his voice and said, "I heard Kristina and Viki said something."

Scott took a sip of his coffee and said, "Great."

Scott drove straight to Country Light after he finished his coffee and tucked a note on Viki's windshield.

Viki saw the note flapping in the wind as she headed to her car to pump her breasts during her lunch break. She preferred the quiet sanctuary of her car with her own music playing than the nosey talkers in the nurse's lounge. She planned to breastfeed for a year but now that she was back to work, her supply seemed to get smaller each day.

She hoped it was an advertisement, but based on the 3x5 memo lined paper, she knew it was from Scott.

She scanned the parking lot for any signs of him then read the words written. 'Do you hear a bird chirping?' A pair of eyes wearing glasses were drawn on the paper.

She tore the paper in half and tucked it in the cup holder. "Screw you Scott McKylie" she yelled. She slammed her hand on the steering wheel, then took a deep breath and turned the key.

She stopped at a payphone to call her supervisor. "Hi, sorry to do this to you, but Tori is sick and I need to call out for the afternoon."

She sped into the William's driveway and rang the bell. Mrs. Williams came to the door. "Viki, what's wrong? Are you okay?"

"Scott knows I said something. I don't know how but I got this note." She handed the torn up piece of paper to her. Viki paced the floor. "I have to get out of here. He is going to kill me."

Mrs. Williams picked up the phone and called her husband to tell him Viki was at the house. "I'll be right there. Keep her calm, and get Gerry over to the house. He said.

Gerry was on his portable PlayStation. His shift as a flight attendant gave him plenty of time to play the new version of Dragon Slayer, especially when his roommates weren't home hogging the game. Video games were a childhood pastime that he became obsessed with in high school. He dreamed of one day making his own video game but for now whenever he had downtime, he jumped in a game.

He lived seven miles away and with no traffic lights, it was an easy and quick ride. His dad was already there. "I called the DA yesterday and he sent an Agent Amy Ashlyn to assess our situation. She is on her way now."

Mrs. Williams explained about the note and Viki shook with fear on the couch. "I can't lose my daughter."

Amy arrived within a few minutes and said, "Listen Viki, Mr. Williams has told me what is going on. I appreciate and understand why you felt you couldn't say anything. But we need to get Scott for this crime. You are the only person that can put him with Jessica that night."

"But that makes me an accomplice or something. I can't lose my daughter. He has taken enough from me."

"We will work out as many details as we can. Are you willing to tell me what you told Mr. Williams about your relationship with Scott, and what happened that night, and now today?"

Viki nodded. Mr. Williams said, "For the record, I will be representing her." Amy nodded and said, "Then I ask your counsel if I can record this conversation." Viki followed Mr. Williams nod.

Amy placed her recorder on the table and repeated the date and time, as well as the location into the recorder and they had a conversation. Viki told Amy everything. Mr. Williams didn't object to any of the details. He wanted Viki to share her story and he knew it would help his son if it came down to it.

Amy listened and reassured Viki she was doing the right thing. Mrs. Williams cringed at the visual of Viki recalling nights of their role playing game. Viki took a photo out of her purse and showed them Tori and her blue eyes. "I don't ever want her to know who her dad is, he is a monster."

Amy explained what she felt the DA would do with this information. "Until then, we can offer you protective custody at a private shelter."

At first Viki wanted to ask how they would provide protective custody without Scott finding out, but when she heard the words "private shelter", she had to ask, "For how long?"

"Well, at least until his arrest, and perhaps even until the trial."

Viki said, "What about Tori?"

Amy shook her head, "I cannot offer that until I talk with the DA. Is there anyone she can stay with? Have your family watch her, tell them you have a job interview out of town for a few days, at least until we can come up with a more permanent reason for your absence."

With her head in her hands, she listened to Amy and shook her head, "I don't have any family around here. They don't even know about Tori."

Mrs. Williams said, "I will take care of her."

"Yes, make us Tori's guardian." said Mr. Williams. "Better yet." He paced the floor and said, "Hear me out, if Gerry was her father, he would have legal rights to have her."

"But he isn't her father." said Viki.

"Regardless, you said it yourself that you told Scott he wasn't the father, if Scott challenges that Gerry is her father, then he will have to prove he is her father." He looked at Amy, "This could work. Viki can take a leave at work and tell them she has to go to court in another state to apply for sole custody. I have a friend that works in the family courts."

Viki was confused. She knew the Williams wanted to help her, but adding Gerry's name to Tori's birth certificate seemed wrong. But then it kind of felt right.

Mr. Williams walked over to Victoria and said, "Actually, if Gerry agrees to what I am about to suggest, you wouldn't have to leave Tori." Viki raised her eyebrows.

Amy looked at both of them, as Mr. Williams turned to Gerry and said, "If you and Victoria got married, no one would have to file for guardianship, and Viki could stay here with Tori while working with me to prepare the case. It could be a win-win-win, because as a married couple neither of you could testify against each other, nor could anyone take custody of Tori."

"And I wouldn't have to go into protective custody?'

"No." said Amy.

"But what about Scott?"

Gerry had been staring at his father. "It really could work." said Mr. Williams. "But that is up to you son."

Gerry paced the room, "But what if Jessica wasn't pregnant?" He looked at his mother, "She could be completely crazy and just trying to get me to confess to something that isn't even true."

Mrs. Williams motioned for him to follow her to the kitchen. "Even if Jessica wasn't pregnant, the truth is this girl is in trouble. This is a huge call to duty and I will respect whatever decision you make."

"But what if something happens to Viki and I really am left with sole custody of Tori? I don't even know her! I can't be a father."

"Honey, children are a blessing and Tori deserves to have a loving family around her, especially if something happens to her mom. Would you want her shuffled around between foster families for the next sixteen years? Think about all you have been through. This could have been you. Adoption is a gift. You are the greatest blessing to me."

He knew she was right. It was the right thing to do. Being a single mom was what his own mother intended to do until she overdosed when he was three. If it weren't for the Williams, who knows where he would be.

AM Grout

~~~

The dew of the morning creates the water of the roses.
The fragrance lasts longer than the bloom ever will.

Petals fall displaying its core.
Memories linger painting a portrait.

No thirst can be quenched by only the Rosewater.
When intact, the petal's message is stronger.

Daylight passes for the bloom to unfold.
Trusting the scent will find its way home.
~~~~~~

~32~ A BULLET WITHOUT A TRACE

Over the next few days, Amy worked with Viki to write her statement. Mr. Williams called his childhood friend, Reverend Charlmae. Reverend Charlmae was on retreat until the weekend. He left an urgent message for him to call immediately when he returned.

Amy met with the District Attorney. She discussed providing protection for Viki until Scott could be arrested. Sully was impressed that Gerry and Viki agreed to Amy's suggestion of legally marrying.

Sully was concerned. "If Viki is lying, then Gerry will be an accessory after the fact." He told Amy that this was her call. Amy said, "Viki has nothing to lie about, and even if she is lying, she is at least setting Tori up to avoid child services."

Sully agreed. If Viki was telling the truth, he wanted Scott off the force immediately but he also needed to proceed properly. He said to Amy, "Update Chief Robinson that Viki avoided a paternity suit by marrying Gerry. Then talk to her roommate. Someone has to know that Scott is Tori's father. Find someone."

Amy update Chief Robinson. He understood the necessity to push for information regarding the paternity of Tori. Robinson agreed she should pay a visit to Kristina at Buckley's. She asked if Dave should come with her. Robinson

273

said, "I reassigned him to another case. This is too close to home for him, and he had to have some surgery, so I took him off the case." Amy understood.

At the bar, Amy got Kristina's attention and the two walked to the far end of the bar where no one was sitting.

"Kristina, can you tell me something about Tori's father?"

Kristina asked suspiciously, "Why?"

"Gerry is claiming to be her father and wants paternity."

Kristina's eyes widened, "What? Gerry is Tori's father? I don't believe it."

"Why not?" asked Amy

Kristina's mind raced to the night Jessica left with him, then to the next morning and then to Viki meeting him here the other day. "I live with her. I would think she would have told me."

"She never mentioned who Tori's father was?"

"No, I once asked about it, but" Kristina looked in the direction of the office. "I kind of assumed it was Scott."

"Why did you assume that?'

"Well." She hesitated. "It's just that once I asked Viki if Tori's dad had blue eyes because Tori's eyes remind me of Scott's"

"What did Viki say?"

"She said no. I never really believed her but I didn't question her. But I saw the way those two flirted when I went to the bar. The rumors back then were that they had an affair before Tori was born." Kristina sighed. "To be honest, I've often suspected they still saw each other on the nights I worked. The house smelled of cigarettes when I would get home. I never asked Viki and secretly hoped she was a closet smoker."

Kristina wanted to ask her if she was working the night Jessica went missing but she knew she could look that up in the report. Plus she needed to stay focused to help Viki.

"Viki never mentioned her relationship with Gerry?"

"No. She just ran into him the other day here." She pointed to the area where they met. "Uh, now it makes sense why he was so angry at her." Kristina thought about how he called her crazy. "She must have told him about Tori."

"I don't know about that." Amy didn't want to confirm any details. "Can I ask you if you remember a day when Viki was attacked at the nursing home by a patient?"

Kristina's eyes dazed in thought, "Ya. She was covered with marks on her neck and scratches on her arm. She told me the patient was having an episode and she just got caught in the crossfire. She said he was having a psychotic reaction to his meds or something. I asked her if she was going to press charges but she said it was part of the job. What does this have to do with Gerry?"

"It has nothing to do with him."

"What does Gerry want?"

"Well, I heard that he is seeking paternity."

Kristina shook her head, "Wow, that's a heavy news flash. I need to call her."

Scott walked in. Amy reached for her keys. "Tell her to call me when you see her." Kristina nodded.

Scott came around the bar. "What was that about?"

Those blue eyes never looked more like Tori's than in that moment. "She wanted to know about Viki. Apparently, Tori's father is in town and seeking custody of her."

Scott raised an eyebrow and said, "Really?"

"Yea. Truth be told, I always thought you were Tori's dad." Kristina felt dazed as she reached for the bar towel and began to wipe the bar. "I don't get it. She never told me about him."

"Who is he?" asked Scott

Kristina looked down and shrugged her shoulders. She didn't want to see his eyes piercing through her. "I don't know."

"Lucky her. Maybe she can get some money from the baby daddy." He said looking out of the corner of his eye as he counted the twenties in the register. Kristina kept wiping the counter. She couldn't look at Scott. He closed the register and said "You should have enough change for tonight. I'll be back later."

Kristina said, "Ok."

Scott drove by Viki's house, her car wasn't in the drive way. He sat at the end of her street for a few hours. When her car turned down the street, he turned his lights on. She refused to pull over and made a U-turn in the cul-de-sac at the end of her road. He followed and forced her to drive off the road into the field of a farm. She got out of her car and screamed at him, "Stay away from me!"

She was shaking, Tori was in the back seat. "I told you to stay away from me!" He smacked her in the face. "I thought we had an agreement. Why you flapping your lips about Tori's daddy?" She put her hand to her cheek and with fire in her eyes she said, "I haven't told anyone."

He looked at Tori in the back seat, then leaned close to Viki's ear and said, "Kristina knows." Viki kneed him in the groin and quickly jumped back in her car. Her tires spun in the grass as he banged on the window, "Open this door bitch or I will fucking break it." She peeled away.

An oncoming car was headed towards him, and swerved to avoid hitting him in the middle of the road. He screamed at the driver, "Slow Down!"

Kristina's suspicious look at him was burned into his brain. He drove back to Buckley's. She was locking up. He planned to press her with questions about what she knew about Viki's paternity suit but he went into the office and opened the safe. Kristina headed out the door to her car when she heard him call her name.

"I want to tell you something important." Scott moved closer to her.

"What's up? Did I forget to do something?" she asked.

He replied, "No. But I want to share with you something about Jessica's murder, that maybe you can explain."

Shivers ran over her body, "What is it? Is it about Gerry?"

"No one knows this but there is a tree that someone carved with Victoria's initials and Gerry's name." Kristina was confused. "What?"

"Yes. This is why that agent was asking you questions. Viki's was jealous that Gerry slept with Jessica so she killed her."

"I don't believe you." said Kristina.

"Follow me."

She followed his cruiser to the entrance to Stonewood Extension. She hesitated to get out of her car. Scott opened her door and reached in his pocket. He quickly pulled the trigger close to her head. The bullet went thought her hair and she fell back into the car. He place the trigger holder on her thumb, closed the door, and drove away.

Victoria was sleeping on the bed when she heard the lock on the backdoor. Scott walked into Victoria's bedroom, stopping to take a towel from the bathroom. She jumped when she saw him. "How did you get in here?" she asked.

"There have been some break-ins in the neighborhood. You should get your locks changed." He then pushed her against the headboard and said, "Why did you run from me today?" She tried to push him off her but he was too strong. He put the towel across her face and slapped her hard. "Are you going to make me silence those lips?" She shook her head and yelled, "No."

Tori began to cry. He moved the towel and smacked her with it. Then he punched the towel as it laid on her chest. She tried to roll over. She whimpered, "Stop, please."

He pushed her off the bed onto the floor and kicked her in the ribs. She begged, "Please stop. Kristina will be home soon."

"Don't worry, she is working late tonight."

Scott played resisting arrest with her as she wriggled around trying to really fight for her life. "Let me check on

Tori." She begged. He ignored her and began to choke her. She blacked out. When she woke in the morning, Tori was screaming in her crib. "Kristina?" Viki tried to yell with her faint voice.

Dazed and battered, Viki dragged herself past Kristina's room to Tori's. She picked Tori up and consoled her. She changed her diaper then carried her to the kitchen and picked up the phone.

"Mr. Williams, I need help. He was here last night. I have to get out of here."

Mr. Williams listened to what happened. He put one hand over the bottom of the phone and whispered to his wife to call Amy on the other line. Mr. Williams said, "Viki, take a breath, I have Amy on the other line. Talk with my wife for a minute, we are going to take care of you. Breathe."

Mrs. Williams took the phone from him and said, "Viki, I don't know what is going on, but I promise you, we will help." Viki calmly held Tori as she listed to Mrs. Williams reassure her.

Mr. Williams gestured to talk with Viki again. Mrs. Williams handed him the phone. "Listen, Viki, Amy is on her way over to your house."

AM Grout

~~~

Strangers case the place where I once was.
The uniform was a friend.

Now I feel so alone.
The morning dew quenches my skin.

The cool breeze sends shivers through my head.
Today brings a revelation that dampens the festivity for years to come.

I don't understand.
In front of me, I see a friend.

The colors of the rainbow swirl to blue.
A rainbow embraces my faith once again.
~~~~~~

~33~ SILENT PASSING

Amy arrived on the plant covered porch and knocked loudly. "Viki, Viki?" Viki jumped at the sound and came to the door holding Tori still in her pajamas. "Viki, you have to pack your bags now. I have to get you out of here."

"Why? What's going on?"

Amy looked at the red marks on Viki's neck. "Did he do this to you?'

Viki nodded her head.

"When?"

"Last night."

Amy didn't want to tell her. Not now, not here. "Viki, I'll give you ten minutes. You have to pack, I have to take you and Tori out of here."

"Where too? He will kill me if I leave. He will find me."

"You have to trust me. Scott will not find you. I talked with Mr. Williams. Gerry is signing the marriage certificate. Mr. Williams and the DA have a judge ready to put Gerry's name on Tori's birth certificate, they only need your signature. You have to trust us. Tori will be in safe hands."

"I can't leave her. She needs me, she needs my breast milk still."

Amy reassured her, "I can bring it to Mrs. Williams and you will have to wean her. After we have your complete statement, and Scott is in custody, we can bring you and Tori together."

"Where are you taking me?"

Amy looked at her. "Protective custody. We have a connection with a facility in the next state. We will have you examined by medics to assess you." Her eyes went to the welt on her cheek. "To document Scott's abuse. The DA will need to match Gerry's DNA because it will solidify your statement. They are in the process of obtaining it."

"How?"

"We have ways to get DNA under the radar. The match wouldn't hold up in court so we are doing it under the radar."

"But will Gerry be charged with murder? He didn't kill her! I can't let him be blamed."

"He won't. Like I said, obtaining his DNA without a warrant would force his lawyer to contest it, making it not useable for the case. I talked with Kristina. I think I can get her to testify that Scott is Tori's dad."

"But she doesn't know Scott is the father. I never told her."

"She has always thought that, and that could be enough grounds for obtaining his DNA. Once Kristina gives us her statement, Scott will have to prove otherwise. And once his paternity is matched, your lawyer will file a restraining order at which time Scott's misconduct will be investigated. You have to trust me. Mr. Williams has already reached out to the president of the American Bar Association. They say you have a great defense of entrapment, never mind the abuse."

Viki rocked Tori back and forth repeating, "Oh, Tori, I am so sorry." She kissed her and handed her to Amy.

Amy followed Viki to her room, "Just pack the essentials, we can have someone pack all your things and forward them to where you will be relocated to."

"Forever?" Viki asked.

Amy's beeper went off. She pulled it off her hip and asked to use the phone.

Viki filled a suitcase with Tori's clothes and toys, and diapers, then she went into her bedroom and opened her top drawer. In it was the news article of Jessica's obituary. She tucked it into a small music box and put it in her own suitcase. Amy walked in and said, "Viki, sit, I have to tell you something."

Amy hesitated and said, "Kristina's been shot."

Viki heard the words in slow motion. She mouth the word, "What?" then staring into the distance, she whispered, "Scott?"

The phone rang once then it stopped.

AM Grout

~~~

The silence began at the sound of the bell.
Hesitantly I answered yes to a demanding request.

Why argue, why protest.
The threats, the beatings, and the fear was real.

No one to call except for you.
You were protecting me? But I was protecting you.

Nothing stop from hearing her cry.
Mistakes are made but lies create so much more to hide.

The calls have stopped. I see the fate.
No right is wrong when I saw your face.

You were protecting me.
I thought I was protecting you.
~~~~~~

~34~ TESTAFIABLE LIES

Mr. Williams arranged to have Amy bring Viki and Tori to the chapel at the Hinsdale Hospital. Gerry and his mother were already there. Viki hugged Tori and cried as Mrs. Williams took her. "Viki, I promise I will take good care of her. It will only be for a few days."

Viki cried and looked at Gerry, "Do you really want to do this?"

Mr. Williams and Gerry exchanged a look. "Yes, if something happens to you, I promise I will help take care of Tori. My own mother overdosed when I was born and if it wasn't for the Williams, who knows where I would be today. I can be a good father to Tori and well, together we can get through all this." He squeezed her hand gently.

Reverend Charlmae entered the room and Mr. Williams introduced Viki to him. He explained that he has known Gerry all his life. "He is a good man. We all make mistakes but when one can step up to help another, which is the call that only God provides." Viki was shaking. "I can't believe you are doing this for me."

"For us." said Gerry. Mr. Williams nodded his head and Reverend Charlmae began to have them recite the vows.

AM Grout

After the vows were exchanged, Mr. Williams excused everyone from the room saying, "I'd like to talk with my clients alone."

Mr. Williams said, "Listen, with this marriage contract, neither of you can testify against each other. Viki, you cannot say you knew of Gerry's relationship with Jessica, nor his paternity of Jessica's pregnancy. And Gerry, you cannot mention Scott, nor anything Viki told you about the night Jessica came to her. Let the DA investigate, and until Scott talks, you both are safe." They nodded at the same time.

Amy came and took Viki to the facility in the next state, Viki wept. Amy hugged her. "You are doing the right thing." she said.

Viki gave her deposition for the following three weeks. Each day, Amy would retrieve less and less breast milk and bring it to Mrs. Williams; returning with updates on Tori and photos for her. On the twentieth day, Amy convinced Viki to contact her family on the west coast. Viki's dad had remarried. He was working at Edwards Air Force Base in California, and Amy knew this could be helpful for a relocation process.

Viki contacted her father and explained what was going on in her life. He agreed to help her. Amy found Viki an apartment in Lancaster, a few miles from the Air Force Base and arranged for her to have employment at the clinic on the base.

Reverend Charlmae traveled with Viki to California and helped her settle into her apartment. Each day driving the ten miles through the gates to the clinic, Viki cried missing Tori. It was fall back home, Viki knew from Mrs. Williams that Tori was excited to go pumpkin picking. After over six week of not seeing her, Viki demanded to visit.

Amy didn't think it was safe but even Father Charlmae felt mother and daughter needed to be reunited. Viki came back and stayed with the Williams for one night to pack Tori's things and then moved her to California against the recommendations of the District Attorney but she couldn't be without her daughter.

Back in Tymingsly, Scott shared stories about Kristina suffering from so much grief she took her own life. He told Robinson he was shocked to learn Kristina used the gun from the petty cash safe that night.

He shared that Kristina had taken the gun one other time when she felt threatened in the bar. Scott assumed that is how she had the gun that night. After a quick investigation, it was confirmed to be a self-inflicted gunshot wound.

Scott seemed genuinely sad to have to replace her. Until then, he worked the bar listening to the rumors surfacing that everyone had thought Scott was the father of Viki's child. Scott laughed it off.

He told everyone, "She was a coke whore that I should have never fucked. It ain't my kid and she isn't getting any money from me."

A few weeks after Kristina's funeral, Jessica's roommate, Kathy pulled Joe aside and said, "I know you don't want to hear this, but I know for a fact Jessica did date someone else. I told the police. Kristina knew too. I think she felt guilty not telling them or you. Now with Kristina gone, I just want you to know I never meant to hurt you. And Jessica didn't want to either."

"Do you know who it was?" he asked.

"His name is Gerry Williams." Kathy said. "The police said he had come forward already and his alibi checked out. He didn't kill her but she did cheat on you with him."

Joe was numb and he was done. His girlfriend was dead, everyone talked about how she had wanted to break up with him and was afraid. That motive made him the prime suspect. He couldn't even find relief in knowing the truth that he always suspected. He knew she cheated, he just didn't know with whom. Ted denied knowing Gerry when Joe asked him.

"Ted, I just don't get it. Everyone thinks I am a bad guy. They think you are hiding something and truth is Jessica was the one hiding the truths. Everyone is talking about how wonderful and innocent she is, but what the fuck, someone killed her, raped her and all I know is she cheated on me. Is that fair? Fingers pointing everywhere except at who really did this? I'm done. The police have my DNA, my fingerprints, my statement, my alibi, they can't need more from me. I'm telling her parents that I want out of all this. She didn't want me in her life anymore, so why should I bother to stay."

"Whoa; buddy, relax. Jessica really cared about you. She cared about everyone, she never wanted to hurt you which is why she was so afraid to break up with you. I'll be honest. She told me New Year's Eve, she was thinking of ending it with you but she didn't know how we could all maintain hanging out still."

Joe glared at him and said, "Well we can't."

Scott shouted, "Joe, wait. Listen, Teddy was just trying to protect you, and Jessie. You got to give him a break."

Joe flipped Scott off and walked out.

"I can't blame him. I lied to him. Best friends don't lie." Said Ted.

"You didn't lie, you just didn't tell him what could hurt him. And that is a good thing." Scott winked. "Some secrets are meant to protect. You know what I meant."

Mike Piccard walked in at that moment and said, "What do you mean?" he demanded in a playful voice. Scott glared at him and said, "I was just telling Teddy here not to air any dirty laundry. Get it rookie."

Mike looked at Scott and winked, "Chill dude, it was a joke."

AM Grout

~~~

The world looks different at another angle.
The world shines light with a help of an angel.

Somethings so sacred you can't share with anyone.
Then somethings bring fear so we never lend an ear.

The ones that help, understand the view.
The reporters, only report the news.

There are details that are awful.
There are truths that will always remain unclear.

Yet within these wings is nothing but love.
Some things to forgive and much more to give.

A prayer for help is always heard.
Years never erase when you are gone too soon.

I want to cry. I need to sigh.
Reaching for my hand, the lady understands.

My memory restored with a moment of darkness.
Then the light interrupts this reconcilable pause.

Colors swirl as I find my place.
Knowing you will remember my face.
~~~~~~

~35~ HONORING TRUTH

The wait staff was setting tables for the first of the summer's outdoor dinner show. Mrs. Teggotta was in her office sorting program booklets. She saw Ted walk by her office. "Ted, Ted, come in here a minute."

Ted hung his head defeated as he answered, "What is it?"

She reached into her desk drawer and handed him a business card. "This girl came in here asking questions about Kristina's roommate, Victoria Mallard. I don't know her. Do you?"

"Not well." He said taking the card from her.

"Well, this girl wants you to call her, she says it's urgent. Something about wanting to ask you about her husband." Ted felt the raised letters on Amy Ashlynn's business card. He headed down to the foyer to use the payphone, quietly repeating, "Viki's husband?"

Amy asked if she could meet with him at Rosewood. She arrived thirty minutes later.

"Apparently, Gerry and Viki were married. She left him before Tori was born. Rumor is she filed a restraining order against him."

AM Grout

Ted's eyes widened, "What?" Amy was good at using loose facts to leak information. She needed Ted to tell her about Viki and Scott.

Amy nodded, "Viki says he was stalking her. We think maybe he was stalking Jessica. We are thinking maybe Jessica knew this information and refused to tell Gerry where Viki was living. And when Jessie wouldn't tell him, he got angry and well, you know the rest. Viki is in trouble. Her husband has admitted to her he was involved with Jessica. Viki feared for her life and left town, leaving Tori with his parents."

"That is ridiculous. Viki wasn't married." Teddy's stomach turned. "She worked for my cousin Scott for a few years, she had a reputation of being a coke whore. I wouldn't believe anything she says."

"Really, well, what if I tell you she says you brought Jessica to her house the night she died. And we have an eye witness that saw Jessica in her living room with you."

Ted shook his head. "They are lying."

"Ted, listen. I know you didn't do anything. Viki told us you only dropped her off so she could help her. We need you to corroborate her statement. She has been badly beaten. It happened the night Kristina died. She claims Scott McKylie did it to her. And we need you to just tell us what happened that night."

Teddy shook his head and said, "I don't believe you. I told the police everything about that night. I gave my DNA, I have nothing to do with Jessica's death."

Amy interrupted, "Well, if Viki's story checks out, then you may just be more involved than you think." She put a manila file on the table and opened it. Inside was a photograph of Jessica's body covered with maggots and dried blood lying in the snow. "He did this to your friend."

"No." said Teddy. "He told me he only gave her a ride home. Viki's husband was the one that did this to Jessica. He followed her home."

"Where did you hear that?" asked Amy.

"Scott told me." Teddy closed the file. Tears welled in his eyes. "How could he have done that?'

Amy took the file and retrieved a photo from the back and put it in front of Teddy. The photo was a specimen jar labeled APR-1L. "This is the DNA found in Jessica." She said. "We know it doesn't match you, but if it matches Gerry, he will go to jail for her murder. Can you live with that?" Amy glared at him.

Teddy sat silent.

"Would you like me to read you your rights?"

"Am I under arrest?" he asked.

"Not yet."

He folded his hands and said, "I think I need to talk with a lawyer."

"Absolutely." said Amy. She handed him Mr. William's card. "You might want to talk with him."

Back at the station, Amy told Chief Robinson and the DA that Teddy was getting a lawyer. Robinson was frustrated. He didn't have enough to charge Scott or Teddy with anything until Viki's story checked out. Looking at her bruises in the photographs and knowing the rumors he knew about Tori infuriated him.

"If we can prove Scott's paternity, then Viki's testimony will get him indicted. Without that, we are done. And if we get Gerry's DNA before that, then Gerry is done."

~~~

Spirt melts into oneness.

The oneness of creation.
The oneness of grief.
The oneness needing peace.

Be not the jury nor the judge.
Be the change in the creation.
Be the comfort in the grief.

Spirit knows the truth.

The truth of love.
The truth of trust.
The truth of forgiveness.

Be not afraid of love.
Be the seeker or truth.
Be the wisdom of light.
~~~~~~

AM Grout

~36~ ONE WAVE

Lara McKylie didn't expect to see Chief Robinson when she stopped at the post office. He was buying stamps. It was his day off. Robinson knew her father had just passed away. He planned to attend the services but was out of town with his own family that week. He paid his condolences to her.

Lara thanked him and began to walk away but something stopped her. She looked at his gentle schoolboy face and said, "I need to ask you something."

Robinson lowered his head as they walked outside the building and stood next to the mailbox.

She took a deep breath. "I'm sure you heard I filed for divorce."

Robinson had heard. Scott came into his office last week and requested some time off. Scott looked genuinely upset.

Lara adjusted the box she was carrying and said, "I don't know what is going on with Jessica's case but if you tell me he was involved with that girl too, I'll kill him myself."

Shocked by her tone, Robinson said, "Lara, he wasn't involved with her. He is on that case, that's all. I don't get involved with the social life of my men."

Her eyes darted at the woman getting a child out of her car. Then she said, "Well, I know he cheated on me.

Several times. I didn't have any proof but if I get any, then I'll nail the bastard in my divorce settlement. Do you know how many women called our house? Hanging up when they heard my voice. He said it was his Whitneys, I don't believe it."

"What did you know about his Whitneys?" Chief asked.

"I've seen him with a few at the coffee shop, and ignored them. The one that called the house a few times was a woman named Viki."

Robinson's tilted his head and asked, "When was that?"

"It was almost a year ago. She sounded in trouble so I talked with her. I don't think he messed with her. She was a respectable nurse and not a coke whore like the others."

"I don't know much about his Whitneys."

"Well, I can tell you one thing. I asked him why he keeps calling someone in the 604 area code. I saw it on the phone bill. Am I being paranoid or could he have an informant in California?"

The box she was holding was heavy, she set it down on the ground. "I know undercover work can't be talked about, but I am begging you to tell me if he has another woman there?"

"I will look into it." said Robinson.

Robinson called Amy. "I know you can't tell me where she is. But is it any interest to you that Scott has called the 604 area, and is currently out of town."

Amy was at the courthouse now with the DA. Teddy was giving his deposition. She couldn't tell Robinson where

Viki was but the 604 area code was where the Naval Base was located. Amy knew Mr. Williams had ties with the Navy. She called Mr. Williams.

Mr. Williams didn't like the fact Amy was telling him Scott was out of town. "Where is he?" he asked. Amy said she would find out.

Mr. Williams had served in the navy until his retirement. He had friends at Edwards Air Force Base. He urged the relocation knowing she would be protected. She resumed her nursing career at the triage clinic, while Tori attended the day care in the next building.

Mrs. Williams visited a few times bringing paperwork for the Briggs case. It allowed Mrs. Williams to spend time with Tori. Tori got more and more excited each time she visited. "When is Grandma coming back?" she asked her mother each time she left.

Viki took a half day, fully intending to get her grocery shopping done and get a manicure before picking Tori up at daycare. The receptionist offered to take a message. The man simply said, "No message. I will try her at her apartment. Have a good day." Mr. Williams had called the office many times. The receptionist didn't recognize his voice.

Mr. Williams called her apartment and left a message on her machine. "Viki, this is your father. Please report back to work as soon as you get this message. They are looking for you and have called here looking for you. I will meet you for dinner later tonight." He hoped she would understand the urgency. He contacted his wife and had her get them tickets for the 2pm flight to California.

Amy's beeper went off. She removed the beeper from its holder which was fastened under her shirt on the right side of her belt. She recognized Mr. Williams's number. The double asterisk after the number indicating an urgency for her to call. She quickly requested a recess from the deposition citing personal reasons. Using the pay phone again, she called Mr. Williams. "What's up?" she asked.

"I need you to find out exactly where Scott is. My wife and I are headed out of town in a few hours."

"Is everything alright?" asked Amy knowing his impromptu trip must have something to do with Viki.

"Just find out where he is. If I don't hear from you before I take off, I'll call you when I land."

"I'm on it. I'll call you back." She said adding, "Good luck with your trip."

The DA was organizing papers when Amy gestured for him to talk to her. "Mr. Williams just called. He is going out of town on a family emergency and he requested we find out Scott's location."

Sullivan's eyes widened. He nodded and said, "Where are they headed?"

"I think Viki is in danger. I told him about Scott's phone calls to the 604 area code. I know there is a Navy Base there. My hunch is that is where he's relocated Viki, and maybe that is where Scott headed?" Her eyes fiercely confirmed everyone's suspicion.

Sully made a few phone calls and checked his computer. Within ten minutes he confirmed Scott boarded a plane yesterday for California. They knew his location. He contacted the Lancaster sheriff's department and requested to have a visit paid to Scott's hotel.

Mr. Williams contacted Gerry and informed him that Viki might be in trouble. He said, "Listen, I have all your statements in an envelope on the kitchen counter. Come take them and keep them in your possession until I get back."

"Why?" Gerry asked. He had written those statements months ago regarding his one date with Jessica and included his visit to Greenways the night she went missing. The police had copies on file, he didn't understand why he needed them.

"Just do it. If, and I stress if, something happens to Viki or the sheriff's department shows up at your apartment, leave them for them to find."

Amy and the DA returned to the deposition room. Teddy was exhausted. Amy walked over to where Teddy and his lawyer were sitting and said, "We just got word that Scott knows where Viki is. He left town yesterday." Teddy's eyes widened.

The judge reentered and resumed Teddy's testimony. The DA again asked Teddy what his relationship with Viki was. Teddy had consistently answered "I only know her as the bartender at Buckley's. I know Kristina lived with her but I never really socialized with her." Teddy refused to confirm any details about Viki's relationship with Jessica or Scott, pleading the fifth.

The DA glared at him in the eyes. Teddy whispered to his lawyer. His lawyer said, "Off the record for a moment." He nodded to Teddy. "I was at Viki's house that

night." He lowered his eyes. Teddy explained how Scott
requested he give Jessica a ride. "She was in a lot of pain.
Viki is a nurse, she only was helping Jessica." He said.

"Scott is my cousin, he is a good guy. He didn't do
anything to Jessica. He told me he brought her home that
night." Teddy began to cry and he admitted he always
thought Scott could be Tori's father. He repeatedly said, "I
brought her to Viki because Scott told me to. I thought he
was helping." He began to cry.

Back in California, Scott was detained in the hotel
lobby by the local sheriff's department. "Scott McKylie?"
Scott turned towards the man in the sports coat. The man
showed his badge and said, "We have a few questions for
you."

Scott wanted to run but he sat with the two men in
the hotel lobby. They asked what brought him to California.
He explained his wife filed for divorce because she though
he was having an affair. He came out to get away and think.

"Any chance you planned to share your thoughts
with a Victoria Mallard about your divorce?"

Scott's poker face told the men all they needed to
know to arrest him. "Who?"

They showed him the restraining order that Viki had
filled out in California when she arrived. It boldly announced
a No Trespassing Order against Scott McKylie. Scott rolled
his eyes.

"We highly suggest you head back home."

Scott nodded. The man folded the no trespassing
order and put it in the inside pocket of his blazer. He nodded

at Scott and said, "Good day." The other man bent his fingers into a childish goodbye wave.

Scott headed to his room. He wrote an address on the pad and packed his bags. The sheriff wasn't smart. The no trespass order listed Viki's home address.

It had been almost a year since Viki disappeared. Scott took notice when Mrs. Williams left town. He hired a private investigator to follow her and hit the jackpot when the PI gave him photos of Mrs. Williams with Tori and Viki. He researched where she was working and now finally got her address.

Her apartment building was a three family house. The entire place was in desperate need of a makeover. Pieces of scaffolding littered the front yard and was assembled on the driveway side of the house. Not much progress could be noticed except the overflowing dumpster which suggested one of the apartments was being gutted.

Scott parked his rental across from the front door and entered the building. The first floor apartment was unlocked and opened. The construction was in the demolition stages. He opened the door leading to the upper floors. On the second landing was a wicker basket with yesterday's paper and a few discarded magazines. The mailing label on the magazine was addressed to a Peter Faulkner. Scott continued up the stairs.

A stroller leaned against the wall to the right of the door. He knocked. No Answer. He picked the lock and waited. Her answering machine blinked with the message from Mr. Williams. An hour later, Viki entered carrying groceries. She put them down and saw Scott. "I hear you are trying to save your husband." He emphasized the word husband. She ran to her bedroom and locked the door.

He tried to stop the door from closing but she quickly locked it. She had taken his advice and gotten better locks. She even installed a deadbolt on her bedroom door. With the door locked, she opened her nightstand and grabbed Mr. Williams' business card.

"Did you tell him what you did to Jessica?" He yelled pounding on the door. Viki tucked the card into her bra and opened the window.

She jumped onto the scaffolding outside her window just as Scott pushed the door open breaking the lock. The curtains blew out the open window. Looking down he saw Viki climbing onto the second floor, she lost her balance, screamed, and fell.

The neighbor outside mowing his lawn saw her fall. He looked up to the window where Scott was standing.

When the paramedics arrived, there was no man in her apartment and the groceries bag was spilled on the floor. The neighbor couldn't describe him. Said he didn't look long enough because he ran to see if Viki was okay, then ran into his house to call 911.

~~~

He has been free.
He has lived a life.
He has given life and mine is over.

He stole my rights.
He violated my will.
The family, the community, the world will never be the same.

We need redemption, so many need peace.
Peace on the streets.
Peace in the way life is meant to be.

No hatred.
No violence.
No killing will ever rectify what he did in his life.

But on Earth as it is in Heaven...
This light on him will forever change or forever destroy him.
~~~~~~

AM Grout

~37~ A CANDLE IN THE NIGHT

Mrs. Williams took custody of Tori as Viki remained in a medically induced coma for two months. With the construction on Viki's apartment building on going, Mr. Williams had Viki's things moved to a storage facility on the Navy Base.

Mrs. Williams brought Tori to the apartment to pack her things, Tori went into her mother's room and started playing with a music box on the night stand. Mrs. Williams was startled by the music. Tori handed her a paper folded inside. It was Jessica Briggs's obituary.

Mr. Williams didn't allow Gerry to travel to California. "Let your mom handle it, Tori has enough changes going on; and if Scott made connections in California, then you will be putting yourself in jeopardy."

Mrs. Williams moved to Santa Rosa, California, a few miles from the hospital Victoria was at. She cared for Tori as Viki underwent several surgeries, and visited Viki every day updating her husband on Viki's condition.

When Viki came out of her coma, Amy headed to see her. Viki was heavily medicated as she recalled what happened at the apartment. The DA has informed Amy that he made a motion to indict Scott on witness tampering and it was granted. He told Amy, "The grand jury will convene within the year. I need Viki's and Gerry's deposition."

Amy knew they had Gerry's DNA but since it was obtained without a warrant, it would not be allowed in as evidence for the time being. She knew the key to proving Scott's involvement was in proving his relationship with Viki, which they needed Tori's DNA. The DA instructed Amy, "Get Viki to sign consent."

Victoria shook her head no. Amy explained how having Tori's DNA would validate her statement. Viki refused, repeating, "I don't want her involved. She doesn't need to ever know who her father is. I told her it was Gerry. She knows Gerry's mother like her own grandmother. It would change everything for her."

Amy empathized with her. "I understand, but there is no other evidence to establish the basis of your relationship with Scott." Viki refused.

Within a few weeks, Viki's lungs collapsed for a second time and she didn't survive the next surgery." Mr. Williams explained to Amy that in California law the rights of a minor far outweighed the facts of the case in Tymingsly.

With Viki now dead, their witnesses were dwindling. Sullivan was pissed. "I cannot let this Brigg's case remain unsolved when we damn right know what happened. Williams should file a wrongful death lawsuit, which might get suspicion on Scott, enough for us to move forward."

"I don't think he will go for that. At his point, he just wants to protect Tori's rights and honor Viki's wishes. And there is no way to prove Scott was in her apartment."

"If I get Gerry's DNA legally, his son will be charged. His only out will be if a jury believes Viki's statement without her testimony."

Sully secured a warrant and called Mr. Williams. "We are serving Gerry tomorrow." he warned.

Mr. Williams booked the next available flight which wasn't until the morning. He instructed Gerry to stay at their house that night. Mr. Williams didn't want Gerry at his apartment when they came to serve.

Gerry's roommate, Dan Braden, answered the door in his bathrobe. Shocked to see four officers at the door. He explained

Gerry wasn't home. He said, "He is probably at work, I don't know his schedule." They left Gerry the DA's business card with a two words written on it, "Contact ASAP." When Gerry arrived home, the business card was taped to his door with a note. "Cops were here looking for you, what is going on?"

Gerry called his father for instructions on what to do. Mr. Williams was in route from the airport. He said, "Leave the file containing your statement with a note for your roommate to give to the police. Then head to Huffington Hospital. Go to the emergency room, tell them you think you are having a heart issue, and they will keep you for observations. I will be there ASAP."

The DA had no jurisdiction at Huffington, he would have to file an extradition across state borders, and even with connections the paperwork would take at least a week giving Mr. Williams plenty of time to file enough motions to delay and even get the subpoena dismissed.

AM Grout

~~~

The river flows gently at my feet.
A man stops to share the news.
We chat about what happened.
It wasn't his fault.

He did the best he could to be a friend.
When all went wrong, as it often does.
He covered me so my fear would be safe.
He followed his instincts hoping to do what was right.

When the water washes over him.
Next to the river my feet remain.
And my hand touches the bridge of faith.
Together we cross the raging waters.
~~~~~~

~38~ A BLUEJAY KNOWS

Dan Braden was confused when he saw Gerry's note on the table. 'Please bring this envelope to the police', Gerry wrote, 'I've been avoiding this for a long time, but it's time to face the music. Sorry to involve you.'

The envelope wasn't sealed. Dan opened it. The details of his date with Jessica Briggs, including the fact he slept with her. Dan was shocked.

Dan remembered when Jessica died. It was all over the news, his own girlfriend at the time wouldn't drive at night in fear there was serial murderer. Dan sat at the table and poured through the pages. He didn't want to give them to the police. He believed Gerry's words. Gerry didn't do anything but Dan knew these papers could incriminate him. He called Mr. Williams and asked him what to do. Mr. Williams said, "Do what Gerry requested."

Sully opened the envelope, and the statements. He called Mr. Williams and arranged a closed door meeting with Gerry, Amy and Robinson. Sully guaranteed that everything would be off the record for the moment. He shared Teddy's deposition and shared that without Kristina's statement, her comments to Amy would be hearsay in court.

 Sully said, "A judge will need more than Teddy's suspicion that Scott and Viki were in a relationship."

Robinson suggested Lara McKylie testify. "Her testimony could prove he had been unfaithful throughout their marriage.

She remembers Viki calling the house. She even talked with her once." he said.

The DA shook his head. "No, that would be circumstantial. We need proof. Getting Tori's DNA is the only way. There is no motive for Scott to have disposed Jessica and helped cover up for Viki. Without Viki to be cross examined, a defense would discredit her statements in a heartbeat, and believe Scott. Once a jury hears Gerry fathered a baby with Jessica, there would be more than reasonable cause for him to have murdered her."

Mr. Williams interrupted, "But he has an alibi. You have the flight record from his job. He wasn't even in town."

The DA pointed to the photograph of Jessica's body as Bob Baxter discovered her in those woods so many years ago. "Yes, and then all charges would be dropped and Scott gets away with that. I can't let that happen. Besides, once a jury receives the evidence APR-1L, they will know Gerry was involved. The press would have a field day."

Amy opened the file containing the medical reports on the six week old embryo found in Jessica's right fallopian tube. A report with the word MATCH was attached to a photograph.

Gerry's eye became wet when he saw the photograph of APR-1L. The reality of Jessica's death. His baby. He never knew. He wiped his eyes and said, "Just take my DNA. I'll take my chances. Jessica never intended for anyone to know about the pregnancy. If I have to be a monster to protect her truth, I will."

Mr. Williams objected. Turning to Gerry he said, "If she had told you and gotten an abortion, you would not be held accountable. If she kept the child, and never told you, you would never know. She decided not to tell you, that is her business. Let them work at proving you are the father."

Amy exchanged looks with the DA and said, "Jessica may not have even had the confirmation that she was pregnant. And without confirmation of the pregnancy, APR-1L shouldn't even be entered into evidence."

Sullivan tapped his finger on his chin a few times then said, "APR-1L has to be entered into evidence, without establishing the father, the defense has a better case at arguing reasonable doubt. And Teddy only puts Scott at Viki's house, which he will deny it."

Sully began to pace the room. "I don't like it. I want Scott. What he did to her body isn't justifiable. I think we need to prove he is Tori's father. Get Tori's DNA entered as evidence."

Robinson looked at Amy. She was thumbing through Viki's file. A photograph of Tori and Viki was stapled to the front inside jacket. It was taken the day Amy told her about Kristina's death. He reached for the file and said, "We asked her for it then. But she refused." He looked at Gerry, "But in light of the fact that she is no longer with us, that makes you the sole guardian of Tori; and you could approve the test."

Everyone stared at Gerry. "And what if I agree, and Scott doesn't get put away?" Gerry looked at his father. "Could he gain custody?"

Mr. Williams looked at the DA and nodded to his son. "If this gets out of hand, I will file a motion to suppress the evidence based on the rights of the child."

"Understood." said Sullivan.

For the next several weeks, Sullivan presented the case to the grand jury, including the circumstantial evidence that Tori was the daughter of Scott McKylie. The judge denied the hearsay.

Sully introduced the photos of Viki taken after he attacked her the night Kristina died. He made several motions to the grand jury including five counts of witness tampering (Teddy, Viki, Wyatt, Kristina, and Gerry); three counts of assault and battery (Victoria, Jessica and APR-1L); two counts of intent to commit murder (Kristina and Wyatt), one count of involuntary manslaughter (Victoria), one count of murder felony (Jessica, APR-1L), one count of destruction of evidence (Jessica), one count of illegal disposing a body (Jessica), and five counts of obstruction of justice.

Sullivan knew he didn't have enough evidence for the grand jury to prove Scott had any involvement in Wyatt's or Kristina's deaths but for the record he wanted it noted. The grand jury subpoenaed Scott's DNA. It didn't match APR-1L and the charges were all denied for lack of evidence.

Teddy pleaded guilty to obstruction of justice and was sentenced to community service. The evidence marked APR-1L disappeared from the evidence room the following year.

Seven years later, Mr. Williams passed away and was buried next to Tori's mother. Amy Ashlyn attended the funeral. During the graveside service, several birds chirped in the distance. Viki's stone was etched with a pink ribbon honoring her mother's battle with breast cancer. Tori reached down and picked a pink rose from among the flowers at her grandfather's grave.

As she leaned to place the rose on her mother's stone, she overhead Amy whisper to Gerry, "I commend your commitment to being Tori's father. Your family has been so great to her and Viki."

Tori tuned out the birds and looked towards her father. He mouthed the words "Thanks" to Amy. A bird landed on the casket and everyone gasped. Tori looked at the bird as Gerry smiled and said. "God works in mysterious ways."

"Yes he does." Amy said.

~~~

Time has not passed long here.
I've waited to feed your soul.
But peace came with a price.

I didn't plan to sit idly by.

He did not do what he did to me, to you.
But what he did to you was try to protect you.
That was wrong and now you hear me.

A little too late for me, but not for you.

I only tried to do what was right,
But death came in the dark of the night.
I felt the blame, you gave him a name.

Your heart feels more pain than me.

We want you to heal.
Even if I am wrong.
It might set something right.

Life deserves so much more than feeling the rain.
~~~~~~

AM Grout

~39~ THIS ONE IS FOR THE CHILD

Over the years, Tori held her mother's jewelry box and reread the obituary for Jessica. She had been told that her mother was friends with her. Tori often included Jessica in her prayers, wondering what happened to her.

After her grandfather's funeral, her mind raced thinking about how often her grandmother would be on the phone with her grandfather over the years. Talking secretly and always apologizing to her that he had to be away with work so much. Tori knew he was a lawyer but his cases were always in Tymingsly, the hometown of Jessica Briggs.

When Tori was beginning her college search, she wanted to consider going where her mother went. Her grandmother insisted she could study nursing in Santa Rosa but Tori wanted to see Hinsdale.

Gerry met her at the airport, and they toured the campus. The college had changed, it was now a private university, expanded over forty acres. Tori noticed a memorial wall. Names of deceased alumni were listed. She slid her finger down the M column until she saw her mother's name.

As they left the college, Tori asked her father to show him where her mother had lived when she was attending Hinsdale. Gerry drove her by Victoria's old house. The house had changed too. It had been renovated and the porch removed.

Gerry slowed by the house, then made his way past the nursing home and onto Buckley's Bar. "That is the nursing home my grandmother first met your mom." He said pointing to the Tritown Rehab sign. The place looked exactly the same.

As a child, Tori often asked her grandmother to tell her the story of how her parents met. Mrs. Williams told her that her mother-in-law, Mae set them up on a blind date.

Tori was told her father worked to pay off all of her mother's medical bills, which is why he wasn't home very often. Every night Tori said her prayers which always included, "And please watch over daddy and keep him safe in the air."

As Gerry pulled his car into the parking lot of Pitcher's Sports bar, he said, "This used to be Buckley's but it has changed owners since your mom worked here." Tori asked if they could go in. Gerry got out of the car and took a deep breath. The last time he was here was the day he met Viki.

Seventeen years later, he sat across from Tori. Three television screen lined the wall behind the bar. Gerry faced Tori ignoring the ad paid for by the Trump campaign. They placed two orders of the fish and chip special; and ordered two ice teas.

Tori took one sip of her drink before changing the subject about the new layout of the bar. Clearing her throat she said, "Dad, there's been something on my mind since Grandpa's funeral." Gerry's stomach knotted as he asked "What?"

Tori explained, "I overhead Amy Ashlyn say something to you at grandpa's funeral. She said it was great you were so nice to me and mom. It confused me and got me thinking. I mean you were never home when I was a child and grandma raised me after mom died. I've been trying to figure out why Amy said that. Then one night after watching an episode of The Big Bang Theory, I considered that maybe I wasn't your daughter. I mean, where did these come from?" She pointed to her eyes. "Studies say they are from the father's side of the family. Grandpa didn't have blue eyes and well, I got to thinking. I sent a swab into one of those DNA testing sights, these are the results."

Gerry didn't touch the envelope she placed on the table. She put her hand on his. "Why Dad?" she asked. "Why did mom and I really have to move to Roseland?"

Gerry nodded toward the front door. Tori turned around and saw the paper asking for tips in the unsolved murder of Jessica Briggs. "Because of Jessica?" she asked.

He nodded and said, "Tori you have to understand, your mom wanted to protect you."

Tori's mind raced, she glared at him and said, "From what? You?" She stormed out the door grabbing the flyer as she left.

That night, Tori called the tip line and said she might have a tip regarding the Jessica Briggs case. She met with the DA. Sully explained the circumstances to her and showed her the deposition her mother gave before they left for the protection Edwards Air Force base offered. "Tori, you have to understand, your mom was trying to help Gerry but when Scott threatened her, she feared for her safety and yours. Gerry's family helped her to escape and helped to protect you all these years."

"Where is Scott?" Tori asked.

"Still working here in Tymingsly." Sully said.

"I want to meet him." Said Tori.

Sully said, "Let me talk to Amy and make it happen."

A week later, Amy arranged for Tori to be wired. They were hopeful Tori could get Scott to admit he was her father. Tori walked into the coffee shop where he was sitting. Her heart raced as she took the stool next to him.

"Excuse me, are your Officer Scott McKylie?" she asked in a quiet voice. He turned and said yes.

She extended her hand and said, "Hi, I'm Tori." His smile faded as he squinted to recognize her.

"Tori Mallard, Viki's daughter." She said firmly.

He furrowed his eyebrows. "Who?" He asked.

"Viki Mallard, the woman you fathered a child with nineteen years ago." Tori raised her voice.

Scott quickly stood up and reached for his radio. "Ma'am, I think you have me confused with someone else. Have a good day."

She followed him into the parking lot. "Wait. Please. I found a letter she wrote to you."

Scott turned and said, "A letter?"

Tori said, "Its right here." She reached into her purse to hand him the subpoena. The DA and Amy Ashlyn stepped out of an unmarked car. "Scott McKylie, you have the right to remain silent." They cuffed him and read him rights.

Sullivan refiled his motions from years ago. The jury refused to indict Scott on Kristina or Wyatt's murder. Scott's lawyer filed a motion to dismiss the DNA search but the DA filed a motion to get DNA samples from all suspects, including Scott. The motion was granted. Scott and Gerry both matched just as Viki Mallard said they would.

The reality that Gerry fathered the pregnancy that killed Jessica sent shivers through him and seeing the reality that Scott was responsible for disposing Jessica's body so violently turned his stomach. Tori held her father's hand throughout the trial as her own stomach knotted learning the truth of her biological father.

Scott's lawyer called Mike Piccard to the stand to testify that he witnessed Scott dumping Jessica's body. Mike began to corroborate Scott's testimony only to have the DA file charges on him as an accomplice. The judge quickly agreed and when the discovery of Mike's black notebook from that week was entered into evidence it solidified the charges. In it, Mike wrote "SM made me defile the oath."

The DA interrogated him and Mike broke down on the witness stand admitting that the initials were Scott's. Mike cried,

"It violated everything I understood about being an officer. Scott called me a rookie. I knew he had pull to get me removed. I wanted to be an officer since I was a boy. I watched him plunge my knife into her, slicing her belly like a deer. He removed her uterus and tossed it into the woods. He told me I would no longer be considered a virgin when it came to hunting."

Scott glared at Mike. "I have the knife still. I told him I tossed it but I buried under the bridge during the reconstruction. Tossed it in the cement as it rushed into the pylons."

Sullivan made a motion to charge Mike as an accessory. He pleaded guilty before they even read him his rights. The following day, the jury came back with a guilty verdict for Scott. The courtroom was silenced by the betrayal. Sullivan shook Amy's hand and extended hugs to the Briggs family.

Tori tapped Gerry on the shoulder, "Can we visit Jessica's grave?" she asked. Gerry said he would take her there. As they entered the cemetery there was a farm stand selling fresh cut sunflowers. Tori bought two and gave one to Gerry.

Jessica's stone was covered with coins, and a patch of miniature pink roses bloomed in front of it. Tori placed her sunflower on the coins and hugged her father. "If that baby never died, then we would all be in different places right now."

"Yes we would." said Gerry. "Yes we would." He knelt down and placed his sunflower next to Tori's.

Only the blooming buds at the base of the stone recalled the day they were planted. It was when the evidence labeled APR-1L went missing. Mike Piccard parked his cruiser next to her stone, his heart raced hoping no one would catch him planting the rose bush. He dug a small whole, emptied a container of water in it and planted the rose bush in it. The only thing is it wasn't only water, it was a container marked APR-1L.

AM Grout

~~~
Welcoming us through the gate.
The long path grows shorter as the trees lead to the garden.

Blue delphiniums stand tall among the rose bushes.
Every shade of pink imaginable.

And there in the garden is a single flower standing tall.
A sunflower reaching for the sky.
Stretched beyond its comfort with petals perfectly peaked.

There are flowers gifted to grow.
And there are flowers gifted for us to know.
The meaning, the fragrance, the beauty to be fully embraced.

When God opens the gate.
The light of love illuminates the space.
~~~~~~

AM Grout

~40~ A MALLARD'S STATEMENT

Tears fell from Tori's eyes as she listened to her mother's words during the trial.

I, Victoria Mallard, admit that I treated Jessica Briggs on the night she went missing. Scott McKylie called me for help. His cousin's girlfriend was possibly having a miscarriage and he asked me to help her. I didn't want to but wasn't given a choice. Teddy Teggotta dropped her off at my house around 9:00.

My baby was asleep. I tried to reassure Jessica everything would be fine. She went into the bathroom, took off her skirt and put on my roommate Kristina's bathrobe. Scott arrived with some medical supplies from the clinic above Buckley's. I used to work there and assisted Dr. LaVallee with private procedures.

Jessica was running a fever and in severe pain. Upon examination there was so much blood that Jessica gave me consent to extract the pregnancy. It would have been dangerous to let her bleed like that. I couldn't call the police because I had been warned in the past. Unfortunately, as I was performing the menstrual extraction, Jessica went into what I thought was cardiac arrest. She died at 10:48 that night.

When Scott arrived back at my house sometime after eleven thirty, he told me he would take care of things. I didn't know what that meant but I knew it meant he would protect me from being charged with anything connected to her death. He told me no one would ever know she was at my house.

Days after the autopsy, Scott called me to tell me Jessica died of an ectopic pregnancy. I felt relieved to learn it wasn't my fault, but I also knew she needed more medical attention than what I was equipped with at my house in the middle of the night.

When Scott found out Kristina suspected him as Tori's father, he thought I told her about Jessica. He was paranoid and violent. He threatened me and beat me on numerous occasions. My lawyer, Mr. Williams, will have those details.

I hired Mr. Williams after coincidentally finding out Gerry was the father to Jessica's baby. The night Jessica was at my apartment, she told me about the one night stand she had with Gerry. She never mentioned his last name but when I ran into him at Buckley's and Kristina introduced him to me as Jessica's friend, it just clicked.

It was then I knew he would be found guilty of Jessica's murder. I contacted his parents by researching their address at Country Light Nursing Home. I happened to have been Gerry's grandmother's discharge nurse. I looked up Maye Williams' file and the family's address.

I did not know Mr. Williams was a lawyer when I told him that Gerry was in trouble but it so happened that God works in mysterious ways, and the Williams family offered me and Tori protection. I am forever in debt to Gerry and his family.

My wish is that Tori never learns the identity of her biological father. Scott McKylie was a married man, and I should have never gotten involved with him. I am so sorry for withholding this evidence. I feared I would be prosecuted; and I could not leave my Tori alone in this world.

If you are reading this, I am probably dead so please tell Tori how much I love her. Please tell her I did my best. I made decisions that I thought would keep us both safe. Everyone makes bad decisions but no one did it to intentionally hurt Jessica. Gerry has beat himself up over the years for not wearing a condom that night. And well, I know I should have just brought Jessica to the hospital. I didn't then and I am sorry. I wasn't thinking straight.

Please tell the Briggs family how sorry I am and tell Scott McKylie that as much as I know he was trying to protect Jessica's secret and me, that is not the way to protect and serve in America.

I made a huge mistake ever getting involved with Scott McKylie but the best decision I ever made was keeping Tori as my baby. RIP Jessica Briggs, I am so very sorry that I didn't do the right thing for you then.

AM Grout

It was signed by Victoria and dated a few months after Jessica's murder.

THE END.

"They have taken my Lord away," she said, "and I don't know where they have put him." At this, she turned around and saw Jesus standing there, but she did not realize that it was Jesus. He asked her, "Woman, why are you crying? Who is it you are looking for?"

Thinking he was the gardener, she said, "Sir, if you have carried him away, tell me where you have put him, and I will get him." Jesus said to her, "Mary." She turned toward him and cried out, "Teacher."

Jesus said, "Do not hold on to me, for I have not yet ascended to the Father. Go instead to my brethren and tell them I have gone to the Father, our Father; to my God and your God."

Mary Magdalene went to the disciples with the news. "I have seen the Lord!" And she told them that he had said these things to her.

On the evening of that first day of the week, when the disciples were together, with the doors locked for fear of the Jewish leaders. Jesus came and stood among them and said, "Peace be with you!" After he said this, he showed them his hands and side. The disciples were overjoyed when they saw the Lord. Again Jesus said, "Peace be with you! As the Father has sent me, I am sending you." And with that he breathed on them and said,

"Receive the Holy Spirit. If you forgive anyone's sins, their sins are forgiven, if you do not forgive them, they are not forgiven."

-John 20:13-22

AM Grout

Acknowledgements

The passion to write is air to my lungs, unconscious, active and often a struggle. I am forever grateful to my friends and family who provided me with oxygen when I was most in need of airing these words. Kay, Kristen, Charlene, Sara, Erica, Erin, Sarah, Annah, Abbe, Jenn, Wendy, Nancy, John, Darcy, PJ, Kellye, Chris, Molly, Maggie, Lily, all my Katies, Kate, Tricia, my cousin Mark, my Aunt Marie, Anna @ MOT; Jake from State Farms (aka ATI); Danny E@ the Majestic, Kim, Mellissa, and Karin K. I have one angelic and amazing support team; and it keeps going...

To my fabulous editing crew, proofreaders and prayerful friends including the Kelsult team at AFS; Donna Trask, Kim Dotiwalla, Melissa Lizardi, Maggie Grout, Vicky Connors, Pam Tully, and Gary Grout. Thank you all for your compassion, enthusiasm, encouragement, and inspirational conversations. Special thanks to Donna, Kellsey, Theresa, and the guides that have gifted their expertise to guide this story on track and on time.

Special Thanks to my husband, Gary for his belief in me and this story. You gave me space to think, to write, and to work on this project. I am blest to have you as my partner, desk builder and bookshelf mover. I love you.

To my daughter Maggie, thank you for coaching me to balance the reality of life and dreams. You constantly shine light that dreams come true. You are my dream come true. May you reach for the stars because you are one!

AM Grout

To my daughter Molly, thank you for teaching me about character voices. Your lessons are invaluable to me and I know you will be a great author one day. Your stories are amazing!

Thanks to Jenn, Sarah, and Erin for the ladies nights to erase the gray areas when my head was itching with ideas. And to Rodney, for the memorable story at the lake and the vision to focus on the trees; thank you.

Thanks to my Emmy Winning cousin, Steve Kwas, for being a text away when I was ready to walk away.

To Bean for the dream of the screen and the reality to witness the struggle. To Ron & Jake Wieners, and Robert Mitas for enthusiastically receiving my first pitch.

To Jenny McNulty, and Mary Kay Ash for proving dreams are achievable; thanks for all the beautiful wisdom you provide me in so many ways.

Thank you to the Springfield Museum for hosting Creative Writing with Theresa Chamberland, her guidance has allowed my journey with writing to evolve into more than just scrambled notes.

To Sir Tim Berners-Lee, thanks for putting Wikipedia, MassLive, Google, Reddit, Crime Watch Daily, Web sleuths, The Guardian, and the world accessible to my fingertips.

Special thanks for the advice from the Google Hangout Crew of Jonathan Kesselman, Herschel Weingrod, Mark Bomback, and Dean Craig. Thank you so much for your encouragement, and belief in getting a final draft. It may not be in the draft form we discussed but your words of wisdom gently guided me to where I needed to be. Thank you!

To all the Facebook/Internet coaches that have provided me with much needed wisdom cheering me to tap the keys through this writing process: Joe Mercado, Megan Barnhard, Ashley Scott Meyers, Jerry Jenkins, Oprah Winfrey, Steve Jobs, Albert Einstein, and Saint Augustine.

To JAMES PATTERSON, Dan Brown, Margaret Atwood, and Judy Blume, my Amazing MasterClass instructors. Your teaching techniques brought this story out of my head and onto the page. Judy Blume was my 1st and favorite author...she has taught me character assessment and the sanctity of my own notebook. Thank you.

To the many spirits that cross paths with the flower fairies; I empathize with your journey, your sorrow, your pain, and your silence. May you sing with the angels that brought you to safety, and may your life and your spirit always reflect the gift of love.

To Shelley, thank you for sharing quotes from the greatest story ever written and reminding me the authors never knew their audience. Your words echo my call "someone may need the story."

To my mom, and Carol ~ you told me to have faith and trust that God will handle my worries, I do. And Dad thanks for teaching me about record keeping and remembrances, it has allowed for me to journey into my imagination knowing who I am regardless of the stories I venture to share.

To everyone that supported this project, thank you for encouraging me especially when I was discouraged. You

AM Grout

recommended books, stories, mediations, and even gave me paths to research that benefited this story and my own personal journey.

Finally, and most importantly, I am eternally thankful to God, the Master builder and creator of everything seen and unseen. And to Mother Mary and all the saints, whose guidance is loving, gentle and persistent. Knowing you are in every story gives courage to choose love over fear.

Life is a gift and inspiration is everywhere, sometimes in the scariest and saddest moments of our life, we must turn to our imaginations to find an answer to soothe our soul. Bad things have happened to good people, but at the end of our life, it doesn't matter what has happened to us, it matters our reactions which leaves a ripple effect for future generations.

The one thing I have always known is God does not forget the pain on our hearts. He wants us to heal, he wants us to forgive, and most importantly he wants us to live. Humans make mistakes, and God strives to repair, teach and continue to shine light even in the darkness.

Finally, THANK YOU... the reader, for reading this story and shining your own light in this world. A writer is nothing without a reader, I humbly thank you for giving me time to share a story.

I wish you peace and happiness.

AM Grout

AM Grout

About the Author

AM Grout is a graduate of Western New England Universtity in Springfield, Massachusetts; and has studied creative writing with James Patterson, Judy Blume, Aaron Sorkins, Dan Brown, Margaret Atwood, Emily Stoddard, and Theresa Chamberland.

A member of the Springfield Museum's Creative Writers Group; and a passionate Catholic, teaching faith for over thirty years, concentrating in confirmation.

AM Grout successfully completed a Protecting God's Children® Program offered by the National Catholic Services, LLC; and holds certificates of completion for various VIRTUS programs.

A Certified Reiki healer inspired to bring healing to all God's children. With an appreciation for the rosary and passion to pen stories to entertain reflections of life's mysteries.

AM Grout

Printed in the USA
CPSIA information can be obtained
at www.ICGtesting.com
LVHW070343180923
758487LV00025B/301